EVAN

LOVING A WINSTON BOOK 2

STACY EATON

CHAPTER ONE

EVAN

"Oh, my gosh! Evan, did you see the new pictures that Cara posted of Luke?"

"I did." I grinned at my sister, Coral, as she pushed my to-go coffee over the counter. "He's a cutie."

"He is soooooo adorable! I can't wait to get down there and see him. I can't believe he's already three months old." She glanced around the café as if making sure she didn't say something she shouldn't in front of the wrong people.

Her check made me glance over my shoulder. We had to be careful when it came to my sister, her new husband, and their baby. To people around here, her husband was dead.

Coral shook her head and handed me a small white bag with two lemon Danishes in it. One for me and one for Nicole, my co-worker who was almost as addicted to them as I was.

"Time is flying, that's for sure," I replied as I took the bag. "You have a good day, Coral."

"You too, Evan," she called before she turned her attention to the next customer in line.

After getting into my SUV, I drove onto the main roadway and thought about my oldest sister, Cara, for a few minutes. She had gone through a lot when she first met Ryan. He was in an outlaw motorcycle gang, which was bad news in these parts. From the moment I met him, I felt that I knew him, and it didn't take long for me to realize precisely why I felt that way and who he was.

His name wasn't Ryan Vigilante, as he had said. It was Bryan Hemlock. When I went through nursing school in Philadelphia, I was best friends with his fiancée, Jeanette. While I had only met him briefly, I had seen a lot of pictures of him, and the day I had confronted him, I had brought one with me. Unfortunately, Jeanette had been brutally murdered, so obviously, he wasn't with her now.

He hadn't denied who he was but told me that I had to keep it quiet because he was undercover and trying to protect my sister. His idea of protection was claiming her as his property to the club. My older brother, Ethan, almost lost his shit on that. Being a county detective, the last thing he wanted was my sister wrapped up with a bunch of drug-running felons.

However, Ryan had done everything that he could to protect not only Cara but our family. Thanks to Cara saving one of the club members after he'd gotten shot by a rival gang, the club owed Cara a favor.

Ryan had gotten shot too, and Ethan and I were the ones who told Cara that he had died.

In reality, Ryan Vigilante had died, but Bryan Hemlock had not. I had called Jeanette's father and asked him if he knew Bryan and if he could tell us if Bryan had any family. He advised me that he was the only family Bryan had and that Bryan worked with him at the FBI. Because of how big the undercover operation was, they brought another medical transport chopper in, and as soon as Bryan was stable enough to move, they flew him out. To everyone waiting, including the gang members, Ryan Vigilante died that night.

It took a while before Cara learned the truth. Ethan and I

had discussed it several times and decided that it was best if Cara thought he was gone for good. I mean, if he had really cared for her, he wouldn't have lied to her and then just left her behind. How could you leave someone that you truly loved? I knew that I couldn't.

We had even talked it over with our father, and he agreed with us, but that decision changed when Cara announced that she was pregnant. We knew that we couldn't keep this from her. She had the right to face him and tell him what was going on.

If he were half the man Jeanette had said he was, he would at least talk to her and hopefully figure out a way to be in the child's life—despite being a walking ghost.

The night that she dropped the bomb about being pregnant, we had sat her down and explained it all. Cara took a while to decide what she wanted to do, and finally, she called in her favor with the club and asked them to release her and our family for good. They did, and she left town under the guise of starting someplace new after losing Ryan.

We flew to Texas to confront Bryan. She wanted to go alone, but I told her there was no way I'd let her do that. Ethan had wanted to come too, but he had a significant investigation going on and couldn't get away.

Things worked out for Cara and Bryan, and now they were happily married with a child. The only problem was that Bryan could never come back to town. It would put him and our entire family in danger if he did. Was it worth sacrificing everything that you knew for another person?

Cara believed so. She had once told me that she felt as if she had fallen in love with him the first time she saw him at an accident scene. Cara had looked into his eyes and had felt a connection. She said it was as if two pieces clicked, and no matter what, she couldn't deny the chemistry they had.

I thought that was a whole lot of horseshit. Love at first sight did not exist. People could say it did all they wanted, but it would be a cold day in hell before I believed it.

I parked in the employee lot and collected my stuff before heading into the hospital. I worked on the fourth floor in the ICU. I loved my job. I even loved the long hours that I worked. Maybe that was because I didn't have much of a life outside these walls.

There was no one special in my life right now, and other than going out with friends or family for dinner, bowling, movies, or drinks at the tavern, I didn't get out much these days.

It was hard to meet people when you lived in a small town, and I had lived in Millerstown my entire life. I pretty much knew everyone, and the dating pool was severely lacking. By my age, most people had gotten married and were having kids. There weren't many single women left out there—at least ones that I would be interested in building a relationship with.

I wanted a woman who was devoted to helping people. A woman who understood long working hours and didn't complain if I missed a holiday or event because my shift required me to do my job.

I wanted a woman who loved family, someone who could blend into my large family, and wanted to add members to it. She had to be someone who liked to snuggle in front of the fireplace, and it wouldn't hurt if she enjoyed cooking. Not that I expected my woman to do all the cooking. I knew my way around the kitchen, and I enjoyed making meals. Thanks to my mother, I could even make a mean peach pie with a crust from scratch.

I frowned as I hit the elevator button. My mother had been dead almost two years, and I missed her every day. She had died of that ugly C-word: Cancer. Sadly, it had gone untreated too long and had taken her from our lives way too quickly. There wasn't a day that I didn't think about my mother, and I knew I wasn't the only one. My siblings and I constantly talked about her with my father to keep her memory alive.

I rode the elevator up and then got off on the fourth floor, stepping around a woman with long brown hair who was talking on her phone. I made my way to the unit and slipped into the small break room/locker room. Nicole was just closing her locker.

"I have a Danish for you," I called out.

Her head snapped my way. Her brown eyes grew wide with excitement. "Lemon?"

"Is there any other flavor?" I grinned at her as I dropped the bag on the table and set down my coffee so that I could open my locker.

"No, well, the peach isn't that bad, but the lemon is always perfect," she replied as she made a beeline for the table and practically ripped the bag open to get the sweet treat.

"One!" I called out to her sternly, and she rolled her eyes.

"As much as I'd like to ignore your command and have both, I am watching my waistline."

I snickered. Nicole was forty-seven years old and fighting that premenopausal period where her body weight didn't want to cooperate. She wasn't overly heavy, but she did have an extra twenty pounds that she was forever trying to lose.

"You know that you are beautiful just the way you are."

She tsked, shaking her head. "If only you were fifteen years older."

I chuckled. It was a long-running joke between us that she said if only I were closer to her age, she would have swept me off my feet and taken me off the market for good. She'd also have to be divorced since she was happily married and had been for twenty-five years.

I loved Nicole dearly. She was one of my best friends, and I confided in her almost as often as I did my brother and Huntley Young, my best friend since high school. Well, maybe even longer than that since our families grew up doing everything together.

Our parents had been best friends, and each of our families had six children. We had two boys and four girls, and they had four boys and two girls. My older brother Ethan was married to Huntley's Irish twin sister, Riley, and they had a daughter.

"You know I love you just the way you are, and so does Bob."

She rolled her eyes as she took a large bite of her breakfast treat, then spoke around her food. "Of course Bob does. He has to. He's married to me."

The door opened, and Rebecca peeked her head in. "Hey, Evan, you have a new patient in four. She came up about thirty minutes ago. I wanted to make sure that I had a chance to talk to you about her case before I left." She glanced at her watch. "And I have to take off as soon as I can."

"Give me five minutes, and I'll be at your disposal, Rebecca."

"Great!" She disappeared out the door, and I glanced at Nicole to find her eyes closed as if she were savoring the flavor of her food. I chuckled as I put my lightweight jacket into my locker, grabbed a new pair of scrubs, and began to change.

I could have gone into the restroom changing area, but there were no secrets here, not after working with these people for so many years. I slipped them on, collected the rest of my things from inside, and then grabbed my coffee cup off the table. I eyed the bag with the pastry and wondered if I should shove it in now but decided to hold off until break time.

Nicole had already gone to check in with Teresa, the nurse she was relieving, and for the next thirty minutes, Rebecca and I discussed not only the new patient but the other three that I would be overseeing on my shift today.

ICU was a bit different than working on the main floors. These patients were critical and required more of our attention. Vitals were constantly monitored, medications were adjusted, and doctors were in and out more regularly. We were only assigned four patients, five at the absolute most, and those patients kept us busy through our twelve-hour shift.

It was exhausting some days, but I didn't mind. The most challenging days were the ones where we'd lose a patient. Sadly, since this was ICU, that happened more often than I cared to admit. We saw our share of death in this unit, sometimes an overwhelming amount, but we would see miracles too.

Rebecca had explained that the new patient was a domestic violence victim and had been stabbed four times, allegedly by her husband. She had undergone emergency surgery and lost half of her liver along with half a lung. She had also coded on the operating table, not once, but twice.

She would be lucky to survive the day. If she did, her chances would be much better. Rebecca stated that she probably wouldn't have visitors either because she didn't have any other family in the area—except for his family, and they were not allowed in the room.

I was okay with that because that meant I didn't need to explain every single thing I was doing. Or worry about upsetting someone if the patient began to go downhill.

So, ten minutes later, when I stepped into the room to do my first check of her, I was surprised to find a woman standing beside the bed. While we did have glass walls that allowed us to see in, I hadn't noticed her.

"I'm sorry. I didn't know her family was here," I said softly, and she turned toward me as if I'd startled her.

My eyes popped wider, and I leaned back slightly as if a wave had just struck me and I was trying to keep my footing on loose sand. The woman had the most elegant features, and her eyes were the most beautiful array of colors that I had ever seen. They were so bright and vivid—with light green around the outside and a golden brown around the pupil. I had never seen anything like them, and I couldn't tear my eyes away from her.

As she stared back at me, I felt something inside of me shift, and I wanted to approach the woman in a way that I had never wanted to do before. How crazy would it be to walk up to her and pull her into my arms?

Nuts! I would be absolutely nuts! I shook my head, breaking whatever trance I'd gotten lost in as she began to speak.

"I'm sorry. I just slipped in to let Mary listen to something."

"You're not family?"

She shook her head. "I'm not family."

"Then you aren't allowed to be in here." As I said the words, I wanted to tell her I'd overlook it if she gave me her number.

She nodded. "Yes, I know, but her children can't come in here. I'm with the county domestic violence center, and the kids recorded a video. I wanted to play it for her. Maybe it will help her fight more." She turned to look at the woman lying unconscious in bed. "She deserves to live."

"Oh, well, okay, that's fine. You can do that."

"Thank you," she said softly, and when she graced me with a smile, I felt my knees grow slightly weak.

I quickly turned away from her and focused on the computer. As I did, I wondered if this was what Cara had been talking about when she met Bryan.

CHAPTER TWO

LANEY

"I've been at the hospital since I got the call," I told Joyce, my supervisor at the domestic violence center that I worked for, as I stood in the lobby near the elevator on the fourth floor. "She's in ICU, but I haven't had a chance to try and see her yet. I'm not sure they will even let me in."

"How are the kids? Has CYF shown up to get them?" I shook my head even though she couldn't see me. I was too tired to think straight after being at the hospital all night long, and I was trying to rattle the cobwebs off.

"Yes, finally! They arrived around five-thirty this morning. They took custody of Ben and Barbie."

"Okay, well then, why are you still at the hospital?"

"The kids made a little video for their mom. I want to see if I can get into her room long enough to play it for her. She coded twice in the operating room, Joyce. I think a part of her wants to give up. God knows that after all she has gone through, I would want to also, but I hope if she hears their voices, it will remind her why she was fighting in the first place."

"I hope it does. Mary is a sweet woman."

"How long have you known her?"

"Well, the first time she called was about six years ago. I was the one who took the call that night. She wasn't ready to leave her husband, but she asked many questions, and we stayed in touch for a while. About six months later, she called for emergency help and came into the shelter with the kids for three days, but then she went back to him."

"Do you know how many times she left him?"

"She was in emergency intake four times since the initial one."

I sighed. That was five times too many. No woman, or man for that matter, should be abused by their partner. I hoped there was a special place in hell for those that did.

"I wish she had stayed," I commented as I looked down the long hallway and watched a man disappear around a corner.

"You know that sometimes it can take them six or seven times to cut the strings finally. Her case was difficult because he was the breadwinner, and I'm not talking about white bread here. He has a high six-figure salary. He held that over her head since she was a stay-at-home mom. He controlled her money, questioned every penny he put into the household account, and even dictated when she was allowed to drive their car." She paused. "The man had software on her car that would notify him if she left the house and would report every place she went."

"Are you kidding me?" I was flabbergasted. "What an ass."

"Yes, I agree." She sighed heavily into the phone. "Okay, well, see if you can share the video with her and then go get some sleep."

"Do they have him in custody yet?"

"Not that I know of. The last I heard, the police are still searching for him."

"You know, I would feel much better if he was locked away."

"You and me both, but as I said, he has money and means to

avoid authorities. I wonder if he's even still around here. If he were smart, he would have left the state."

"Yeah, well, I hope they catch him fast."

"We can both hope for that." We finished the call after that, and I found a restroom where I used the toilet, washed my hands, and stared at the haunting image in the mirror.

Taking this job had been a difficult decision. On the one hand, I wanted to do anything to protect those being controlled, manipulated, physically and mentally abused. On the other hand, it was a constant reminder of how I had failed my sister, Lindsey.

I had been blind to what was happening to her. Absolutely ignorant of the disastrous circumstances that she was living in. Lindsey had always been more reserved than me and our older brother, Lawrence. She had never wanted the spotlight, never drew attention to herself, and after she got married, no one noticed that it got worse. If anyone should have, it should have been me.

By the time Lindsey got married, both of our parents had passed, and it was just Larry, Lindsey, and me. I was busy focusing on my future and the work Larry and I did for our family's company. Larry cracked the whip daily as he ran the show. He tried to prove to everyone that he was just as incredible as our father and grandfather had been. Sadly, he didn't seem to realize that he could never be as good as either of them —not on his own.

Lindsey met Matt while she was in college, and in her third year, the two of them eloped. Larry was furious and demanded she get an annulment, but Lindsey refused. Our family's image was everything to Larry and having his baby sister run off and marry a guy who was a wannabe musician was mind-boggling to him. I hadn't seen him that angry in forever.

But Lindsey didn't care. She loved Matt and wanted to be by his side as he rode the wave to stardom. He took her to all his performances, and Lindsey talked about the fun and parties they had on the road, but things began to change once Lindsey found out she was pregnant. Sadly, she ended up losing that baby—and the next.

Looking back, I had missed so many signs, and I knew that no matter how much I beat myself up about that, I could not do anything to rectify her untimely demise.

I gathered my shoulder bag and let myself out of the restroom. I headed toward the entrance to the ICU and was about to hit the buzzer when an aide exited. I slipped through the doors before they closed as if I knew where I was going. I peered into a couple of rooms as I walked down the hallway and reached the central nurses' station, where a male and female nurse discussed patient charts.

On the wall behind the station was a board that had last names, only one box had the initials DM and beside it was the number four. I was pretty sure that was for Mary Davidson.

I skirted the nurses' station and easily found room number four. As I stepped through the glass doors, I froze. Mary lay there with multiple wires attached to her and a ventilator in her mouth to help her breathe. I was instantly transported to the night my sister died, two years and eleven months ago.

I had received the phone call from the hospital that Lindsey was fighting for her life. At the time, I had been living in Santa Monica, California. The call was from a hospital in Portland, Oregon. It had taken me six hours to get to her, and once I did, I had missed her by fifteen minutes.

I was devastated to arrive after she had died. It wasn't enough that Matt had hurt her, but during that talk with the doctor, I learned that Lindsey had sustained multiple fractures, several concussions, and a host of abrasions over the last few years. The doctor said he had checked with other hospitals near her home address when he started reviewing test results and noticed the past injuries. He found many visits with reports of injuries about falling because she was clumsy, had not paid attention, or walked in her sleep.

I knew for a fact that she was not clumsy. She had been a ballet dancer for over twelve years and had been amazing to watch with her grace and beauty. She also didn't sleepwalk.

The doctor said he had seen the list of injuries many times before, and his heart went out to my sister. Sadly, there was no way to save her life. They had done everything they could, and he was writing a detailed report about her injuries and what he had found so it could be used for prosecution. He also told me that he'd be willing to testify in court to the extent of her past injuries.

At that time, I was unable to process the past. All I could think about was the future—a future without my baby sister. I also wanted to know where Matt was, but the police said he had taken off before they arrived, and no one had seen him. It had taken six months before they had captured him, and he ended up taking a plea bargain instead of going to trial.

Personally, I wished that he would have had a trial. I wanted nothing more than for him to get life in prison, or the death penalty would have been better. However, he took a plea for twenty-eight years behind bars, with a chance of probation at eighteen years.

Eighteen years wasn't long enough. As it was, a little over two years had passed since his incarceration. That meant that in another sixteen years, that scumbag would have a chance to walk free. Something that my baby sister would never be able to do again.

I forced myself to walk toward the bed, and I leaned down beside Mary. "Mary, my name is Laney Marshall. I'm a friend of Joyce's." I opened my mouth to speak, but a man's voice rang through the room and startled me.

"I'm sorry. I didn't know her family was here."

I turned to study him, immediately taken with the wide,

expressive brown eyes that stared back at me, and noticed that he seemed to jerk back slightly as if he were the one that was startled. I shifted my gaze to the brown scruff that ran along his jawline, and my hand instantly itched to see if it was as soft as it appeared.

The two of us kept staring at one another for a few seconds as we appraised one another. He was a handsome man in his early thirties, about five foot nine or ten. I wasn't sure why it surprised me that he was a nurse. I guess I never pictured an extremely handsome man being a nurse. Most men I knew who were attractive were way too arrogant to work in this industry.

As I told him that I wasn't family, he commented that I wasn't allowed in her room, but after I explained who I was and that I just wanted to play a video for Mary, he seemed fine. In fact, he dismissed me quicker than I had expected and focused on the computer.

I took a few seconds to ogle the shoulders that filled out his scrub shirt perfectly. He also had a very sexy booty too, and I found myself nibbling my bottom lip for a second before one of the machines in the room beeped, and I jumped.

Oh, my God! Here I was ogling this hot male nurse, and a client was lying here clinging to life. Ugh!

"Mary, I have something to play for you. I was with your kids earlier while you were in surgery, and they wanted me to play this for you so that you knew they were alright." I logged into my phone and brought up the video as the nurse stepped over to one of her IV bags and checked something. "I know you can't see this, but I hope you can hear their voices."

The nurse was staring at the monitor on the other side of the bed, a frown on his face. His eyes cut to mine momentarily. "Did you want me to leave?"

"No, you don't have to do that."

I hit play on my video player and held it closer to her ear. Ben's ten-year-old voice rang through my speaker. "Hey, Mom.

I know you're in the recovery place, and we can't see you because we're just kids, and they don't let kids in there. We just wanted you to know that we are okay. Laney is really cool, and I told Barbie that we were going on an adventure while you get better. Don't worry about us. We will be okay, and I promise to watch out for my sister. We love you, Mom. We need you to get better."

There was no movement from Mary, and when I glanced at the nurse, I saw his gaze locked on the monitor.

"Her pulse dropped lower when she heard her son's voice." He smiled briefly at me, and I changed the video to the next one.

After a few seconds, a perky but tired seven-year-old spoke. "Hi, Mommy. I wish I could hug you. Laney bought us cheeseburgers and fries, and I even got a milkshake in the middle of the night! Ben and I are going to a friend's house to sleep now, but we'll be here to see you soon. Get better, Mommy! I love you."

I glanced at the nurse who was watching Mary. "Well, her pulse was nice and low both times, so that's good. I was concerned it might cause her anxiety, but it looks like it didn't."

"That's good. Mary has gone through enough."

The two of us fell into silence again as we watched one another, and I self-consciously tucked a lock of hair behind my ear. "Well, I should go."

"Yeah, you probably should," he replied, but neither of us moved from our spots.

I couldn't remember a time when I had felt such an attraction to someone, and I was wondering if it was just because I was so damn tired. That had to be it. I finally tore my eyes away from his dark-chocolate ones and shuffled toward the door.

"Hey," he called, and I turned. "Could you send me those videos? I could play them for her later, see if she reacts to them."

"Um, sure. I can do that. Do you want me to email them?"

"No, can you text them to me?"

"I don't see why not. I'll do that before I leave the hospital so that I am still on the Wi-Fi."

"Great. I appreciate it."

I nodded, and we continued to stare at one another. I laughed. "I need your number to do that."

"Oh, yeah, that's right." He grinned, and I swear my heart sighed. Yep, I was exhausted and turning into an idiot.

He quickly rattled off his number, and I typed it into my phone and attached the first video. "Should take a minute, but you'll get it."

"Perfect. Drive safely. You look tired."

"I've been up since five yesterday morning, so yes, I'm exhausted."

His gaze softened as if he were concerned. "Well, make sure to keep yourself awake."

"I only live about ten minutes away, so I should be fine. Thank you and thank you for taking care of Mary."

"You're welcome," he said, and I forced myself to turn and walk out of the room.

It wasn't until I was at my car that I realized that I didn't even know what his name was, and after I received a text reply of, *Got them! Thanks! Drive safe!* I stared at the message and started to delete it, but instead saved the contact as Hot Nurse.

I laughed to myself as I set my phone down and started my car.

CHAPTER THREE

EVAN

I watched her leave. I couldn't take my eyes off her. I even followed her into the hallway to watch her pass through the doors of our unit. After she was gone, I blinked twice and shook my head.

Suddenly, Nicole was beside me. "You okay? You look a little bowled over."

I laughed, the sound slightly unsteady. "I am bowled over. There was a woman in here with the patient. She was from the DV center, and she was playing a video that the patient's kids had made for her, hoping she could hear it and it would help."

"Okay—" Nicole said slowly.

"I don't know, Nicole. She was just, just—"

"Just what?" Nicole crossed her arms over her ample chest and regarded me with a raised brow.

"Beautiful," I blurted out. "But it was more than that. There was just something about her. When she turned to look at me, I froze, and then it was like someone plugged me into a wall socket because every part of my body tingled."

A slow grin slipped over her lips as she nodded slowly. "Ah, okay, and now you have a hot date set up, right?"

"No, I don't even have her number." I laughed and stepped back into Mary's room to continue my assessment. As I did, my cellphone pinged, and I pulled it out and laughed. "Actually, scratch that. I do have her number. She just texted me the video."

"Well, you will have to let me know how that hot date goes." Nicole grinned, then asked me a work question. As the day progressed, the image of the woman came back to me time and time again. What was her name? Man, I didn't even know that. Had she told me and I forgot? I didn't think she did, but for a few moments, I was dumbfounded as I had stared at her. At least I did have her number. Although I wasn't sure what I would do with that.

I played the videos for Mary twice during the day. Both times she responded favorably, and I was glad that I had thought to ask for them. Hearing her children's voices seemed to calm her, and I noticed that she was doing much better by the end of the shift. If all went well, there was talk that she would be off the ventilator the following day.

It wasn't until I was home again that I thought about the beautiful woman I'd seen in the room. I pulled out my phone and looked at the text message. I had sent her a brief thank you after she'd sent the videos, but that was all. Would she think me weird if I sent her a message?

What if she were married, and her husband asked her who I was? Would sending a message to her bother her or get her in trouble? I'd think that if she worked for the DV center, she wouldn't be with a man who would be violent or controlling.

Perhaps if I worded it correctly, it would come across as informative and not me trying to hit on her—not that I was trying to hit on her. Liar, my inner voice said in a whisper.

I started to type. *Hi, I'm not sure you remember me, but this is Evan Winston, the nurse caring for your friend. I met you this morning. I just wanted to let you know that I played the videos for her a couple of times today. She responded really well, and she is healing. We might even remove the ventilator tomorrow if she continues to improve overnight. I just thought you might want to know. Have a good evening, and sorry to bother you.*

I read over it twice, then sent the message. Then I went into the kitchen to find something to eat. Thanks to Brad Young, and his sister Kayley, I had an incredible gourmet kitchen in my house. When I bought this split-level four years ago, I hated how closed the kitchen was. Brad and Kayley opened it up by removing a wall and installing an enormous island. Then Kayley gave me some suggestions on decorating the area and creating a sanctuary to come home to.

Next, I would tackle my bottom floor and the entertainment and family room that I wanted badly, but I needed to save for that project. I was still paying off the loan from the upstairs remodel. What I wanted downstairs wasn't going to be quite as expensive, but once I added in the pool table, the seventy-two-inch flat-screen TV, all new leather furniture, and updated my workout room, it was going to cost a pretty penny.

I stood in front of my fridge, debating making eggs or having leftover stew. I decided it was a stew night and warmed it up. It wasn't until I had sat down on the stool at the island bar that I looked at my phone and saw a reply.

I set my fork down and read it. *Evan, thank you so much for the update on MD. That is good news all around. I'm sorry that I didn't introduce myself to you this morning. I was a little out of sorts. My name is Laney Marshall, and you aren't bothering me. I hope you have a good night.*

I was smiling as I finished and quickly typed back. *Nice to meet you, Laney. I wasn't sure if you might have a husband or boyfriend who would get jealous about another man sending you messages—even though they are about work.*

Her reply was only a minute later. *No husband and no boyfriend either. So, no one to get jealous, and I wouldn't be with a* man who was like that. *Is your wife or girlfriend upset that you are texting me?*

I had never been so happy to be single. *You are talking to a single man. Can I ask you a question?*

Sure, she responded back.

How long have you been with the DV center?

About six months. How long have you been a nurse?

About six years.

I could imagine her smiling as her reply came back. *Looks like we have the six in common, Evan.*

That we do, Laney, I replied and then hesitated before I started another message. *Would you be interested in having coffee sometime?*

I would like that. I'm not sure if you're working or not, but I'm off on Saturday. There is an excellent coffee café in town. I'm sure you know Coral's, right?

I laughed. *Oh, yes, I know Coral's very well. I work tomorrow, but I am off Friday through Sunday. Saturday would be perfect. What time works for you?*

Would ten o'clock be okay?

Ten would be excellent.

Great, I will see you then. Thanks again for the update. I look forward to coffee on Saturday.

I do too. Have a good night.

Night, Evan.

Night, Laney.

I set my phone to the side and took a couple of bites of my food as I thought back over the conversation. It looked like I had a hot coffee date with Laney. Saturday couldn't come soon enough.

On Thursday, Mary made remarkable improvements, and we did remove the breathing tube. She also woke up early afternoon, and I called the detective working on her case to let him know. He arrived a few hours later, and beside him was Laney Marshall.

It had been a rough afternoon as we'd lost a nineteen-year-old, and the family had been inconsolable as they had been here when he died. It had taken up a good portion of the afternoon, plus dealing with all our other patients, and I was ready to punch the clock as soon as seven rolled around.

Seeing Laney's beautiful eyes and her serene smile brightened my day in a way I never thought possible. I could barely tear my eyes from her as the two of them stopped in front of me.

"Hey, Evan," Adam Brewer said as he stuck his hand out to me. Adam worked with my brother Ethan, and we had hung out many times at the tavern together.

I forced myself to give him my attention. "Adam, I didn't know that you were assigned to this case."

"Your brother was supposed to take it, but he got tied up with another case, so I was next on the list."

Laney spoke up. "Your brother is a detective, Evan?"

"Yeah, Ethan Winston."

"I've met him," she said with a smile that reached her incredible eyes and made my heart beat a little faster.

Adam looked between us. "You two know each other?"

"We met yesterday," I replied as my eyes remained locked with Laney's.

He nodded. "Okay, so is she awake?" I finally peeled my gaze from Laney and shifted it to Adam. "I'd like to get a statement from the vic. Not much of one. I know she's serious and all, but we need her to confirm some information about the incident, and then we can get a more detailed statement later."

"Okay, but I'm going to be there, and if I see her struggling, then I'm going to stop it. I can't have her regressing."

"That's fine, but be aware that if she says something important, you could be called to testify as a witness, especially if she doesn't make it."

"That's fine."

He nodded and turned to Laney. "Do you want to go in and talk to her first? Maybe let her know that I am going to ask her some questions."

"Absolutely," she replied and stepped away to head toward Mary's room. As she left, I didn't miss how Adam's eyes checked her out from head to toe.

He whistled softly. "Man, that is one gorgeous woman."

I turned to watch her behind the glass. She stood next to Mary's bed and leaned forward slightly. "Yeah, she is."

"I heard there was a really hot woman working at DV, but this is the first time I have seen her in person. I plan on asking her out to dinner after we finish here."

I clamped my teeth so that I didn't snap, *back the hell off.* I didn't have any right to say that. Laney and I barely knew each other, and even though I was seriously attracted to her, I had no idea if she felt the same.

Before I could come up with any type of response, Laney lifted her head and locked eyes with me. She waved us in. Adam arrived in the room before me and stood close to Laney on the right side of the bed. I went to the opposite side and glanced at the monitors to make sure her vitals were stable, then I touched her hand and smiled at her.

"Mary, I'm going to stay here with you. I want to make sure they don't upset you too much. We can't have you regressing now that we got you on the mend. Alright?"

She nodded slightly.

I nodded to Adam, and Laney introduced him to Mary. I

stepped back and out of the way but kept a close eye on the monitors.

"Hi, Mary. I'm glad that you are doing better. I'm sorry about what happened to you, and I know talking about it is going to be difficult, but I do need to ask you a few questions." Adam's voice was softer than usual but still professional.

She nodded but didn't speak.

Laney looked down at her, then at me, and moved around Adam and to the other side of the bed where she could hold Mary's hand. She lifted her face to mine momentarily and smiled almost shyly at me. I winked back at her.

Why did I love it so much that she changed positions so that she could hold Mary's hand and be a reassurance to her? I didn't know, but I did.

"Mary, can you tell me who hurt you? Who stabbed you?"

She closed her eyes, and Laney spoke softly to her. "It's okay, Mary. He can't hurt you now. You're safe."

"My husband, Rick."

"Rick Davidson? He's the one that stabbed you four times?"

She nodded. "Only four? It felt like a hundred." Tears trailed from the corners of her eyes into her brown hair.

"Yes, only four times. Mary, do you know why he stabbed you?"

I glanced at the monitor and saw her heart rate beginning to accelerate, her blood pressure too.

"He said he wanted to kill me."

"Why? Why did Rick want to kill you?"

"Because I didn't pick up his dry cleaning and he had to leave for a business trip."

Fury rushed through my veins at her softly spoken words. How could any man do this to someone they vowed to protect and cherish? Over dry cleaning? Jesus! Let me meet this man. I would teach him a lesson.

Adam asked a few more questions, but Mary's vitals began to

climb too much, and I cut him off. "That's it for now, Adam. You can come back tomorrow and try again. She is getting upset and needs to rest."

I moved to the cabinet near the bed and unlocked it, removing a sedative and filling a syringe. When I closed it, I turned to find Laney observing me.

I approached the bed, and Laney stepped aside so I could reach Mary. "You did a great job, Mary. You need to rest now. You're safe here. I'm going to give you something to help you calm down and sleep, okay?"

She nodded, closed her eyes, and welcomed the oblivion I administered to her while Adam sighed in frustration.

I pointed to the door, knowing he was angry with me for stopping his questioning. He had a job to do, just like I did. Right now, mine was more important.

When I stepped out, he glared at me, and I snapped, "Look, you might want to pin homicide charges on her husband, but I'd prefer they stay as attempted homicide charges. That means I have to look out for her health. She told you who did it. You know approximately what happened. You can update your criminal complaint at the preliminary once you arrest the guy."

"Does anyone know where he might have gone on his business trip?" Laney asked.

Adam frowned. "You don't think that he stabbed his wife, then packed a travel bag for work and went out of town as if nothing happened, do you?"

Laney shrugged a slim shoulder. "Maybe. He most definitely would if he is as narcissistic as I think he is. He will probably try to blame it on some random home invasion."

Adam thought about that for a minute and nodded. "Hey, do you want to grab a bite to eat tonight? We could talk more about the case. You seem to know a lot about these cases."

Laney shifted back slightly but kept her chin up and her eyes focused on Adam. "Thank you, but I'm sorry. I have other plans."

Adam shrugged. "Okay, well, then another time. I need to get going. I'll walk you out."

"Thank you, Detective Brewer, but I have to visit with another patient in the hospital. Please give me a call if you need anything further with Mary."

I said my goodbyes, and the two of us watched him walk away. Laney turned to me after he was gone and smiled. "I don't really have another patient to visit. I just didn't want him to walk me out."

I barked out a short laugh. "Nice. Well, do you have plans tonight?"

She shook her head.

"I get off around seven. Most of the time, I'm out of here at around seven-fifteen. Do you feel like getting a bite to eat with me?"

Her smile widened. "I'd love that."

"Okay, I could meet you someplace local around seven-thirty. How does that work?"

She nibbled on her bottom lip for a moment, then smiled. "I know just the place if you're in the mood for a home-cooked meal."

I grinned at her. "Who would want to miss that?"

"Great." She pulled out her phone and typed something, then grinned at me as my cellphone notification went off. "There is my address. I'll see you at seven-thirty, Evan."

With that, she spun and walked away, leaving me speechless. She was going to cook me dinner. Come on, seven!

CHAPTER FOUR

LANEY

The day I met Evan, I considered sending him a message at least a half dozen times. I kept telling myself it was to check on Mary, but deep down, I knew it was because the sexy nurse intrigued me.

I had always been the type of girl to go for what I wanted, but recently I had forced myself to hold back and stay in the shadows. Maybe it was time to change again.

Yesterday I managed to get about six hours of sleep before I was roused to deal with another situation. While it was serious, it wasn't anywhere as dire a situation as the night before. However, I didn't get home until almost midnight, and sleeping was difficult as a kaleidoscope of thoughts kept me awake.

My mind shifted from memories of my sister to what Mary went through, to several other victims, to my brother, my father, and then back to my current job. Nurse Evan would appear in my thoughts every once in a while but quickly spiral away with a new one.

After only getting about three hours of solid sleep, I was in my office at the center the next day and promised myself an early night tonight to catch up on my rest. My job was too stressful not to get as much rest as possible. I needed to be wide awake and aware while dealing with the women, children, and men coming into our system.

Joyce popped her head through the door to my tiny office. "Did you get any sleep? I heard you got called out again last night."

"I did, kind of," I told her as she leaned against the doorframe.

"That's good. I spoke to Detective Brewer at county detectives a few minutes ago. He wants to question Mary this afternoon. I heard that she was awake now. Do you think you could go over and meet him there? I don't want Mary to talk to him alone, plus I'd like to learn about anything that she has to say."

"Sure, what time?"

"I don't know yet, but probably around four or five. The detective said he wanted to do it on his way home since the hospital was on his way there. I gave him your number."

"Oh, that's fine. I'll make sure to answer my phone." Not that I didn't typically answer it. There were only a few numbers that I neglected to pick up. One was my brother. The other was his office. There was a third, but I hadn't seen that one in a while.

"Alright, well, I'll let you catch up on mail. Keep me updated on Mary. I'd like to see this case blow up in the media, although I have a feeling that he will find a way to keep it under wraps." She sighed wearily.

"I promise you that when the time comes, I'll be right there shouting it from the top of the building. Let him come for someone who is not afraid of him."

"I hear that, sister." She gave me a slight wave and disappeared out the door to allow me to catch up on what I had missed earlier today.

My job was vastly different from when I lived in California. Mergers, acquisitions, real estate investments, corporate investments, stock options, meetings, and more meetings. A little wine and dine a client here, a little stack the deck with some extra options there, and then rush on to the next client to oversee their money and build portfolios while growing our company.

When I had first started, I had loved it. I had grown up hearing my father tell stories about business and building his empire, and I had stared into his eyes and thought that I would work side by side with him one day. Of course, that never happened, but I did attend college and graduated with degrees in finance and business.

For several years, I thrived on my job. I loved the hustle and bustle, the I'm-gonna-rope-in-the-next-client-and-bring-in-another-million-bucks, or more. I lived for the chase and celebrated the capture.

And then Lindsey died, and everything changed.

For six months, I sat in my office, practically ignoring every phone ring or electronic notification on my phone and computer, and stared out the window of the high-rise over the city.

It all kept moving. The world kept turning. The city kept going. People hustled and bustled, stole and cheated, loved and lived, and my baby sister was buried six feet under in a gorgeous mahogany box with ultra-fine silk lining.

I couldn't work. I didn't want to work, and it irked my brother something fierce. I didn't care. One afternoon, almost six months to the day that Lindsey died, I got a text message from an old college friend, Vincent. Vin apologized for not being there for me but said he'd been out of the country and just got back and heard the news.

In a split-second decision, I asked him if I could come to visit. He didn't even hesitate but told me that he no longer lived in New York City and now worked in a small town in Pennsylvania called Plattsville.

Two days later, I packed two bags, locked up my house, and got a ride to the airport. I hadn't been back since.

My cellphone broke me out of my reminiscing, and I answered it. "Hello?"

"Hi, is this Laney Marshall?"

"Yes, it is."

"Hi, Laney, Detective Brewer here from the country detective's office. Joyce told me that you'd be able to meet with me later at the hospital to interview the victim from last night's assault."

My jaw dropped. "Assault? That was an attempted homicide, Detective."

"You're right." He quickly backpedaled. "Well, an attempted homicide, I mean, if she was close to dying. Otherwise, it's just an aggravated assault."

"*If* she was close to dying?" I was suddenly angry, and I was pretty sure my voice reflected that. "She did *die*, Detective. Twice, in fact. While she was in surgery, she coded not once, but *twice*."

"Oh." He paused. "I wasn't aware of that."

"Well, maybe you should do your homework better."

He sighed. "Look, don't get yourself in a tizzy here. I'm sorry that I didn't know that detail. How about you meet me at the hospital, and you can share everything that you know? Would that make you feel better?"

"My feelings have nothing to do with this, Detective Brewer, but I would be happy to meet you so that I can make sure *you* have the correct information."

He snickered as if he were indulging me. "Very good, then I'll meet you soon."

We decided on a time and a location to meet, and I promptly hung up. I didn't like that man, and I was pretty sure my opinion wouldn't change once I met him face-to-face.

I was correct. My impression did not change when I met Adam Brewer. Truth be told, I liked him even less after he undressed me with his eyes and started the conversation with, "Wow, yeah, I'm pretty sure I have never worked with someone from DV that looked like you."

I internally rolled my eyes because I was used to those kinds of stupid comments from sex-crazed men. I had recognized the lust glaring from his eyes the moment he saw me. Men like him thought that a beautiful woman was better in the bedroom than in the boardroom. I had no trouble showing those men that I could do both—although the boardroom is where I mostly faced off with them.

I was picky about the men I slept with, and before I moved here, I had been with one man for almost three years. We were engaged to be married three months after my sister's funeral. I couldn't even process her death; how could I consider a future with a new husband? Despite him pushing to keep it on that date, the wedding had been called off—indefinitely.

In the last few years, I dated a couple of men but hadn't found anyone who hit the mark on the kind of man I was looking for. I wanted someone down-to-earth who didn't look at me like I was arm candy but knew that I had a brain and wanted to make the world a better place, especially for those who needed help. I wanted a man with whom I could share my hopes and dreams and build a future.

In the past, my only goals had been to take over the next company, or the subsequent merger, the next big sellout. I had no real dreams other than to increase my wealth. But since I had stepped away from the corporate world and the glitz and glamour of million-dollar homes, I had my eyes opened to how the everyday person lived. I liked how they lived, and I found a way to incorporate myself into their world.

I forgot about my one hundred pairs of shoes and my sixty

designer purses. I didn't miss my two-hundred-square-foot closet or my shopping sprees. Okay, maybe I did miss those just a little bit, but I was a woman, and I did enjoy shopping.

Speaking of my shoes, the detective was eyeing me from head to toe again like he was wondering where to start licking first. Gross. It didn't matter if he was handsome; I didn't like the vibe he put off, and I sure wasn't going to entertain his sexual interest.

I might have used that against him at one time in my life, but those days were long gone.

We sat at a corner table in the cafeteria, and I explained the details that I knew from the night before. Ben called 911 after his father fled the house. Then I explained how Ben told the police that he had witnessed his father stabbing his mother and hidden him and his sister under the table. I also said that Ben admitted to having seen his father's abuse many times over the years.

I proceeded to explain that Mary and the children had been clients of the center for several years and had been in emergency housing five times.

"Why do women go back to those shitheads?" he growled. "I don't get it."

I frowned. Had this detective never gone through domestic violence training? I thought that all law enforcement went through such classes these days. How could he not understand the amount of mental abuse some of these women went through?

"I do agree; it is hard to understand sometimes why they return home, but it's from years of conditioning by the abuser, and in this case, he held financial stability over her head, along with taking her children away from her."

"Still doesn't make any sense. These women can't be that dumb."

I smiled at him, even though I wanted to lash out. I hoped that my smile wasn't as condescending as it felt. "Well, it's a good thing you don't have to decide for them. How about we go upstairs and see if we can talk to Mary?" That way, I can get the hell away from you sooner, I thought to myself as I got to my feet.

"Sounds like a plan." He followed me to the elevator, and when we started to step into the car, he had the audacity to put his hand to my lower back. I made sure to shift away from him the moment I was inside and turned so that there was space between us as I took out my phone and pretended to check for something.

I could tell he was watching me from the corner of my eye, but I ignored him. This interview couldn't be over quickly enough, and the only saving grace was seeing Evan standing at the nurses' station as we came around the corner. I smiled brightly at him, immediately thankful that he was here.

I wasn't sure why I felt that way, but I felt safe. Perhaps Evan's presence would keep the detective from making any more rude comments or advances. Not that he had done anything other than touch my back. Well, except leer at me like a wolf about to pounce.

I was surprised to find that Evan's brother was Ethan Winston. I had worked on a case with him a few months ago when I first started here. He was a compassionate man, much nicer than Detective Brewer, and I silently wished that I had gotten him instead.

As I listened to the two men talk, I noticed that Evan did look similar to his brother. They were both very handsome men, and neither had made me feel as if they were undressing me with their eyes. Come to think of it, I'm not sure Evan even looked at any other part of my body but my face since we met.

I appreciated that. I was also thankful when Evan stepped in and said that was enough questions for Mary. She looked tired, and I noticed that her numbers were climbing on the machine behind her.

When Detective Brewer asked me to have dinner with him, I couldn't decline fast enough. The last thing I wanted Evan to think was that I was interested in a man like Adam Brewer. Not that I was overly interested in Evan.

Okay, that was a lie. Evan intrigued me, and I looked forward to having coffee with him on Saturday. So much so that I made sure he knew that I had fibbed to Adam. I was surprised and rather happy to have him ask me to get something to eat with him after his shift.

Now, if he were as tired as I was, he might enjoy a quiet meal where we could talk and get to know one another. I was going to take a chance here and see. As I walked away from him after texting him my address, I felt a sliver of excitement slip through my veins. It had been a while since I was excited to have dinner with someone.

Now I just needed to figure out what to fix. On the way home, I stopped by the store and picked up a few things that I knew for sure I didn't have at home. When I got there, I took a shower, dressed in comfy slacks and a blouse, and went to prepare dinner.

It wasn't anything crazy—baked chicken, roasted vegetables, and pesto pasta. Hopefully, Evan wasn't allergic to tree nuts. That would be horrible to kill the guy with pine nuts in the pesto sauce. After thinking about it, I decided to send him a text and ask.

Do you have any food allergies?

Less than a minute later, he replied, *Nope, I can eat anything.*

Perfect. See you soon.

I was grinning as I set my phone down, and at seven-thirty on the dot the doorbell rang, and I wiped nervous hands down the sides of my slacks as I glanced around my house.

It was a lot more modest than where I came from, but it was still elegant and expensive for this area. I immediately wondered what he would think of it and winced as I realized I probably should have met him someplace public instead.

Too late now.

I smiled at him through the glass door and unlocked it before pulling it open. "Did you have any problems finding it?"

"No, but when I pulled down the driveway, I wondered if I had it correct. Do you live here alone? This is a huge house."

I chuckled. "Yes, I live alone. Remember, no boyfriend, no husband."

"No sugar daddy either?" he asked with a lopsided grin.

I laughed a bit harder. "No, no sugar daddy. I learned to invest well when I was young. Home is my sanctuary."

He nodded. "As it should be." He held up a bottle of wine. "I wasn't sure what we were having, but I'm not sure you can go wrong with a Merlot."

"Nope, you sure can't. Come on in."

I took the wine bottle, and he followed me to the kitchen. After setting it on the granite counter, I removed a wine opener from a drawer and put it beside the bottle. "Would you like to do the honors?"

"Absolutely, and dinner smells delicious."

"It's ready whenever you are."

"I'm ready."

I began to fill our plates and knew that Evan's attention was split between me and my place. I allowed him to indulge his curiosity, and it wasn't until we sat down and started eating that the two of us began to talk.

I knew that our dinner conversation would probably revolve around getting-to-know-you questions, but the first one he asked was a doozy.

"What made you decide to work for domestic violence?"

I finished chewing what I had in my mouth and then wiped

my lips with my napkin before setting my hands beside my plate. "My sister was killed by her husband."

Immediately, Evan reached over the table and laid his hand over mine. I felt the pain and guilt that I held for the last several years begin to fade in one brief second.

CHAPTER FIVE

EVAN

"Seriously? This is where she lives?" I gawked out the window at the two-story house with a beautifully manicured garden and walkway leading up to a tall glass entryway.

I was a little in awe and wondered again if she was married. Maybe she had been married, and she got this in the divorce. Only, I had lived around here for a long time, and I'd never seen her around before. I tried to remember who this house previously belonged to but couldn't. Kayley Young might know, not that it was important right now.

While I tended to know most of the people around, some were in a class all by themselves. They were the wealthy and elite members of our community who used their houses only part of the year. They typically kept to themselves when they were around. Was that why I had never seen her before? Perhaps.

As I stepped into her house, I attempted to keep my awe under wraps, making a joke about her maybe not telling me about a husband, partner, or wealthy older man who was helping her with her house. I was so thankful to hear her say she had learned to invest well.

I hadn't learned to do that until I was older, but I did have a retirement and savings account that had something in it—not a whole lot, but something.

I gazed around her kitchen, realizing it was at least three times the size of mine. It even had double ovens and two sinks. I could visualize my entire family in here cooking Sunday dinner together. What a difference it would be from cooking in my childhood home where you couldn't get more than three people in there without feeling overcrowded.

I would have to bend her ear and learn more about investing. Not tonight, but someday in the future. Apparently, she was good at it, and I hoped she would give me some sound advice.

But before I did that, I needed to get to know Laney better. So as we sat down to eat, I asked a question that I figured would have meaning. I just didn't realize how deep the importance ran.

"My sister was killed by her husband."

She said it with a voice devoid of emotion, but that didn't mean I didn't see the pain in her eyes. I immediately reached out to Laney and covered her hand with mine, squeezing it gently.

Her shoulders shifted as if the weight she had been holding on them was somehow removed by telling me that.

"Laney, I am so sorry to hear that. How long ago did that happen, if you don't mind me asking?"

She shook her head. "No, I don't mind. We are actually about to come upon the third anniversary of her death." She frowned. "I had always thought that anniversaries were for happy events, but I guess in a way, this is a happy event."

"Why is that?" I asked as I squeezed her hand once more and slowly pulled it back.

"She's not hurting anymore. Not being abused."

I closed my eyes and frowned. "Damn, Laney, I'm so sorry. I can't even imagine how difficult that must be. All of my siblings are still alive, and I can't even contemplate how I would feel if one of them died. It was hard enough when my mother passed two years ago from cancer."

"Thank you. I'm sorry to hear about your mother. How many siblings do you have?" I realized that she had changed the subject, but that was alright. I was sure the last thing she wanted to talk about was the death of her sister, especially to a stranger over dinner.

I happily took the question and began to elaborate on my family. "I have five siblings. You said you met Ethan, and then we have four sisters."

She smiled, her eyes brightening back to the way they were before she spoke of her sister. Her irises were so intriguing with the levels of color that I knew I could stare into them for hours and not get bored. "Four sisters? Where are you in the line of them?"

I chuckled. "I'm the baby."

"Well, there were only three in my family, and I was the middle child," she commented and then asked, "So Ethan is a cop, and you are a nurse. What do your other siblings do?"

"My oldest sibling, Cara, was a paramedic and helicopter pilot."

"Was?"

"Yes, she recently moved to Texas and had a baby. Right now, she has a part-time job as a chopper pilot for an oil company that has three helicopters in its service. She wanted to stay home for a while with her son before she went back to work full-time as a paramedic."

"Your family is very civil service-oriented."

I laughed. "Not all of us. Coral owns her own business; Carmen is a child psychiatrist, and Candy is an engineer."

"Wow, and are any of them married?"

I paused, wondering what to say about Cara. I decided to brush over her. "Yeah, Cara is. Ethan is married too. He's married to Riley Young. Not sure if you have met any of them, but our family was really close to theirs when we were growing up. We are still very close to them. Over the last two years, all six of them have fallen in love and gotten married—lucky them. Riley to my brother, and they have a daughter named Corey."

Her eyes had been wide as she listened. "Another family that has six children? That's unheard of from where I come from." She chuckled.

I nodded as I cut another piece of chicken. "Yep, Wesley Young is a pediatric emergency room doctor in Summersville. He's married to Charlotte, and they have a couple of kids. Henley Young is a paramedic. Henley's married to Roxanne, a wedding planner at the country club. They are expecting their first child. Huntley is a firefighter; he's married to an author. Her real name is Daniella. Then there is Kayley, and she is married to Cameron Sexton, and they have a baby boy named Brett. Cameron is a cop, and they also have guardianship over a young lady in college. Kayley works with her older brother, Brad. He owns a construction company, and he's married to a woman named Nolan, who is a teacher. Between them, they have four kids."

Laney sat with her eyes wide and her lips parted. "Okay, wow. You realize that I will probably never remember all of that, but it was fun to hear."

I chuckled. "I promise there won't be a test."

"So, you have lived around here all your life?"

"Born here and will probably die here too." As I said that, I wondered, though. Cara had repeatedly said she would never move away, but look at her now. I put food in my mouth and chewed it as Laney pushed hers around the plate. "I am going to assume that you are not from around here since I have never seen you around town, and I'm pretty sure we are close in age."

She eyed me carefully. "I'm thirty-two."

"Thirty-four."

"No, I am not from around here."

I had a feeling that she didn't want to tell me where she was from, and that was fine—for now. "What brought you here?" I paused and leaned back as a thought occurred to me. "Your sister didn't live around here, did she?"

She shook her head. "No. Lindsey didn't live here. After she died, life kind of lost meaning. My career meant nothing to me, quite honestly, and one day a friend of mine called, and I asked him if I could visit him just to get away from home. He lives in Plattsville, and when I arrived, I fell in love with this area."

She took a sip of her wine, and I hung on her every movement. "I struggled for a while, trying to make sense of it, and then Vincent, my friend, suggested that maybe I volunteer for a domestic violence center. That maybe it would help me understand, so I did. I was a volunteer and quickly began to learn what was needed, and I went back to school, got another degree, and then landed the job as one of the senior support staff at the center there and moved here to Millerstown about six months ago."

"You've been in town for six months, and I haven't run into you. That's surprising." I thought for a moment. "Actually, it's surprising that my sisters didn't talk about a new attractive woman being in town."

She laughed, the sound musical. "Do they do that normally?"

I snickered. "They have been known to."

"Well, I tend to work long hours, and I am a bit of a hermit and haven't met that many people, so I don't have a social life."

"What about the people that you work with?"

"They are either young, like right out of college and going out and drinking all night, or they are older with families. I don't particularly fit into either of those categories."

"Well, how about I take you out one night and introduce you to my sisters and some of the Young siblings. They are all in their thirties, and while some do have families, they still go out and enjoy life. You know what? I think Saturday they are all going to the tavern in town. I know we had plans for coffee in the morning, but what would you say to doubling back on Saturday and doing dinner, too?"

"That's very sweet of you, Evan, but you don't have to. I don't want to monopolize your time."

"Laney, I want to." I paused and wondered if I was wrong to say what I was thinking, but I had never been one to hold back. "I'm gonna be honest here, and maybe this is way too early to say something like this, but the minute I saw you, I felt something. You probably think I'm stupid for even saying that, but I never have been one not to say what was on my mind. So, suppose you're up for the possibility of getting to know me better. In that case, I am one hundred percent interested in allowing you to monopolize every single minute of my time on Saturday."

She cocked her head. "You felt something when we met?"

I nodded. "Yes. Is that weird? Did I just freak you out?"

She shook her head slowly. "No. I did too."

A thrill raced down my spine, but I tried to remain calm. "Then say yes."

She hesitated a few seconds, then lifted her chin as her eyes sparkled. "Okay, then yes. I would very much like to get to know you, Evan, and I would love to have breakfast *and* dinner with you on Saturday."

I wanted to burst from my chair and pump both hands in the air as I shouted hot damn! I didn't, though. That would have been childish, and I already felt stupid for how much I was grinning at her. I forced myself to nod and then forced myself to pick up my fork and knife and continue eating.

After dinner, we refilled our wineglasses, and Laney led me out on the balcony that overlooked a lush garden with a small stream winding through it and a relaxing waterfall focal point near a firepit. "Wow, this is amazing. If I lived here, I think I would want to spend all of my time right here."

We stood at the railing, looking down at the great space. "I know. I spend so much time here, especially now that it's warm. I like to put a fire in the pit and curl up and read a book." She turned to me. "This is another reason I never go anywhere. Why should I when I have this?"

"That is very true. I could get used to an area like this." I eyed her. "I can see you sitting over there reading. What I can't figure out is what types of books you like to read."

She tossed her head back and laughed. The sound was so riveting that I couldn't look away. This woman was incredible.

"Well, I'll have you know that I read quite a lot of different things. I might be reading a spy novel or a self-help book. It could be a book on finance or business, a book about helping victims, or even a juicy romance." She shrugged. "It all depends on my mood."

"Well, I like that you read a variety of things, and now I can picture you sitting there paging through one of Veronica Raven's novels."

She gave me a confused look. "How do you know Veronica Raven's novels?"

I grinned. "I have four sisters, remember?"

"Ah, yes, that's right, you have sisters."

"And—I know her too."

"Who?"

"Veronica Ravens."

She spun toward me. Her eyes burst wide with excitement. "You do not!"

"I do. I know her very well."

"Very well? As in you dated her or something?" Her jaw dropped. "Oh, my god! You dated her! Is she as sexual as she writes?" She threw her hand up. "Wait, don't answer that!"

A bark of laughter exploded from my lips. "Um, no, I did not date her, and I do not have any idea about that last part. My best friend might be able to answer that, though, since he's married to her." I paused. "Her real name is Daniella. She's married to Huntley Young."

"Oh, my god! What a small world! Is she one of the ones that will be out on Saturday night?"

"I'll check with Hunt, but usually she is. Unless she's in her writing cave crunching a deadline."

"I adore her books. I would love to meet her."

"Stick with me, kid, and I'll get you that introduction."

She stared at me for a long silent moment, and all I could think of was how glorious her eyes were and how much I wanted to kiss her beautiful lips. "Is that the only reason I should stick with you?"

I shook my head slowly as my feet shifted a little closer to her. "No, I might be able to come up with a few other reasons."

"Yeah? I think I recall you saying that you thought I was attractive."

I glanced over her head as I recalled our earlier conversation at the table. "I might have said that."

"Well, I think the same of you."

I couldn't help myself. My hand reached out slowly, and I brushed a knuckle over Laney's cheek. "I have never been one to rush anything, but right now, I am trying hard not to lean forward and kiss you."

She lifted her chin a bit closer. "Would it make it easier or harder to resist if I said I was too?"

"Harder, much harder, Laney."

Laney surprised me by leaning forward and pressing her lips to mine, and the mere touch of them sent my heart racing. I curled my hand around her neck and held her face there as the kiss deepened, wondering how this could feel so right, so perfect. I barely knew this woman, and yet, I didn't ever want to stop kissing her.

CHAPTER SIX

LANEY

*E*van's lips on mine caused my body to sigh as it leaned entirely into him. I had never been shy about taking what I wanted, and I had wanted to see if the sexual chemistry that surrounded us would get more substantial or vanish into thin air the moment our mouths met.

Well, it sure as hell didn't vanish.

I clung to him with one arm, wishing I had set my wineglass down, as Evan wrapped his arm around my body, holding me as tightly as I was clinging to him. I was dizzy as the kiss continued, and I was glad that he was holding me up. If he hadn't been, I would have slipped to the ground in a boneless heap.

I wasn't sure how long the kiss lasted, but if it had lasted longer, I wouldn't have complained. Evan stared down at me with those warm brown eyes, looking as blown away as I felt.

"Wow," he breathed toward me.

"Yeah, wow."

His lips lifted in a smile so sexy it made me shiver. "I don't know about you, but I think I might need to sit down or risk my legs falling out from under me."

I giggled, something I hadn't done in so many years. "Let's go sit by the firepit. I'll turn it on and show you my other favorite thing about down there."

Evan laced his fingers with mine. "Sounds like a plan." His thumb brushed over my knuckles and sent a thrill right up my arm. I felt like a teenager with her first crush, all giddy with a smile plastered on my face that I could not hold back.

Downstairs, I set my wineglass on a small teak table and pointed at a cushioned couch nearby. Evan took a seat while I turned on the gas firepit and then collected another remote control and brought it over to where he was seated. I curled up beside him, my legs under me, and he rested his hand on my thigh as if it were the most natural thing to do.

The funny thing was that it seemed like that was precisely what he was supposed to do. It felt comfortable, and it had been a very long time since anything had felt that way.

"What's the remote for?" he asked.

I glanced around, noting that it wasn't quite dark enough to get the full effect. "Just wait. I'll show you in a few minutes."

"Okay," Evan said before he sipped his wine and relaxed back into the seat. I watched him as he scanned the area. "It is beautiful here. I envy you with this area. Did you build this?"

"No, it was here when I bought the house. It was one of the main reasons I bought it."

He grinned widely at me. "And the kitchen was the other, right?"

I laughed. "Well, I think the kitchen was the third. The second was the master bathroom with its heavenly shower."

As the words left my mouth, I could instantly visualize Evan in there with me. I quickly put my wineglass to my mouth to stop myself from nibbling my bottom lip—or inviting him to join me.

"You'll have to show me that sometime."

"I will, but it might have to wait a little while."

"Why is that? You having work done to it or something?"

I shook my head, trying to hold back a smile as my playful side began to emerge. "I'm afraid that if I showed it to you, I wouldn't be able to let you leave until after you tried it out."

His brows jumped, and his thumb that had been making lazy movements on my leg stilled. I watched him swallow. "Would you be trying it with me? Or is that something I would do alone?"

"Oh, I don't think you'd want to be alone," I replied in a low, seductive voice. My god! I was playing with fire here, but I wanted to let him burn me with his flames.

"Ah," he said and looked away, his head moving up and down in a continuous nod for a few seconds. "I'm going to take your word on that."

He stared into the fire for a long moment, then turned to face me. "Where are you from?"

"California," I answered.

"Do you surf?"

I laughed. "No, I most certainly do not. I never was very good with balance. Growing up, I had a lot of friends that did, and I tried it a few times, but I could never stay upright on the board. Now, my sister, she was great. Lindsey had so much grace and balance. She was a ballet dancer for years, and she was a natural on the surfboard."

"Tell me about your sister," he said as he shifted a bit more to the side to see me better.

"Well, she was three years younger than me. Where I had dark hair, she had light. She had similar eyes to mine, not quite as vivid."

"Your eyes are intense," he commented. "I think they are incredible."

"Thank you. Honestly, I think they are my best feature."

His eyes slipped down my face to my body and then flashed back to my face. "If you say so."

I laughed and ignored his comment. "Anyway, she wasn't anywhere as outgoing as I was, or Larry, our brother. She was more of an introvert. She danced and studied and hung out with her close friends, but she wasn't into going out all the time or partying or even dating a lot of people."

"Did she seem happy?"

"She was growing up. She was always happy. Even when she started dating Matt, she was happy. She was in college when she started dating him, and our parents had both passed, so it was just the three of us. When she started seeing Matt, my brother wasn't pleased about it. He didn't think that Matt was the right kind of guy for his sister. He tried to put a huge wall between them and even threatened Matt to break it off with Lindsey. But neither of them were going to listen to my brother. Just to spite Larry, Lindsey eloped with him."

"She did that to spite your brother?"

"Sadly, I think she did. Don't get me wrong, I know she cared about Matt then, but I don't think she ever would have married him if my brother hadn't made it such a big deal."

I finished my glass of wine and noticed that his glass was almost empty too. "Would you like more wine?"

"I'll take a little more. Do you want me to go get the bottle?"

"No, you stay here. I have a few over at the bar down here."

He turned and looked under the balcony where I had a long bar. "Well, look at that."

After grabbing a bottle that I had opened the night before, I returned, filled our glasses, and then took a seat. This time, Evan didn't let me curl my legs under me but pulled them onto his lap.

"Did your sister and brother ever get things ironed out?" Evan asked once I was situated.

"Sadly, no. Lindsey wouldn't even talk to him. She barely spoke to me, but then I was working full-time, and she was traveling with Matt all the time from show to show."

"Show to show?"

"He was a musician, and his band did opening acts for larger bands while they waited for their big break. I heard them once. They were decent." I stared at my wineglass for a minute, eyeing the red liquid. "She got pregnant, and I think that is what started to change the relationship. Matt was a selfish pig. When he realized that he would have to compete with someone, he didn't like that idea. He had already become a lot more controlling. He didn't let Lindsey work, even though she had a degree in marketing. He made her travel with him all the time. She ended up losing the baby, and I remember the night she called to tell me, she was distraught, saying that she blamed Matt. A few days later, when I spoke to her again, she denied saying that."

"Do you think he caused her to lose the baby?"

I shook my head. "I have no idea. In my heart, I think so. Especially now that I know some of what she went through. After that, I barely saw my sister, and her texts and emails were few and far between. The two of us drifted apart." I stared at the fire. "Then one night, about eighteen months later, I received a call from a hospital in Portland, Oregon, and I rushed there. I arrived fifteen minutes after they pronounced her dead, and she had already been taken to the morgue. Matt had beaten her, smashed her skull, broke all the ribs on one side, probably by stomping on her while she was down. She had a lot of internal injuries, but it was the head injury that killed her."

"Ah, damn, Laney, I'm so sorry. Tell me he got arrested."

"He did, and he is serving time, but he only got twenty-eight years, with a chance at parole at eighteen."

"Seriously? The guy should have gotten life."

"I agree." I lifted my gaze to find Evan observing me. "Do you know what my brother said when I told him?" Evan shook his head. "He said, 'I tried to warn her that he was no good. It was her own fault.'"

Evan's jaw locked, and I saw a muscle begin to tick quickly in his jaw as his eyes turned to slits momentarily. "Please tell me you're joking—or he was."

I shook my head. "Nope. I haven't spoken much to him since then."

"Jesus, if that were me, I wouldn't have either. No offense, but your brother sounds like an ass. How could he be so cold and callous?"

"Because he is. That's Larry, and I agree with you. That's the way he has always been. He is all business, and that's it. He has no emotion, and he's not capable of caring for anyone."

"I assume he's single."

"Yes, or at least he was the last time I spoke with him."

"When was that?"

I tilted my head as I thought about it. "I think it's been about two years now since we spoke personally."

His jaw dropped. "You haven't spoken to him in two years?"

"Nope, as you can see, my family dynamics seem to be a little different than yours."

"Yeah, that's for sure."

I realized as I sat there that it hadn't been as hard to talk about it with him as it previously had with other people. Was that because it was Evan I was talking to, or because I had finally come to accept her death?

I guess it didn't particularly matter. I glanced around and noted that it had gotten darker. I retrieved the remote control from the table and grinned at Evan. "You ready to see this?"

"Absolutely," Evan said, and then he reached for my hand and pulled me so that I was closer to him. "And thank you for telling me about your sister. I cannot imagine what you went through. What you do now makes a lot of sense."

"Thank you," I said softly into the space between us. Evan leaned forward and brushed his lips over my brow.

"Now, show me this." He pointed at the remote. "Wait, you aren't going to make it rain or something?"

I laughed. "No rain." I remained upright, sitting beside him with my legs in his lap, and rested my arm along the back of the seat behind him as I turned off the main porch lights.

"You wanted to show me the dark?" he said in a whisper. "Don't tell me you're shy, and this is how you're going to start making out with me."

I giggled. "No, hold on, silly. I forgot what button it was in the dark." Just then, I found the one I wanted and pushed it. Fairy lights began to glow all around us, shifting from soft yellows, pinks, greens, blues, and then back again.

"Oh, wow!" Evan exclaimed. "This is incredible, Laney."

"Isn't it? I couldn't have designed this area any better myself." We grew quiet and listened to the sound of the small water fountain and the babbling stream, along with the sounds of insects in the night. It was perfect, and I stared at Evan's profile. He had a partial smile on his face, and his eyes shifted from one place to another.

He turned to me. "Laney, this really is incredible. If I had this, I don't think I would ever want to leave either. I'd have to change my job so I could stay home all the time."

I lifted my hand so I could touch him and let my fingers drift over the back of his head and his soft brown hair. "I know the feeling."

The two of us watched one another, and then Evan set his wineglass down before taking mine and setting it beside his. When he turned back around, he cupped my cheek. "This place is the perfect background to doing this again."

He didn't let me respond and took my lips with a passion

that I hadn't had in years, if ever. I clung to Evan and slowly lowered myself back on the seat, pulling him with me so that he was lying partially over me as the two of us kissed slowly and allowed our hands to drift over one another.

There was no rush, no urgency. It was as if we both knew we had all the time in the world, and there was no need to go fast. I inhaled his natural musky scent, filling my lungs over and over because I couldn't get enough. I loved the feel of his short beard on my face and neck, and his lips and tongue put me into a daze each time they returned to my mouth.

Several minutes later, his phone began to ring, a song from the Doobie Brothers playing as the ringtone, and Evan pulled back, reaching immediately for his phone. "Sorry, it's my father, and he doesn't normally call me this late."

Evan sat up and helped me into an upright position as he answered his phone. "Pop, are you okay?"

The look of concern vanished, and he chuckled as he shook his head. "Yeah, Pop. Do you want me to fix it tonight?" He listened. "I'm actually not home, so I could do it on my way."

Evan glanced at me. "I'm kind of on a date."

Evan laughed. "No, it's okay. I was about to head home anyway." He paused. "No, I don't mind. I'll see you in a little while."

He said goodbye to his father, and I suddenly missed my father. It had been so long since I had been around a father figure.

"Everything okay?"

"Yeah, he's having trouble with the garbage disposal. Knew I didn't work tomorrow, but if I don't go fix it tonight, he'll spend all night trying, and he's not as agile or strong as he used to be."

"Then you should go."

"Sorry to cut this short," he said as he stood.

I got to my feet and stood in front of him. "I think it was

probably a good idea for us to stop. Otherwise, I might have kept kissing you all night."

He nuzzled my nose with his. "You know I wouldn't have minded kissing you all night, Laney."

"Something to look forward to another night."

"You got yourself a date," he stated huskily, and I hoped that our double date on Saturday turned into a double date with a bonus overnight stay.

CHAPTER SEVEN

EVAN

$\mathcal{I}$t was a good thing that my father called. If he hadn't, I'm not sure I could have made myself leave her arms. Not when kissing her felt like my only purpose in life. At least at that moment.

Even though I felt a connection with her that I'd never had with anyone else previously, I didn't want to rush things. I was pretty sure that we were both on the same track with that too. Yeah, we could have wound up having sex right there under all those tiny, twinkling lights with the babbling of the water as the background noise, but we hadn't. I was both proud of myself and disappointed that it hadn't happened.

As I drove to my father's, I thought about her outdoor living area. It was incredible, and I could see now why she didn't go out very often. Hell, if I had a house like hers, I'd stay home every chance I had. I'd probably invite people over to enjoy it with me, though.

That made me think about how she said she'd been here for six months but didn't particularly know anyone in the area. I was glad that she agreed to go out with me on Saturday night.

Perhaps she could find some friends out of whatever this was between us, if nothing else.

I pulled down my father's driveway and parked. What did I want this to be? I sure hadn't been looking for anything. Wasn't that what people said? Stop looking, and what you are secretly looking for will find you? Is that what the saying was? I guess it had. I mean, Laney was in my patient's room. It wasn't like I had gone out and found her someplace.

I liked the idea of thinking that Laney had found me. Had she been looking for someone? Was she interested in even having someone in her life? I guess that was something that we could discuss on Saturday during one of our two dates.

I was grinning to myself as I climbed the stairs to the front door. As I reached for the screen door handle, the inside door opened. "Evan, I'm sorry for interrupting your date. I feel terrible about that. You could have stopped by tomorrow."

"Dad, it was perfect timing," I told him as I stepped in and squeezed his shoulder. "I needed to get going before things got any more intense."

"Intense? Were you two disagreeing about something?" he asked as he followed me into the kitchen. His shuffling foot-steps sounded louder in my ears than usual. I turned to look at my father as we reached the kitchen counter.

For the first time in a long time, I studied him. He looked tired. Worn down and weary. His eyes were red-rimmed, his skin pale. His gray hair needed more than a trim, and his clothes were a bit of a mess, with a gravy stain on the left side of his shirt.

He was staring at me like he was waiting for a response, and I tried to recall what he had asked. I laughed as I shook my head. "No, we definitely weren't disagreeing."

"Ah," my father said in a husky chuckle and a grin that made him look instantly better. "I didn't know that you were dating someone."

I turned to look at the garbage disposal, which seemed intact. Tools were lying haphazardly over the counter, and I wondered what he had been trying to do.

"I'm not dating anyone, not really," I said somewhat absently as I turned on the water and then flipped the disposal switch. It started right up, and I frowned. "I thought you said that it's not working."

"No, I said that I think something is wrong with it."

I turned it and the water back off. "Why did you think something was wrong with it?"

"Because it's making a funny noise."

"I didn't hear a funny noise just now. Maybe there was something stuck in it, and it broke loose." I studied him. "You weren't putting pistachio shells down here again, were you?"

"No," he growled. "I learned my lesson with those." He turned and walked away from the sink. Again, I noticed his shuffling steps and the way his shoulders seemed to roll further forward than before.

I collected a flashlight from the counter and shined it down the hole, looking around and not seeing anything. I turned the water on again, and then the switch, and watched the blades spin, but there was nothing in their way. I turned everything off.

"Well, whatever was there is gone now."

My father took a seat at the table, and when he spoke, his voice sounded dejected. "I'm sorry for tearing you away from your date for nothing."

"Dad, I told you that it was alright."

"Well, thank you for coming by. You have a good night," he said, lifting his chin and giving me a smile that didn't go anywhere near his eyes.

"Mind if I sit for a while?"

"You don't have to do that, Evan. I know you worked today. You are probably tired. It's after ten."

"I'm off tomorrow, and I can sleep late in the morning. You and I don't get all that much time to talk these days."

He nodded, more of a smile coming to his face. "That is very true. Do you want a beer?"

"Sure." I chuckled. I might have been worried about my dad drinking beer with the medications that he was on for his heart and blood pressure, but I also knew that Dad would take one, maybe two sips of it, and that's it. He liked to hold the bottle in his hands and pretend that he was drinking.

The two of us went into the living room with our beers and took opposing chairs.

"So, tell me about this girl you were on a date with," he said after taking his first sip. His eyes looked brighter now, his shoulders taller as he sat back and waited, and then it hit me. My father was lonely.

My mother had passed almost two years ago. He had seemed to be doing alright, but how much of that was a show for us?

"Well, I met her yesterday. Her name is Laney, and she works for the domestic violence center. She was at the hospital with a client, and that's how I met her. She came back this afternoon with Adam Brewer to interview the woman, and she invited me over to dinner."

"Well, that's very nice."

"Hey, Pop, do you know anyone who lives over on Phillips Street?"

His brows jumped, and he blew out a short breath. "Well, that's an expensive area. I did some work over there a few times, but I can't say that I have any friends that way. Why?"

"Because Laney owns an incredible house over there."

He whistled. "Really? And you said she works for the domestic violence center?"

I nodded.

"Huh, then she has some money in her family."

"How expensive are those homes over there?"

"Well, I don't know, but I remember Kayley talking about a house that went up on the market over there earlier this year, had a fancy garden in the backyard."

"Did it have a water fountain and stream?"

"Yeah, I think that's what she said."

"That's the house that Laney bought. She bought it about six months ago when she took the job here."

"Wow, I remember Kayley going on about how the house was listed at almost two million. She said something about wishing she was the listing agent on that. Five percent commission would have given her almost one hundred thousand."

"Two million?" I echoed, feeling my eyes pop open wide. "That house costs two million?"

My father chuckled. "I guess you didn't know she was that wealthy."

"Yeah, well, I mean, I could tell the house was exceptional and well out of my price range. Her kitchen is over three times the size of mine, and that backyard garden is amazing!"

"Did she mention where she got her money?"

"No." I frowned at my father. "And that's not something I would ask her on a first date."

"Well, that is true. Are you sure that she's not married?"

"She said she's not, and she doesn't have a boyfriend or a sugar daddy." I grinned at him. "I actually asked her that."

My father laughed. "Well, that's good to know. Maybe she inherited the money."

"She said that she invested well."

"Invested, huh." He nodded. "I don't know too many women who do that. Good for her. Are we going to get a chance to meet her?"

"I'm taking her out again on Saturday. We're going to meet for breakfast, and then I thought I would take her to dinner and then meet up with everyone on Saturday night."

A shadow fell over my father's face, but if I hadn't been

looking at him, I wouldn't have seen it. He smiled, but his eyes weren't as bright as they had been. "Well, that's good. She will get to meet your sisters."

"I can bring her by to meet you if you'd like."

He waved a hand. "Don't worry about that. I'm sure if this turns out to be something, I'll eventually get to meet her."

"Yeah, you will," I replied, but in the back of my mind, I was trying to figure out how I could broach the subject to Laney about coming to see my father on Saturday.

Wasn't it a big deal to meet someone's parents? Maybe to other people. In a small town, meeting a parent was kind of a given if you didn't already know them. However, Laney wasn't from here, and I didn't want to push her into something she wasn't comfortable doing. I would have to wait and see how things went on Saturday.

For all I knew, either or both of us would wake up tomorrow and wonder what we were doing. I hoped that Laney didn't, but one never knew.

My father and I chatted about my job and a few things going on with my siblings for a few minutes, and then my father yawned. "Well, it's past my bedtime. I should get on up there."

I glanced at my watch to see it was after eleven. "Hey, Pop, you mind if I crash in my old room? I'm pretty tired myself."

His smile brightened. "By all means. You are welcome to stay in your old room anytime. However, you'll have to throw fresh sheets on there. The old ones will be dusty."

"I can do that," I told him and stood, collecting his beer bottle and taking his and mine to the kitchen. I think he had only had his initial sip tonight, for the bottle was full. I took a long pull off his bottle, wincing at the bitterness of the warm brew, and then poured it down the sink. As I stood there, I wondered if my father had made up the disposal problem just so that he received a visitor. I was going to have to broach this subject with my siblings on Saturday. We needed to make sure that we spent more time with him.

I was glad that I had decided to come tonight, instead of waiting for tomorrow. I made sure all the lights were off, the doors were locked, and then I made my way upstairs. I found my father trying to get a fitted sheet around the double mattress in my childhood room.

"Pop, I got that. Go get some sleep."

"I was just getting it started."

"I appreciate that." I went around to the other side of the bed and helped him get it on. I let him help me with the flat sheet, even though it would have been much quicker if I had done it. He left the room without a word and returned with a blanket from the closet down the hallway. "Your quilt is probably really dusty. I'll have to have the cleaning lady come up here and refresh the bedrooms."

"Probably a good idea," I told him, then before he could leave the room, I stepped around the bed and hugged him. "Night, Pop. I'm glad I stopped by tonight."

My father didn't hug me at first, but then he held on to me tighter than I expected. My eyes filled with moisture as I realized that my father was hurting and feeling alone, and all of us were too busy with our own lives to notice.

He cleared his throat as he stepped back. "Good to have you here too, son. Get some sleep now."

"You too."

As he shuffled out of my room, I watched every step, and once the door was closed, I sank to the edge of my bed and put my face into my hands. When had my father turned into an old man?

I undressed and slipped under the covers after turning off the light. Then I unlocked my phone and realized that I had a text message that I hadn't seen earlier. It was from Laney, and I quickly opened it.

Thank you for a great evening. I'll see you on Saturday at the coffee shop.

Even though it was late, I typed out a reply. *I should be thanking you for a great evening and a wonderful dinner. Thank you. Looking forward to seeing you on Saturday too. Hope you slept well.*

I was setting my phone down when I got a reply.

Not sleeping yet, but thank you. I'll try to sleep well. Did you just get home?

No, I decided to stay at my father's. We've been up talking. Just came to bed.

Aw, that's nice. I bet your father appreciates you being there.

More than you know.

Why is that?

I'll explain on Saturday.

Okay. I hope you do.

I thought about my next words for a moment and then typed another message. *I know we have plans for breakfast and dinner, but what are you doing the rest of Saturday?*

Lol... Now you want to spend the entire day with me?

Damn, if I didn't want to say that I wanted to spend every minute with her from now until eternity, but I wasn't going to do that and risk freaking her out. *Yes, I would like to spend the day with you, but I was hoping you would do something special with me Saturday afternoon.*

I will consider myself booked for the entire day.

Great! And thank you. Now shouldn't you be sleeping?

I was trying, but my mind kept going back to lying under the fairy lights, kissing this man that I had dinner with.

I grinned like an idiot. *Oh, you were, huh? I hope he is a nice guy.*

I think he is.

Were those happy thoughts you were having, or regrets?

Definitely not regrets.

Good to hear.

I'm going to close my eyes again and try to drift off while I dream of this man more and what might come next—night, Evan.

Holy shit! Her statement sent blood straight to my groin. *Night, Laney. Sweet dreams, beautiful.*

You too, sexy.

I closed my eyes and let my phone drop to my chest. Man, that did not stop the blood flow.

CHAPTER EIGHT

LANEY

*A*fter Evan left, I cleaned the kitchen and sent him a message to thank him for coming to dinner. Then I took a shower before I climbed into bed. The entire time, I dwelled over him. I didn't just think about the impromptu make-out session we'd had, but every moment that we had spent together.

I loved how much he seemed to care about people and how he had pushed Adam out of the room and defended Mary's recovery. That alone had won some significant points in my book—especially if I compared him to men I had previously dated.

I also loved that he came from a large family, and they seemed close. While I was looking forward to meeting them, I was also nervous about it. What if Evan introduced me, and I got along great with them, and then nothing became of Evan and me? Would he have a problem if I spent time with his friends and family?

I didn't think he would, but I didn't know him all that well. I hadn't thought that Matt would kill my sister, but he had done that. It was something to ask Evan on Saturday.

As I snuggled on my pillow, I thought about seeing Evan again. Part of me felt like a little girl who was promised a trip to the circus, and the other part of me wondered what I was setting myself up for. Did I want to invite a relationship with Evan?

It had been a long time since I had been involved with anyone—in fact, since I had left Santa Monica, I had avoided any parts of dating—even sex. I knew I needed to speak with Bas about how I left things—one of these days, but not now. That was about as far up on my list as talking to my brother. God knew I wasn't going to do that anytime soon either.

Come to think of it, Larry hadn't called in several weeks. If I remember correctly, he hadn't even left a message the last three times he did call. Was something wrong with him? I would think that if there was, someone from the Board of Directors would have called me, or at least his assistant.

Even though I no longer physically worked there, I was still a member of the board and a company owner. All of my votes currently were held by proxy. All three of us kids received seventeen percent of the company when my parents passed. We had fifty-one percent between us, giving us the majority vote. When Lindsey died, her seventeen percent reverted to the two of us, and now Larry and I both owned twenty-five point five percent of the Buckworth Industries.

Perhaps tomorrow, I would reach out to Maggie, my eyes and ears there, and see what was going on. With that decided, I dismissed all thoughts of California and my brother. Instead, I closed my eyes to reminisce over the kisses I had shared with Evan.

My god, he was a good kisser. I touched my lips, craving the touch of his again. I had never expected what I experienced in his arms. It was something that I had read about in books— fictional books, like the ones written by Veronica Raven. What I felt when he touched me, kissed me, hell, when he even looked at me wasn't normal—was it? Had it just been so long since I had entertained these ideas that I was in some fairy-tale land?

Perhaps it was normal when you found that one person who was your future—your soulmate. Had my sister experienced that at all with Matt? I hated to think that she could have felt anything like I did with Evan for that bastard of a man she had married.

I was dozing off when I heard a notification on my phone. I had always been a light sleeper, and since I was coming off on-call status, I was still in the mindset to respond to any sound on my phone.

It was Evan, and for a few moments, we chatted by text. It filled my heart with joy that he had spent all this time with his father and hadn't dismissed my message. I didn't think he had, but since things were so new, I was leery to trust that he felt any of what I did.

As I rolled over and drifted off to sleep, thoughts of Evan and a future followed me into my dreams.

Friday was a whirlwind at work, and Detective Brewer was busy with a new homicide case, so we didn't revisit Mary. I did, however, call the hospital and found out that she was being moved to a private room tomorrow. Perhaps Evan wouldn't mind stopping over there with me to check on her now that she was out of ICU.

As with each time I thought of him, a shiver of excitement rushed down my spine. I couldn't wait to see him in the morning and spend the day with him. So much so that I almost called him on Friday evening when I got off work and asked what he was doing for dinner.

It was so tempting, but I refrained. Instead, I went home and curled up on the back porch with the latest Veronica Raven book. Would it be weird if I brought the book with me on Saturday night? Would she sign it? I had met many famous people in my years, and I was never overly impressed.

Perhaps the reason I was impressed now was because I had been out of the glitz and glamour spotlight for a while, and here Evan knew the author of the books I loved to read. It was pretty cool, even if she wasn't a major celebrity.

On Saturday morning, I did my yoga, then answered several emails from Maggie in California about company business. I casually asked Maggie how things were out there and if my brother was up to anything interesting. She knew that I hadn't spoken to him in a while.

After finishing up that business, I excitedly prepared for my day with Evan. Today I wore soft linen slacks and a seafoam-green blouse with strappy sandals. I threw two changes of clothes into my bag and a small makeup pouch, just in case I needed to freshen up later before we went out. I had no clue what Evan had planned, so I wanted to be prepared for anything that came up.

I was about to leave my house when there was a knock at my front door. I was surprised to find Evan standing there, grinning at me through the glass.

"Not that I'm not thrilled to see you, but I thought we were meeting at the coffee shop," I stated after opening the door.

He shrugged. "We were, but then I thought about the fact that you promised me the entire day, so I figured it would be smarter to pick you up, then we wouldn't need to worry about your car."

I grinned at him. "Oh, very true. Did you want to have coffee here? I could make us something for breakfast if you'd rather stay in."

He shook his head. "Nope. If I were to step over that threshold, I'm not sure I would want to leave today, and we have a busy day ahead of us."

I snickered. "Understood. Let me grab my things, and I'll be right out."

"I'll wait by the car," he told me as I closed the door and locked it. After collecting my stuff, I let myself out the side door near the garage and found Evan leaning against the front of his Ford Explorer.

He came around to the passenger door and started to pull it open but stopped and stared at me. "Would it be presumptuous to ask for a kiss from you?"

I stepped closer. "Absolutely not. I've been dying to kiss you since I saw you on my doorstep."

Evan put his hands on my hips and stared down at me. "I swear I have done nothing but dream about your beautiful eyes the last two nights."

I giggled. "Just my eyes?"

"No, but you know what I mean." He leaned forward, brushing his lips over mine once, then twice before he tilted his head further and deepened the kiss. My arms were around his neck, and he wrapped his arms around my lower back. After a few moments, he pulled back.

"Even better than I remembered," he said with a crooked smile.

"Yes, I do have to agree."

He winked and stepped back, opening the car door and allowing me to get settled inside before closing it. Evan smiled as he moved to his door and winked after getting behind the wheel. "You ready for a fun-filled day?"

"I am. What do we have planned?"

"A few things, but nothing that has a time frame. I kinda thought we would move casually from one to the other, starting with breakfast."

"I like your idea, even if I don't know precisely what it is."

As we drove to the café, the two of us shared small talk about our previous day, and I told him I'd learned that Mary was doing much better. He was glad to hear that.

When we arrived at the café, I met Evan in front of his SUV, where he immediately laced his fingers with mine. I loved that he wasn't afraid to show that he was interested in me.

As we turned toward the door, he twisted his head to the side to look over a couple of motorcycles. Did he ride? Before I could ask, the entrance to the café opened, and two men wearing worn jeans and black leather vests stepped out with cups in their hands. One looked a little rougher around the edges than the other, and Evan's hand tightened around mine, although he didn't break stride. What made him tense? The fact that they were bikers? Or was it something else?

Bikers didn't scare me. Honestly, very little did. The two men eyed Evan carefully. The better-looking of the two had sandy-blond hair and warm brown eyes. He jerked his chin toward Evan in a slight nod and then eyed me harder than Detective Brewer had the other day. I lifted my chin and stared back at him to let them know that his scrutiny didn't bother me.

He whistled as we stepped past and said gruffly, "Nice catch, Winston. Didn't know you had it in you."

I figured that Evan would ignore them, but he didn't. He replied loudly without turning around, "Thanks, Bollard."

I chuckled as Evan pulled open the door and winked at me as he held it for me. Inside, we stood behind two other people who were waiting to order, and Evan put his hands on my hips, his chest to my back, and I leaned against him.

"Do you have a favorite?" I asked.

He leaned down and whispered in my ear, "I'm beginning to."

A laugh burst from my lips, and a woman behind the counter flipped her gaze to me, then to Evan, and a surprised expression filled her features. Evan laughed softly against my ear, then kissed the side of my head. "Here come the questions. Get ready."

As we stepped up to the counter, the woman gave Evan a shrewd look. "You've been holding out." She turned her face toward me and smiled widely. "Hi, I'm Coral, Evan's sister."

How had I not put those two things together? Evan had mentioned that he knew this place well, and he had told me that his sister, Coral, owned her own business. Well, duh!

"Hi, Coral, I'm Laney Marshall. I love your café!" I held my hand out toward her, and she shook it energetically.

"It's so nice to meet you. I remember seeing you in here a few times. How long have you and my brother been dating?"

"Two days," Evan and I both answered simultaneously.

Coral was wide-eyed as she glanced between us. "And how long have you known one another?"

Evan and I glanced at one another, and we both started laughing as we responded in unison, "Three days."

"Three days? Oh, my gosh! No wonder none of us have heard this news!"

"Yes, and before you get all wild and crazy, I'm bringing her out tonight to meet everyone. You can relax now, and you can grill her later."

She looked affronted. "Grill her later? Why would I do that?"

Evan shook his head. "Yeah, right. Can we please order?"

"Sure." She took our order, and we stepped off to the side so one of her employees could help the next person while she made our coffee and prepared our breakfast sandwiches.

"Hey, have you talked to Pop lately?" Evan asked his sister in a softer voice.

"Um"—she frowned—"I saw him on Sunday, but it's been a hectic week. Why? Is something wrong?"

"I was over there Thursday night. He seemed really down. I ended up staying the night, and it seemed to help his mood. I think we all need to spend more time with him."

She looked puzzled. "Really? I thought he was doing well."

"Yeah, I did too, but I think he's fooling us all."

"Okay, let's talk about it tonight."

She handed over the coffee and then retrieved our sand-wiches. Evan and I found a table in the back corner and settled into our seats. "I'm sorry to hear your father is struggling."

"Thank you. I'm kind of worried about him. I think we all thought he was doing well. You know he called me the other night because he said the garbage disposal wasn't working. When I got there, it was fine. I think he was just lonely. Actu-ally"—he shook his head—"I don't think. I know. I hung out with him for a little while, and then I suggested that I stay the night. He seemed to brighten up quite a bit. Over breakfast the next morning, he seemed more like himself."

My heart ached at what he said. "I'm sorry he's struggling. I know that has got to be hard for you."

"You said your parents are deceased?"

I gave him a sad smile. "Yes. They died in a car accident when I was in college."

"Oh, Laney, I'm sorry."

"Thank you. I miss my father every day. We were very close." I took a bite of my sandwich and chewed as an idea came to mind. "What is your father doing today?"

Evan stared at me for a couple of seconds. "Why?"

"Because maybe whatever you have planned can wait, and we can go hang out with your father for a little while. I'd love to meet him."

Evan blinked a few times as if trying to hold back moisture. He reached his hand over the table and laid it over mine. "This might sound really wrong and completely unwanted, but I think I kind of fell in love with you right then."

I covered his hand with my other one and smiled tenderly at him. "Good, and no, I don't think it is wrong. I think both of us are experiencing strong feelings for one another. I know I've never felt this close to someone after only knowing them for a few days."

"Me either."

"It's good to know neither of us is alone."

"Yes, it is."

"So, what do you say? Do you want to go hang out with your father?"

He grinned at me. "Who says that's not what I had planned all along?"

I threw my head back and laughed. "I bet you did."

"Would that be alright with you? I mean, honestly? Do you mind going to hang out with him? Pop wanted to clean up the flower garden and plant some new things. What do you think about helping him?"

"I think it is a wonderful idea, Evan. I would love that."

As I stared at Evan over the table, I could feel myself falling, and as much as I might have wanted to stop myself—I knew I wouldn't.

CHAPTER NINE

EVAN

*W*as this a dream? Was it possible that I found someone to build a relationship with—a future? Was it crazy to feel all I did for a woman I barely knew? Was it not crazier for her to return those feelings?

For a few seconds, Laney and I stared at one another. I saw what I was feeling shining brightly in her eyes. Not just the feelings, but the fear that this might not be real. Perhaps we were caught up in a lustful fantasy of love.

Well, shit, if that were the case, I was going to take advantage of the fantasy. I was going to jump off the cliff with both feet and say to hell with a safety net.

We resumed eating, and I told her a little more about my father and my mother and how quickly she had passed. "The thing about it was, none of us had known. Mom and Pop found out, and they were going to tell us, but before she could, she was gone. The only person who knew besides my father was Riley, and that was because Riley saw them coming out of the oncologist's office." I paused. "I have to be very thankful for Riley. She gave my mother a lot of happiness in her last days. Something that she sure didn't get from me or my siblings. All of us were so busy living our lives that none of us suspected anything."

"What did Riley do for your mom?"

"Well, my mother knew Riley was pregnant. She was the only one who knew she was pregnant. Ethan didn't even know then. Since it was summertime, Riley was off work because she's a teacher, so she spent time with my parents and cooked and cleaned for them."

"That was very nice of her to do that."

"It was. It meant a lot to all of my siblings, especially Ethan. He was away at the time in a training class. They were going to tell us all when he got home that day, but she passed before he arrived home."

"I'm sorry that you all never got a chance to say goodbye." She wrapped her hands around her cup. "I know what that feels like. Once I went off to college, my mind was on what I was doing for my future and what I wanted to do to have fun. I didn't think much about my parents, other than missing them once in a while—especially my father. Then my brother showed up with the news that they were dead, and it was hard to come to terms with the fact that they wouldn't be there for me anymore."

"It's a brutal thing to realize. I see people die all the time at work. I have consoled countless people who have lost someone they loved. I think it makes you a bit numb to death until it happens directly to you. Then it's a shock to your system, and it's hard to comprehend."

"Yes, I agree. It is hard to comprehend the finality of it."

"Exactly, the finality of it. When people get sick, you're like, they will still be there, but when they die, they are gone. Just poof. Gone. Maybe it would have been easier to deal with if we had known and had the chance to say goodbye."

"Do you think so? I wonder if it would be harder to know

someone was dying and watch them fade before your eyes. Don't you think that would be harder?"

I put my elbows on the table, contemplating my answer. "I'm not sure. Maybe you are right, but I think I would prefer to be able to say goodbye to someone and maybe prepare myself for what was to come."

"Do you honestly think you can prepare yourself for something like that?"

I leaned back and laughed. "No, I guess you can't."

Just then, Coral arrived at the table. "You guys okay? You looked like you were having a very intense discussion."

"Yeah, we're fine. We were talking about life and death," I stated.

Coral's eyes grew wide. "Why would you talk about something like that on a date?"

Laney and I smiled knowingly at each other. "Laney lost her parents when she was in college, and I was talking about when Mom died. We were trying to figure out if it would have been easier if we had known beforehand."

"Oh, my god! Seriously? You guys could talk about a million things, and you are talking about that? Come on, Evan! Didn't we teach you better? That's not how you keep a woman's interest."

Laney put her hand on Coral's arm. "Oh, he has my interest, Coral, and it was an interesting conversation."

"If you say so," she replied as she gave us both an odd look. "Candy wants to know if you are joining us for dinner."

"I think we might have dinner alone, and then we will meet you all at the tavern after." I turned to Laney. "Unless you'd rather have dinner with them."

"Whatever you decide is fine with me."

I winked at her and found Coral grinning down at me. "Okay, but can you do me a favor, Evan?"

"What's that?"

"Can you find a conversation that is a little more chipper?" She shivered dramatically. "You guys have me all freaked out now."

Laney barked out a laugh. "We'll try."

Coral walked away with a smile on her face, and I turned to Laney. "You ready to go?"

"Yep. Where to now?"

I stood and stepped closer, losing myself momentarily in her gorgeous eyes. "You ready to meet my father?"

She rose on tiptoe and almost touched her nose to mine. "The real question is, is your father ready to meet me?"

Laughter erupted from my mouth, then I captured her mouth with a kiss. "My father has no clue what is about to happen to him." With my arm around her shoulders, we threw out our trash, waved to my sister, and headed out to my SUV.

As we reached the vehicle, Laney asked, "On the way in, those two bikers made you tense. Why is that?"

"Because they are bad news."

"Everyone knows that, but it seemed like something else."

I stared at her after she'd gotten in. "Man, you are astute." I closed her door and went around to the driver's side. Once I was in, I turned in my seat to her. "My sister, Cara, got involved with one of the men in the club. They were pretty serious, and it caused some issues in our family."

"Did they break up?"

"No, he died." Did I dare tell her the truth? No. It wasn't my story to tell, and I had no clue if Laney could keep a secret. She didn't know people around here or who she could trust and not trust with the information.

"Oh, was it a motorcycle accident?"

"That's how they met, but he was shot and killed."

She frowned slightly. "Did your sister love him?"

"She did, but we all know it's better that he's dead. Being

involved with him would have hurt her career and put a major strain on our family."

"That is true," she replied as she stared out the front window. "It's sad that we can't always control those we love. Sometimes we love people that are very wrong for us."

There was a story there, but I let the conversation go for now. Laney remained quiet on the way to my father's house, and I knew that if she wanted to tell me something, she would. Before we pulled down the driveway, I asked, "Are you sure you want to do this? We could find something else to do."

She put her hand on my arm. "I want to. I really do. Unless your father is a total ogre, then we can say hello and goodbye."

I barked out a laugh and assured her that he wasn't as I pulled down the driveway.

"So, this is the house you grew up in?"

"Yep, from the day I was born until I was twenty-seven, I called this place home."

She eyed me curiously. "Twenty-seven?"

"Yeah, after college, I came back here for a few years to save up money, pay off school loans, and then buy a house. It didn't make sense to rent a place farther away from work than this was."

"That is smart and financially frugal. Most men wouldn't want to live with their parents."

"I'm not most men."

She gave me a sexy smile. "You are most certainly not."

"Glad you think so." I glanced up when I saw movement toward the house and found my father standing at the front door. He didn't look as disheveled as he had the other night, and I was glad for that. Perhaps I should have called him to warn him of visitors.

"Well, too late now. He knows we are here," I told Laney, and she popped open her door and climbed out to wave at my father. I was kind of amazed at her. She didn't seem the least bit nervous about meeting him, and most women I knew were concerned over what impression they would leave on my father.

Laney didn't seem to care. She began to head straight to the front door, and I had to take a few long strides to catch up to her. "You in a hurry?" I said with a laugh.

"I'm not going to leave the man waiting," she replied as we reached the porch, and my father opened the storm door, a curious expression on his face.

"Pop, I'd like you to meet my friend, Laney Marshall. Laney, this is my father, Richard Winston."

Laney lifted her hand as she approached my father, a huge smile on her face. "Mr. Winston, it is really nice to meet you."

"Call me, Rich, please, Laney, and the pleasure is mine. Why don't you two come on in?" After we stepped inside, Laney immediately began to skim over the furnishings and photographs with avid interest. "To what do I owe this pleasure?"

"Well, I know you wanted to do some gardening, and Laney loves her garden, so I thought the two of us could help you out a bit. Maybe have lunch together."

"Ah, that's kind of you, but I'm sure you two have better things to do."

"Not at all, Rich," Laney said enthusiastically. "I love to work in the garden. It's a beautiful day, and we don't have anything else planned." She stepped toward one wall where we had a lot of photographs hung. "Is this Mrs. Winston?"

My father made a beeline toward her. "Yes, that is my Rebecca. Have you met the rest of the kids?"

Laney looked into my father's face with eager eyes. "I met Coral this morning, and I have met Ethan previously."

"Okay, well, this woman here is Cara. She's the oldest of the brood and lives in Texas with her husband and son, and this is Carmen, and this here is Candy."

"You have a beautiful family, Rich. I wish I had known Evan sooner so I could have met Rebecca and Cara."

"That's very kind of you. Maybe someday you will get a chance to meet Cara." He turned back to me. "You could take her to Texas on vacation."

I laughed. "Maybe sometime." I didn't think that Laney and I were anywhere near a point in our relationship for a vacation, but it was a neat idea.

Of course, if we went there, I'd have to trust her enough to tell her the truth about Cara's husband.

"Pop, let's go take a look at the garden and decide what needs to be done. Then we can head over to the garden center and pick out some plants before we get lunch."

"Let me just grab my jacket," my father said enthusiastically as he started to step away. I noticed that he had a bit more pep in his step, and after he left the room, I approached Laney, who was still looking at the photographs.

I wrapped my arms around her waist, leaning my head against the side of hers. "You are pretty awesome, Laney Marshall."

She turned to look up at me. "You're not so bad yourself, Evan Winston."

"Thanks for doing this."

"I'm thrilled to do it. Seriously, I am. It's going to be a great day."

I leaned forward and captured her lips. The kiss didn't last nearly long enough before my father cleared his throat and asked, "Should I go take a walk around the yard?"

I snickered as I turned to my father. "No, we're coming." My father was grinning as we joined him at the front door.

We walked around the yard for about thirty minutes and checked to see what needed to be done. I jotted some notes of things that we'd need to complete the project, and once we had a plan, the three of us climbed into my SUV and headed to the garden center.

My father kept Laney entertained with tales of our youth, and I remained mostly quiet, peering at Laney once in a while and feeling my heart expand further and further with each beat. This woman was incredible.

Not only was she beautiful, but she was patient and kind. She was loving and supportive. She had a great sense of humor, and she seemed to fit in immediately with me, with my father. Hell, she had even seemed to fit in with Coral this morning.

All of that just made my feelings toward her that much stronger, and by late afternoon, I was practically ready to drop down on one knee and propose to the woman. I knew that was nuts, but that's how much I liked her.

We were both sweaty and dirty when we finished in the garden, and I suggested that I take her home to shower and change, but she surprised me by saying she had a change of clothes in her bag.

"Well, mind if we go by my house so I can shower and change?"

She glanced back to make sure my father wasn't around. "You going to let me join you in the shower?"

Blood raced to my groin, and I fought like hell to control the hard-on that wanted to explode in my pants. I had been watching her all afternoon, staring at the curve of her ass as she bent over, getting sneak peeks of her cleavage when she leaned forward, and I was all for getting this woman undressed and up close.

"I'd love nothing more than to do that, but if we do, I'm not sure either of us is going to be able to put clothes on to go out to dinner and meet up with my siblings."

"Ah, there is that." She pouted, "Alright, fine, but you know how I promised you an all-day date?"

"Yeah?"

"Well, I want you to promise me that this date will continue until tomorrow morning."

I heard what she was saying, but I was afraid to assume her meaning. "Are you asking me to spend the night with you, Laney?"

She stepped closer, winding her arms around my shoulders. "Yes, Evan. I am asking you to spend the night with me. Your house, my house, I don't care, but I don't want this day to end without having you in a bed."

I cupped the back of her head and kissed her passionately, expressing to her everything that I was feeling in that one kiss. When I pulled back, I said huskily, "I promise you the night." In my head, the promise continued, *and the next night, and the next, and as long as you will have me.*

CHAPTER TEN

LANEY

I could not remember when I'd had a better day. Maybe working in the garden was more of a chore for some, but the company that I had made the activity extremely enjoyable.

Rich was an amazing man. He was kind, intelligent, caring, and humorous. I loved how Evan and his father joked with one another one minute and how they could also speak so seriously a few minutes later. It was obvious how much they loved one another, and a few times during the day, I got emotional as I thought about my father.

I couldn't remember when we had done something together as simple as turning up earth in the garden. Come to think of it, I wasn't sure I had ever seen a garden tool in my father's hands. Our gardens were always immaculate, but that was because we had gardeners that worked full-time on them.

My father was all business, and since that was how I grew up, that's how I thought most families were. Of course, watching movies gave me a sense of how people in middle-class families lived. Since living in Pennsylvania, I had seen not only the middle-class but the lower-class families and the real-life struggles that they endured.

If my family had those struggles, they were never discussed in public or even in front of us kids. I grew up thinking that money solved everything because you hired other people to take care of it. So much I had missed out on in life—like digging my hands in the dirt and planting something that would grow.

While most of my garden was designed and planted by a skilled landscaper, I had done some of the work myself, and I found that I loved it. I also found that I could change lightbulbs and fridge filters.

Moving here had done a lot more than calm my stress and give me a purpose. It had allowed me to see what I had been missing all these years.

Now, as I sat beside Evan and we drove to his house, I found myself excited to see where he called home. I had no visions of grandeur. Not after seeing where he came from and what kind of man he was. Material possessions were not important to him.

My brother would dismiss Evan with one look. He would have no time or interest in speaking to him. If the two of them were in the same elevator, my brother wouldn't even give him a thought after a cursory glance. I turned and studied Evan's handsome profile. How arrogant my brother was. How arrogant I once was.

I frowned as I turned and looked out the passenger window. I had been just like my brother. I paid little attention to anyone that couldn't help me pursue my goals. Of course, I wasn't quite as rude as my brother, but I had dismissed enough people in my day to know that I was no saint.

If I had met Evan four years ago, would the two of us have connected like we were now? Or would I have ignored him if he walked into a room? If someone I loved was in the hospital bed that Mary had been in, would I have noticed Evan then?

My frown deepened because I wasn't sure what the answer

to that question was. The only person I could envision lying in a hospital bed that I would even care to visit would have been Lindsey. If that had been Lindsey, would I have noticed Evan?

Quite honestly, I don't think that I would have back then. Yes, I would have noticed a male nurse, and I would have been polite and respectful, perhaps a bit demanding to know what he was doing and why, but I wouldn't have looked too deeply into his eyes.

I wouldn't have for one moment entertained any thoughts of him. Why? Because I was a powerful corporate woman who busted her ass to close the next deal and add another digit to her bank account? Or was it because he worked in the medical industry where the only ones that got rich were the board members, insurance companies, and a few select doctors that excelled in their fields?

His yearly salary was probably what I made on a single bad deal.

I hung my head slightly for the woman I used to be. I was ashamed of myself for even thinking these thoughts. It's not like I felt that way anymore. I was pretty sure that Evan made more than my meager salary at the domestic violence center—not that I was doing that for the money. I wasn't.

I had told them I would work for free, but they refused to allow me to do that. So, in turn, I made an anonymous monthly donation back to the center for slightly over the amount of my salary.

They didn't need to know I was doing that. No one did. I peered toward Evan momentarily. If he asked, would I tell him? Would I tell him just how wealthy I was if he asked? Would that matter to him? I didn't think it would, but something held me back from saying anything.

Evan glanced at me. "You're quiet. Are you changing your mind about this evening?"

I reached for his arm, squeezing his forearm tightly. "Not at all. I was merely lost in thought."

"I have a few pennies here. Can I buy one of those thoughts?" He gave me a very sexy lopsided smirk to which I chuckled.

"Just one?"

He shrugged a shoulder. "For now. I mean, I don't want to be pushy or make you think that you have to tell me everything about yourself right off the bat."

"Oh, so you don't want to know all about me?" I teased.

He gave me an intense look. "I want to know every single thing about you, Laney, but I'm not in a rush to learn it all. We have time."

I nodded. "I like that answer."

He reached for something on the other side of his steering wheel and then shifted the item to his other hand before holding it out to me. I put my hand out, and he dropped a penny into my palm.

"I guess the main gist of my thoughts was about the stark difference between your family and mine."

He turned on his blinker and glanced toward me quickly. "Yeah, what difference is that?"

"Well, your family seems so down-to-earth. There was always tension in mine." I paused and then tested the waters on a touchy subject. "My family was very well off, so doing things like gardening and cleaning, even cooking, was done by staff."

His brow jumped slightly. "Staff, huh?" He laughed. "So what you are saying is you grew up as a rich kid."

Oh, that was putting it mildly. "Yes, you could say that."

"How rich? Like your family paid other people to come in and do stuff for you, or wealthy as in they lived in your house?"

Damn, okay. Tread carefully on this and feel Evan out. Maybe it wouldn't be a big deal. "They lived in our house."

He turned onto a side street. "Wow, okay. Did you go to private schools?"

"I went to a boarding school."

He laughed, grinning my way. "Yeah, and how was that?"

The tension eased from my shoulders. "It was okay. I was a bit lonely sometimes, but in all honesty, the people I went to school with were my family."

"Did your brother and sister go to the same school?"

"Larry went to a different school. Lindsey was at my school for a few years but transferred someplace else. She said living under her perfect sister was annoying."

Evan pulled into a driveway, and I skimmed over the beige split-level home with the burgundy shutters. "Perfect sister, huh?"

"I can't help it that I did well in school and that the teachers liked me."

Evan turned off the SUV and took my hand. "Well, I like you."

"That's all that matters," I replied as I studied his handsome face. I ran my hand down his bearded jaw. "I have never been into beards, but you do wear it well, Evan Winston."

Evan peeled my hand away from his cheek and kissed my palm. "I'm glad you like it. I'd hate to shave it."

"You'd shave it if I said I didn't like it?" I asked, slightly surprised.

He shrugged. "Yes. It's just facial hair. I've been growing it on and off since I was twenty."

"Well, don't grab that razor just yet," I told him with a chuckle.

Once we were out of the vehicle, Evan waited for me to collect my bag from the back seat, unlocked his front door, and allowed me to enter. I was surprised right off the bat by how open it was. I had recently been to a split-level home for work, and when I stepped in, it felt crowded and dark.

"Wow, this is really nice."

"Well, don't get too excited. I don't have a maid or a cook hiding anyplace, but it should be pretty clean."

I played it out with a laugh. "No, I mean the floor plan. I was at a house very similar to this a few weeks ago, and it looked very different."

He held his hand up for me to proceed him up the stairs. "That's because I had a remodel a few months ago. They took out the wall blocking the stairs and added the safety wires. Now you can see through it up into the living room. Plus, I had this wall removed in my kitchen, and they installed this island. It makes the area look very different."

"I'm sure it does. I love it." I ran my hand over the counter. "This is beautiful granite."

"I wanted something a little darker, but Kayley talked me out of that."

"Kayley?" I asked, wondering if that was a girlfriend who had helped him.

"Kayley Young. She works with her brother at his construction company. While he does most of the construction, she does some, but she likes to work on interior design and the overall aesthetics. I have to agree with her. I think this looks great. Darker might have been too much of a statement."

"Do you like to cook?"

"I love it."

"Will you cook for me?"

"Tonight?" he asked, glancing at his kitchen. "I mean, yeah, if you want, but I'm not sure what I have in here."

"Not tonight, another time."

Evan set his keys and phone on the counter and approached me. "I hope that I get the opportunity to cook for you many times."

I wrapped my arms around his shoulders as his hands slipped over my hips to my back. "I like the sound of that."

"Do you?" Evan asked seriously.

"I do. I know this seems weird, and you might not think the same thing, but this between us feels good. Almost too good, and I want to figure out what it is."

"It feels perfect, Laney, and that's what I want too. I told you this morning I had already started to fall for you. Well, after watching you all afternoon with my father, I've fallen deeper. It scares the shit out of me because I have no clue if you feel the same, and I have never felt this way about someone before."

"Have you been in love before?"

"Yes, but it didn't feel anything like this. This just feels right, comfortable, like it's the start of a future that is building itself, and not something that I have to work to build."

Was it possible for us both to feel the same way so quickly? "I agree, and just so you know, I feel the same way about you. Today has been absolutely amazing, but it's not just because it's new and fresh. It's because it feels different. It's almost like you have been in my life for years, and not days."

Evan cupped both my cheeks, staring into my eyes as he spoke in a husky voice that sent a thrill down my spine. "Let's make it last for years, Laney."

Could we do that? Could this be the future that I never knew I wanted? I had to believe that it was. "Let's make it last, Evan. I want that. I want that with you."

Evan kissed me tenderly and then stepped back. "Okay, now that we have that decided, let me show you to the guest bathroom so you can clean up."

"You sure you don't want to detour to your room for a little while?"

He shook his head and stepped back quickly. "No, because once I get you undressed in my arms, I'm not going to let you out of them for hours."

"Hours, huh?" I asked sassily as I approached him, and he quickly walked backward.

"Yep, hours. Might keep you there all night."

"You better keep me there all night."

"What are you going to do if I don't?" he asked as he stopped beside a door.

"Give you a reason to stay," I replied immediately.

"Trust me, woman. I want nothing more than to be beside you all night. Here is the bathroom. Clean towels are hanging up, and there is soap in the shower if you want to take one or rinse off."

I peered into the bathroom. One sink, toilet, regular bathtub with shower. Nothing fancy, but it didn't need to be. "Perfect. You sure you don't want to join me?" I asked with a perked brow.

"Nope. I'll take you up on that later. Right now, I'm going to go take a cold shower and get cleaned up so that I can take you out to dinner before we meet everyone for drinks."

"Cold shower, huh? You like cold showers?" I asked as I crossed my arms over my chest.

"Nope, hate them, but after being around you all day, I need to cool my blood." He winked and then spun and took off down to the end of the hallway, where he disappeared behind a door without a look back.

I chuckled as I stepped into the bathroom. I would let Evan off for now, but tonight, he was all mine—all night long.

CHAPTER ELEVEN

EVAN

I couldn't get away from her fast enough. Not because I didn't want to be with her. Far from it! I had been a fraction of a second away from crushing her to me. My instincts told me to take her as fast and furiously as I could. I didn't want our first time to be like that, though. I wanted to take my time and treasure every single moment of learning her body.

As I climbed into the shower, I wondered if maybe we shouldn't go out. Perhaps we should stay in, and I could find something to cook Laney for dinner. Then we would be alone, and we could enjoy each other.

I huffed. If we did that, my sisters would be all over me. By now, the news had gotten around that I was bringing someone tonight, and everyone would want to meet her. Even if I told them something came up, and we couldn't make it, they would show up at my doorstep, relentlessly grilling me about Laney.

The only way to handle this was to go to dinner, meet with everyone, and leave as soon as possible. I finished my shower, brushed my teeth, then pulled out a pair of olive green cargo pants and a cream polo.

I stepped into the kitchen and found Laney already there,

looking at something on the fridge. She had changed out of her slacks and into a peach blouse and flowy muted earth-toned skirt. The material stopped in the middle of her calf, and she wore the same sandals as earlier today.

"You cleaned up fast," I said as I approached from behind her and slipped my hands around her waist as I filled my nose with a fresh, light scent of perfume. "Hmm, you smell good enough to eat."

She giggled and pressed her back against me. "Oh, yeah? Does this mean that you changed your mind about going out?"

I brushed my lips over her neck and took a big step back. "No, and we should leave now before I get tempted to do just that."

She turned slowly, and my eyes dropped, immediately noting that her blouse was unbuttoned way more than it should be. Her flesh-colored bra was visible, as was the swell of her gorgeous breasts. I sucked in a quick breath. "You are a vixen. Are you trying to get out of meeting my sisters?"

The sexy laugh that left her mouth caused my balls to throb. "Oh, no. I totally want to meet them." She undid another button. "But I keep thinking about how we will be sitting there—close to one another—wondering when we can leave without offending anyone. We wouldn't enjoy ourselves—not really—because we'd be so focused on what would happen later." Her fingers drifted lower, and she undid the next button.

"Maybe." I croaked the word.

She shook her head slowly. Her incredible eyes shone brightly and were filled with desire. I couldn't fight it. I didn't want to fight it—not anymore.

Before I could say anything, she undid the last button and began to speak again. "So, I think we should have sex before we go. Then we can get that initial excitement out of the way and enjoy the evening."

"What about dinner?" I asked, clutching at straws.

"I can think of better things to eat," she said, and goddamn if my dick didn't try to bust out of my pants. "The tavern has food. We can always get something to eat when we meet with everyone."

She pulled her blouse apart, giving me a full view of her incredible torso. My knees began to shake with the energy it took to hold myself back. She let her shirt fall to the floor and then hooked her thumbs into the waistband of her skirt.

Oh Christ. If Laney removed that garment, I was a goner. I swallowed, unable to speak.

"What do you think of my plan, Evan?" She began to shimmy her hips as she slipped her skirt down. "You interested in skipping dinner and having a little snack now?"

The second her skirt was past her hips, she let it go, and it slithered to the ground, leaving her there in a flesh-colored bra and panties that left little to the imagination.

What the fuck was I waiting for? I asked myself that question as my eyes drifted up her legs, over her panties to her stomach. Laney stepped forward, and my eyes landed on her chest. She reached forward and took one of my hands, uncurling my fist and then placing it on her breast. A groan left my throat, and a moment later, I had my arm locked around her waist as I took her mouth in a demanding kiss—my fight had evaporated.

If she wanted to play this game, I was going to play—and play hard. She clung to me, whimpering into my mouth as she kissed me back with the same enthusiasm that I gave her. I yanked the cup of her bra down, filling my hand with her warm weighted flesh and rolling her nipple between a finger and thumb as she pressed harder into me.

My palm drifted down her back and found she was wearing a thong. I greedily cupped one of her bare ass cheeks and pulled her tighter to me. After a moment, I shifted to pick her up and carried her to the dining room table. I removed the placemats and a few pieces of mail lying there in a quick swipe, and I set her down.

I took her head gently between my hands and stared into her face. Her eyes were lit with a fire that I could never have imagined looking back at me. I kissed her more slowly, twirling our tongues together as if we had all the time in the world. Then I shifted my mouth to skim along her cheek, down her jaw and neck, to her shoulder. I ran kisses along her shoulder as she tugged at my shirt.

I stopped only long enough to yank it over my head and throw it off to the side. As I went back to lavishing kisses on her, her hands worked deftly at the buckle to my pants.

I peeled the straps of her bra off her shoulders and let them drift down her arms as I exposed her other breast, taking them both in my hands and kneading them. Laney looked up at me as I began to push her back to the table, and I was able to lower myself so that I could now suck one of her nipples into my mouth.

The light perfume that she wore filled my lungs and made my cock harder than it had ever been. One of my hands slipped lower to her hip, and I tugged at the thin strap of her thong. She lifted her hips, allowing me to remove them, and I tossed them behind me. I stood, staring down at the most beautiful woman I had ever seen.

She lay there on the wooden surface of my dining room table as if she were a piece of fucking art—exquisite, unique, fucking incredible. I could stare at her forever and never get bored.

I finished undoing my belt and the button and zipper to my pants, then shifted my boxers slightly to allow the head of my cock to peek out as if it needed to see what all the excitement was about. Then I pushed out a chair and sat down. It was time for a feast.

I pulled her to the edge of the table and spread her legs,

groaning at the glistening flesh before me. I ran two fingers down her center, inserting one into her, before pulling it out and doing it again. Her muscles contracted around me, and after the fourth time, I removed my finger and sucked it into my mouth. "Jesus, you taste incredible."

She wiggled on the table, her hand sliding over her belly as if she were going to touch herself. "Oh, no, you don't," I said, stopping her hand just before she touched her clit.

I leaned forward and flicked my tongue over the hard knot, and her entire body jerked as she moaned. "You liked that, huh?" I did it again to prove the point and got the same response.

For a few moments, I enjoyed devouring her flesh. I loved the sounds that she made, the smell that surrounded me, the taste of her body. I felt her climb and worked harder and faster to get her to that prized spot. Her gasps and moans were heavenly to my ears as she hit it.

I continued to lick her until she squirmed and pleaded with me to stop. I wiped my mouth and sat back with a satisfied smirk on my face. I pushed my boxers lower as I stared at her beautiful flesh and grabbed my rock-hard cock. Slowly I stroked myself up and down, and Laney propped herself up on the table, a look of bliss on her face. She watched me jack myself for a few seconds, then licked her lips, pulling her bottom lip under her teeth as she climbed off the table.

She glanced back at the table and then pushed it back slightly so that she could drop to her knees. If I lived to be a hundred, I would never forget the moment she took me in her mouth and locked eyes with me. Those eyes. Those fucking gorgeous eyes.

After a few minutes of her sucking me, I was ready to explode. Her mouth was perfect, her lips incredible, but her tongue. Fuck me! Her tongue was a fucking lethal weapon. I gently pushed her shoulder, but she refused to budge, looking me straight in the eye like she dared me to stop her. Well, fuck if

I was going to tell the woman no if that's what she wanted to do.

I kept my eyes locked on hers until I couldn't control it anymore, and I came with a jolt that almost knocked my socks off. I panted as if I'd just finished running a mile, and my body tingled from head to toe. Laney sat back on her heels, a sassy smile on her lips as she pulled her bottom one under her teeth.

"Now, aren't you glad that we took the time to do that?"

I laughed and sat up, reaching for her. She lifted on her knees and allowed me to kiss her for a few seconds. My hands drifted lightly over her sides and back while her fingers skimmed my chest. When I shifted back, I smiled at her. "Yeah, I'm glad we took the time, but we are far from done."

"Yes, I am aware of that," she said and stood. "That was just the appetizer. We will get to the main meal later. At least we know that it's going to be good."

She grabbed her panties and stepped back into them before she readjusted her bra.

"Good? Jesus, we might kill each other later," I said with a harsh laugh.

She laughed playfully. "We might just do that."

"What a way to die, though," I joked as I stood and fixed my clothing. Laney finished getting dressed and came back to me.

"Now, I'm starving. Think we have time to eat dinner before we meet everyone?"

I glanced at my watch. We were supposed to meet them in just under an hour, but they could wait. "Let's go eat. I'll send Coral a message that we will be a little late."

Laney and I were about to leave my house when she turned and looked at me. "Do you want to stay at my house tonight?"

"If you'd like me to."

"Do you want to bring a change of clothes, maybe a toothbrush?"

I chuckled. "You want me to bring a toothbrush? Will I be able to leave it there?"

She tilted her head to the side as if she were considering that. "I think you should leave it there."

"Alright, give me a minute to throw a change of clothes into a bag." I took the steps back up to the main floor and went back to my bedroom. Damn, I had dated women for months before they even wanted me to stay the night, much less have a toothbrush at their place.

When I came down the steps, Laney was gone. I was about to peer out the window to look out front when I noticed the light on downstairs. "Laney, you down there?"

"I am," she called. I dropped my bag on the floor and went to find her. She was standing in the middle of what would eventually be my family room.

She grinned my way. "Quite a bit different than the upstairs."

"By that, do you mean dark, dingy, and scary?"

She laughed. "Yeah, that's what I meant."

"I had the upstairs done a few months ago. I need to pay back that loan before doing the overhaul down here."

"What are you going to do with the space?"

"I'm going to brighten it up with a lighter color, make this area the family room with a large television and comfortable seating for watching the games or movies. Then on this side, I will put up a wall and close off my workout area. Put in a new floor throughout the area, make that back room a guest room, and update the bathroom."

She nodded. "Sounds like it will be nice."

"I hope so."

She turned and took my hands. "I hope I get to see it."

"I do too." I kissed her slowly and then pulled away and tugged her hand. "Come on, I need food."

The two of us went to a small Italian café and enjoyed large bowls of pasta and sauce while we chatted about houses and projects. I wasn't blind to the fact that my projects were thousands of dollars, and hers were in tens of thousands of dollars. Laney said she had grown up wealthy, and for the first time since I'd seen her house, I began to wonder just how rich she was.

Not that it mattered. I didn't want or need her money. I lived a good life with what I had, and while everyone would like to make a bit more money, I was happy with what I had and where I was in life. It made me wonder what Laney thought about me in regard to that.

I wasn't going to let it bother me, though, at least not tonight. Tonight, I wanted to see how my family reacted to her. She had bowled over my father, and I hoped that the rest of my siblings felt the same.

Despite that she came from a wealthy family in the past, I felt like Laney Marshall was my future. A future that was going to take me places I never expected to go.

CHAPTER TWELVE

LANEY

I didn't know how long it had been since Evan had been with someone, but since it had been three years for me, I was dying to break the ice and get things started. I figured that if things weren't all that great, after dinner and meeting his sisters, I could make an excuse and have him take me home.

Well, no way was that going to happen. Holy smokes! The man knocked it out of the park with one orgasm! My knees were weak when he finished with me, but they didn't have to hold my entire body up to help him reach the same incredible place I had just visited.

Before we left, I invited him back to my place tonight, and yeah, I even wanted him to bring a toothbrush. Perhaps that was jumping the gun—big-time, but I felt something for Evan that I hadn't ever felt before, and I didn't want to waste one minute with him.

If anyone knew how short life could be, it was the two of us, with me losing my parents and my sister, and Evan being a nurse in ICU. I could not imagine the amount of trauma and death that Evan saw daily. How he dealt with that and still appeared happy and sane was beyond me.

With my job, there were many days that I went home depressed or frustrated because I couldn't reach a client or because they went back to the abuser after hearing, *I'm sorry. I love you. I'll change.*

The abusers never did.

That had been a very tough lesson to learn. In the past, if I had warned a client about a potential hazard, ninety percent of the time, they listened to me. Those clients were at risk of losing millions, but my clients now were at risk of losing their lives. Did they think so little of themselves not to feel worthy?

Or perhaps it was because they were blinded by love. Could that possibly be it?

I had been so disheartened with some of the things I had seen that I had almost given it all up. The thought of running back to Santa Monica and the safety of my ivory tower had come to me several times.

I didn't give up on things when they got hard, though. That wasn't how I was raised, and I wasn't going to turn into that type of person now.

As I waited for Evan, I wandered down to the lower floor of his house and stood there. This was more of what I had expected when I first saw his home. This dark area was similar to what I had seen recently with clients.

I was glad that Evan didn't seem upset that I was showing myself around, and I liked what he said he would do to the space. Although I wondered how big of a TV he could fit on the far wall. It didn't seem all that large. I didn't think my seventy-two inch would work there, and if it did, it would be a tight fit.

We finally got on the way to dinner, and if I had been even the slightest bit concerned that things would be uncomfortable between us after what we had shared in his dining room, I quickly found I had nothing to worry about. Evan and I fell right back into the banter of life and jobs.

Our Italian dinner was better than I had expected. Months ago, when I had first seen the small worn sign hanging at an odd angle, I had wrinkled my nose and knew that I'd probably never step foot in the place. Not because I didn't like Italian, but because the sign was so ugly and uncared for, I assumed the atmosphere and food would be the same.

I was happily proven wrong—on both accounts. The interior was authentic, clean, warm, and the food was delicious. It was utterly fantastic, from the fresh-baked bread to the tiramisu that we shared at the end. I was kind of glad that I hadn't experienced this place yet, because if I had, I would have gained about twenty pounds eating it every day. Evan might have ignored me the day he first met me—not that I thought he was shallow like that. I just knew how important first impressions were.

When we arrived at the tavern, Evan removed his keys from the ignition and stared at the place for a long moment. I looked between him and the front of the building.

"You okay?"

He nodded. "Yeah, I was just wondering something."

"Yes, what's that?"

"Would you be offended if I introduce you as my girlfriend?"

A smile burst over my lips, and I reached for his hand. "No, I would not be offended."

"I didn't want to rush anything if you thought I was."

I shook my head. "Evan, I don't think we are rushing anything." I stared at the shadows over his face for a moment, wishing I could see his warm brown eyes. "It feels like we have known each other for a very long time, and I like you much more than I should for only knowing you a few days. I'm not going to look a gift horse in the mouth, and I hope you don't either. I honestly didn't think that I would ever find anything that felt like this. I don't want to lose it. I want to embrace it and take the wild and crazy journey that it takes us on."

Evan released my hand, unbuckled his seat belt, and practically lunged over the console to slip his hand behind my neck and bring my mouth to his. The kiss was passionate and wild, just like I had suggested.

When he had gotten his fill, he leaned back and cupped my cheek, running his thumb over my bottom lip. "I'm so glad that you are thinking this way. I'm right there with you, Laney. It's crazy, I know it, but I also feel like I have known you for a long time. I've never felt this way about someone, even after months with them."

"Then introduce me as your girlfriend and let me be that. Let's take this and run with it. Let's make love, fall in love, build love and a future, Evan."

He seemed surprised and relieved to hear my words. When he spoke, his voice was husky. "How did I get so lucky to find you?"

"Destiny," I breathed toward him before I leaned forward and kissed him again.

A minute later, Evan sighed after we ended the kiss. "Alright, let's go inside and see everyone. I'm regretting this."

"Why? You don't want me to meet everyone?"

"No, I'd rather have kept you naked," he said seriously.

I patted his cheek. "Don't worry, baby. You'll have me naked and all to yourself all night long and for as long as you want me."

He grabbed my hand and kissed my palm. "Promise?"

"Yes, I promise."

He winked, and the two of us got out of the car and walked toward the tavern door, arm in arm. Yes, this was crazy, but life was crazy. I wasn't going to waste a minute of it. I felt freer than I ever had in my life, and I wanted to embrace the feeling.

Inside, Evan looked around and led me through the crowd

toward the back. On the way, I glanced at the bar. Behind it was one of the bikers we'd seen outside the café this morning. He was watching me, and I smiled at him to let him know I remembered who he was. Was he Bollard, or was that the other one who had been with him?

A minute later, I was pulled further into the crowd and lost sight of the bar. Evan pulled me around to his side and put his arm over my shoulders as he came to a stop. Every eye in the group landed on us as the conversation halted in mid-sentence. If I wasn't as confident as I was, I would have shied away from the avid interest on their faces as they surveyed me closely.

"Everyone, this is my girlfriend, Laney Marshall. We met at the hospital. She works for domestic violence, and one of her clients was a patient of mine in the ICU. And yes, we have only known each other for three days, and this is only our second date—even though it has lasted all day." He grinned around the table as I chuckled, along with a few others. "I do believe that answers all the questions that you all wanted to spring on us."

Coral stepped forward, and I thought she would shake my hand again, but she pulled me into a hug. "I hope you two found other things to talk about," she said as she leaned back.

Suddenly a camera flashed, and I blinked at another woman. "Hi, I'm Candy. I had to take a picture to send to Cara. She didn't believe that Evan was actually bringing someone to meet us."

Evan shook his head. "Why is this so hard to believe?"

Everyone around the table started laughing, and then Ethan stepped forward, and we shook hands. "It's good to see you again, Laney."

"Great to see you, too, Ethan."

He pointed across the table. "That's Riley, my wife. You might have heard about the Young family."

I nodded enthusiastically. "Oh, yes. I got the rundown on both your families."

"Oh, good! That will save time, and we don't have to explain so much."

"Hi, I'm Carmen." Another blonde pushed Ethan out of the way. "It's great to meet you. I do some pro bono work for the domestic violence center when they need kids evaluated."

"Are you an attorney?"

"No, I'm a child psychiatrist."

"Oh, wait! Someone was just talking about a Carmen at the office. I bet they were talking about you."

"Probably since I got a referral this week."

"Well, it's great to meet you, Carmen." Carmen pulled me away from Evan and brought me to the far end of the table, where several other couples were seated. "This is Henley and his wife, Roxanne, and this is Huntley and Daniella."

I smiled at everyone but zeroed in on Daniella. "I hear you are an author."

Daniella's head snapped toward Evan. "Really, Evan? You're not supposed to tell anyone!"

He shrugged but was smiling. "I thought that was only for strangers, not girlfriends or people we loved."

People we loved. Those words settled over my heart as Evan and I stared at one another over the table. Yes, I could love that man. Maybe part of me already did.

Daniella laughed, shaking her head, and I tore my attention off Evan and put it back on Daniella. "Yes, I am, but I would appreciate it if you wouldn't announce it. I've had my share of stalkers."

"Yeah, please, let's not go through that again," Huntley said as he put his arm around her shoulders. "Hi, I'm Huntley Young."

"You're a firefighter, correct?"

He nodded, and I turned to Henley. "And you are a paramedic, right?"

"I am."

"And Roxanne, you are a wedding planner."

Roxanne smiled brightly. "Wow, Evan really did give you the rundown on us, huh?" We all laughed.

Henley asked, "Did he quiz you about us, too?"

"No, I'm pretty good with remembering what I hear." I glanced around the table. "There are a few of you missing, aren't there?"

"Oh, yeah, my brother, Bradley, and his wife Nolan are with Kayley and Cam. They went out to dinner but will be here soon. The only other ones we are missing are Wesley and Charlotte, but they live over in Summersville, and Wes is working tonight."

"Plus Cara," Roxanne added. "She's not here."

Henley and Huntley glanced over their shoulders, and then Henley knocked Roxanne's arm with his elbow. "What! It's not like *she* died! She's alive. We can't pretend that she's not. I don't know why you guys get so uptight when her name is mentioned."

I was confused, but I didn't think it was a good time to ask any questions—especially when Ethan approached, gave them all a stern look, and told them to hush.

Roxanne looked contrite for a moment but shook it off quickly and said with a bright smile and evident joy in her voice, "So, when you and Evan tie the knot, you'll let me plan your wedding, right?"

"Hey!" Evan yelled from the other side of the table before he skirted it and came to my side. "Can you let us date for longer than a week before you go marrying us off?"

"She has a habit of trying to rush people into marriage," Henley said with a smirk.

"I do not! I can't help it that I love to plan weddings, and when I see a happy couple, I want to help them make a perfect day."

Daniella lifted her martini glass filled with a drink that looked like chocolate milk. "She sure did plan our wedding quickly. We were thinking of waiting a year, but Roxanne talked us into getting married within four months."

"I didn't talk you into it. You two were almost engaged."

"Wait!" I laughed. "Those two weren't even engaged when you were planning the wedding?"

"No, they were engaged." She shifted in her seat. "I mean, I think they were." She waved a hand. "Whatever. They are happily married now, and that is all that matters."

"Don't mind her. She's around weddings all the time. It's about all she talks about."

"It is not!" Roxanne said forcefully, although she was smiling. She turned her gaze toward me. "Have you ever been married?"

I shook my head. "Nope."

"Oh, good! What kind of wedding have you always thought of having?" she asked, and everyone around the table cracked up. Evan pulled me to his side.

"You can ignore her. She can't help herself."

A minute later, a drink was handed to me, the same kind of chocolate drink most of the ladies were drinking, and conversation raced around the group. Within seconds, I was pulled into them and having the best time that I had had since moving to Pennsylvania. All thoughts of leaving were dismissed, at least for a while, as I laughed harder than I had in a long time, and I made friends with people that I hoped I would know for a long time to come.

CHAPTER THIRTEEN

EVAN

"She's something else," Carmen said quietly from beside me two hours after we arrived.

Since we had gotten here, Laney was immersed in conversation with one person after another. Her face was lit up in a way I had not witnessed yet, and I realized that she must have been starving for this kind of connection with people. Laney had admitted to me about being a homebody and not having many friends in the area, which was a shame. It was apparent that Laney Marshall was a people person. She needed people in her life to thrive.

The way she was thriving now filled my chest with an emotion that I couldn't even begin to explain. "Yeah, she is."

I knew my sister was staring at me, but I couldn't peel my eyes off Laney. "You really like her, don't you?"

"I'm crazy about her," I replied, and I heard Ethan laugh from my other side.

"Yeah, I'm not sure I have ever seen you so taken with someone. Normally, a woman had to knock you over the head to pay attention to them, but you haven't looked at anyone else all night."

I turned my head toward him. "That's not true. I'm looking at you right this minute." Of course, the moment the words were out, my gaze was shifting back to Laney's profile. He slapped me on the back, and we both burst out laughing.

"See what I'm talking about? Well, I hope it works out for you."

"I do too," I said to him, and then I shifted so that I was facing him more and lowered my voice. "When did you know that you loved Riley and wanted to spend the rest of your life with her?"

"When I was seventeen," he said. "Although I didn't do anything about it for years."

"Did you ever question how you felt?"

"All the time, especially when Riley was shutting me down. I wondered why I even bothered. Then when I went away to training, I told myself that it was over for good. I swore to myself that when I came home, I wouldn't see her."

I chuckled. "Yeah, we all know how that turned out."

"If Riley hadn't been pregnant, I'm not sure we would have gotten together, though. I think that's what convinced her that she did love me."

"Do you regret waiting around for her?"

"Nope, not now that I look back. We have our moments when we frustrate each other. I mean, we are talking about Riley here, but I wouldn't trade a moment of my time with her for anything." He studied me for a moment. "This is a pretty serious conversation for you to be having since you just met her a few days ago."

"Yeah, I know, but it's so weird. I feel like I have known Laney for years, not days. We just clicked the minute we looked at one another. It's like I had been waiting all my adult life for that moment when I walked into the room, and she lifted her head to me. Does that sound stupid?"

He shook his head and lowered his voice, leaning closer to

me. "Nope, Cara said something like that. She said that the moment she saw Bryan, she felt pulled to him. No matter how much she tried to deny it, she couldn't."

"Yeah, I remember her saying that."

"You know, you should talk to Hunt. Didn't he fall head over heels for Daniella when they met?"

I turned to study my best friend on the other side of our grouping of tables. Why hadn't I thought of that? "He did. I'm going to ask him about it."

"Sounds like a good idea." Ethan held his beer bottle out. "And good luck. I hope she is everything that you have been looking for and more, but do me a favor and be careful."

"I will. Thanks, Ethan."

In the end, we stayed a lot longer than I had anticipated us staying. I'd stopped drinking after two beers, but I watched Laney throw back at least six chocolate martinis. Needless to say, she was feeling pretty good when we left.

I was opening the door for her to get into my Explorer when she leaned her body into mine. "I had sooooo much fun!" She slurred the words with a happy grin. "Thank you for letting me meet—" She paused, then blurted, "Everyone!"

I laughed at her. "You are very intoxicated, Laney Marshall."

"I know!" she said with a laugh. "I can't remember the last time I got drunk."

"Yeah, well, you might not be so excited tomorrow when the hangover hits you."

"Oh," she said as she slipped past me into the seat. "That's true. Got any tips, Nurse Winston?"

"I might have a few," I told her as I collected her seat belt and strapped her in. "I'll share them with you in the morning. If I told you now, you might not remember them."

"Ah, true." She nodded dramatically, and I closed the door and went around the vehicle. As I got in on the other side, I came to the conclusion that our night might end very differently than we had initially planned. As much as I wanted to get up close and personal with Laney in bed tonight, I would not take advantage of her in her inebriated state. Perhaps I should tuck her in, leave her a note, and go home to my bed so she could rest peacefully.

I thought that over as I drove to her house. Almost there, I realized that Laney was uncharacteristically quiet on the other side of the car, and I glanced over to see if she was sleeping. She wasn't. She sat almost rigid in her seat, staring out the front window.

"You alright?"

"Yes," she stated.

"You look stressed, or like you are expecting something bad to happen. If you are worried that I'm drunk, I'm not. I only had two beers, and that was when we first arrived. I've been drinking Coke and water for the last ninety minutes."

"No, I know you wouldn't drink and drive."

"You know that, huh? How do you know that?"

She turned toward me, a sexy brow raised. "First of all, you are a nurse, and you have seen the results of what can happen firsthand. Second, your brother is a cop. Third, your best friend is a firefighter, and fourth, your other good friend is a paramedic. I think that if you did decide to drink and drive, one of them would have gotten on your case and stopped you."

"There is that," I replied with a soft laugh. "So, if you aren't stressed about my driving, what is on your mind?"

"Nothing." I saw her turn her head away, and I frowned.

"Nothing?"

"Yeah, well, not really. I was just thinking about how much fun I had, and I was trying to remember the last time I had fun. I mean real fun, and I can't remember. Is that weird?"

"Oh, come on, Laney. You had to have had fun sometime recently. I know you said you don't hang out with the people you work with, but didn't you move out this way to stay with a friend? Didn't you guys have a good time together?"

"Yeah, we hung out a little and had fun, but he was busy with his job, and I got busy with going back to school. I was taking twenty credits a semester to finish faster, so I had a lot of studying and work to do."

"Twenty credits? Are you crazy?"

"No, I just wanted to get my degree in social work. I already have two other degrees, but neither of them would help me in this job."

"Two? You have two other degrees?"

"Yes. Business and finance."

Wow. "No wonder you are good at investing." She snorted, and it made me smile, but then my brain started dwelling over her degrees, and I had to ask, "Laney, what did you do before you moved here?"

"Um…" She kept her face turned toward the window. "I helped people invest their money."

"Were you a banker?"

"No." She was quiet for a moment and then sighed. "I worked at a large corporation, and the branch of that corporation that I worked for focused on corporate investments. I helped companies invest their money to make their company stronger, or to help them acquire new companies."

"Wow, that's impressive." I mused over what she said. I had no knowledge of that industry, but it sounded important and very well paying. "When did you know you wanted to do something like that?"

"I guess I got interested in it when I was in high school."

"But you're not interested in it now?"

"No," she said, staring back out the side window. "That's all in the past."

Was it? How did you attend college for years to obtain two degrees and then walk away from all that work? So she had money. Did that mean she had enough that she could throw it out by the buckets? That's kind of what it meant to me. I could not imagine acquiring two degrees and then walking away from them a few years later and going back to school to get another in a field so opposite of what I had been doing. It sounded like she was having a midlife crisis, but she was only thirty-two. Could you have a midlife crisis at thirty?

I wasn't sure where to go with that conversation, and she wasn't adding anything to what she said, so I let it go. Luckily, we were close to her house.

The two of us remained quiet until we got to her place, and then we met in front of my SUV. She glanced at me, then my vehicle. "Where is your overnight bag?"

"I wasn't sure I should stay."

She looked confused and a little hurt. "But why? Did I do something wrong?"

I took her by the shoulders and felt her sway as I kept her there. "I'm not one for taking advantage of drunk women."

She laughed. "Oh, come on, Evan. I'm not *that* drunk. Maybe rather tipsy, but I have my wits about me. I know precisely what I am doing and what I want."

"Yeah, and what is that?"

She stepped closer, wrapping an arm around my neck and pulling my face toward hers. "I want you naked and over me. I want you to make me scream your name and make my toes curl."

"You sure? If you want to sleep, I can leave, or I can stay and just sleep beside you."

She gave me a stern look that almost made me laugh. "Evan Winston, get your bag, get in my house, and get naked. I want to make love to you all night long."

Alright, so maybe she wasn't as drunk as I thought she was. I nodded and stepped away as she removed her arm. I collected my bag and met her at the side of her garage. She unlocked the door and let me into the garage, flipping on the light.

I stopped in midstep when I saw the emblem of the sedan sitting beside her Volvo SUV. "You have a Maserati?"

She glanced at the car and shrugged. "Yeah, but I never drive it. People stare."

Holy crap! Why have a car that you never drove? Wasn't that a waste of money?

I followed Laney into the house and found myself frowning as I glanced around again. The first time I was here, I had been awed by the large beautiful home, but I had been more focused on the incredible woman I was having dinner with. Now, I let my gaze slip around the kitchen again and then the living room area as I followed her further into the house.

The house was like an ad out of the *Better Homes and Garden* magazine. The furniture was modern yet comfortable-looking. The art on the wall looked expensive and not something that you bought off a shelf in a store. The pictures looked like one-of-a-kind pieces that you would purchase at a gallery.

There were glass tables, gold-accented fixtures, elegant throw pillows, and not a speck of dust or dirt in the room. Did Laney clean? I doubted that. Something told me that she had a maid. If she owned a Maserati that she didn't drive, she could probably afford to have someone else clean her home.

Laney went to a bar on the other side of the room, and I was going to suggest that she take it easy from drinking, but after she stood up from behind the bar, I saw that she had two bottles of sparkling water.

"Would you like one, or would you prefer something stronger?"

"Water is fine," I told her, and she brought the bottle over to me.

Laney took my hand and laced her fingers with mine. Then

she pulled me toward the back of the house where the garden was. "Let's go sit under the fairy lights."

"Okay," I told her. While I followed along behind her, my eyes kept moving around the house, and the more I saw, the more I wondered just how wealthy Laney was.

People with money didn't impress me, but I had to admit that I was slightly uneasy about what I saw. It wasn't that I cared that she had money. I just wondered what a woman with this kind of wealth would do with a man like me.

My base salary was seventy thousand a year. The car that she didn't drive in the garage was probably close to double my annual salary. Hadn't my father said that this house sold for around two million?

Downstairs, Laney set her water bottle down and excused herself to use the bathroom. As she walked away, I studied her until she disappeared and then let my gaze drift over the outside living area. She had a table that sat twelve. Plus, two separate seating areas and a grilling kitchen—and it was a full kitchen with the largest grill I had ever seen, a sink, fridge, and more counter space than I had in my kitchen at home. Plus, she had a garden area with a stream and all this incredible greenery.

I frowned as my mind mentally tried to add it all up. Laney's outside living space was probably more expensive than my entire house.

An uneasy feeling drifted down my spine, and I wondered what the hell I was doing here and why someone as spectacular as Laney would be interested in someone so ordinary, like me.

CHAPTER FOURTEEN

LANEY

I excused myself to use the restroom, and after I used the toilet, I stood in front of the mirror and stared at myself. My reflection was a bit blurred, but I was coming down off the alcohol high I had been on at the tavern.

It had been a great night. I adored all of the people that I met, and they had appeared to accept me immediately. Not one of them made me feel uncomfortable or that they were reserving judgment on me.

When was the last time I had been in a group of people and not felt as if I needed to prove something? I couldn't remember. Of course, I didn't feel that way at work, but the people I worked with were so thankful that someone wanted to help victims of domestic violence that they never judged anyone.

Before I came here, everything I did was under a magnifying glass and picked apart by shareholders, clients, co-workers, Bastion, and of course, my brother, Larry.

I thought about the conversation that I had earlier with Roxanne. She had asked if I had been married. I hadn't, but I had been close. Bastion and I were planning our wedding, and it was to be a lavish affair—something that people would talk about for years to come, but I had walked away. Not only from the wedding preparations but from Bastion, too.

Since I had left, I had barely thought of Bastion, and occasionally, I dwelled over the fact that leaving him hadn't been difficult. I guess that showed me just how meaningful that relationship had been to me.

What would Evan say about that? I wasn't sure, but I knew I didn't want to bring it up yet. There would be plenty of time to talk about the skeletons in our closets—although I had a feeling that my closet was a little fuller than his.

I washed my hands, brushed my fingers through my long hair, and then returned to Evan.

He was sitting on the edge of a chair, looking pensive, and I paused a few feet away. "Are you alright?"

His gaze pivoted toward me slowly, and I saw questions in his eyes. "I'm alright, but I started thinking over something that you said earlier."

"What was that?" I asked as I came around him to sit in the chair beside him.

"You said you are from a wealthy family. How wealthy?"

I blinked once, having not expected that question. "Very. Why?"

He shrugged. "I don't know. I guess after you said that you already had two degrees, and then got another one, and then I saw your Maserati in the garage and looked again at your house, I realized what all of this was worth."

"It's not a big deal, Evan. It's just things. They don't mean anything."

"Just things? You have three degrees. Most people can't afford one, but you have three. Two of which you aren't even using, and a car that is over a hundred grand that you said you don't drive. There isn't a speck of dust in your house, so I assume you have a cleaning service, and I would bet a year's salary that the art on your walls does not come from the local chain store."

"So?"

"So, you are more than just wealthy. You are very wealthy."

I frowned. "Does it bother you that I am?"

Evan laughed, slightly uncomfortably. "Does it bother you that I'm not?"

I shook my head. "Not at all. I don't judge a person by their bank account, Evan. I'm surprised that you do."

"I don't." He frowned. "Well, not usually, but having a nice car, nice house, and a little money in the bank is one thing." He lifted his hand toward the house. "Having this level is an entirely different thing."

"No, it's not. I told you I invested well. I could do that, and now I enjoy what I worked hard to earn. Just because I have money doesn't mean I am any different than you."

"Doesn't it?"

I laughed. "Oh, come on, Evan. I can't change the fact that I am financially secure. I won't apologize for that, either."

"I'm not asking you to do that. I'm asking you what are you doing with someone like me when you could have practically any man alive."

"That's not true, and you know it." I chuckled and stood before I moved to kneel between Evan's knees and took his face in my hands. "Don't let what I have worked hard for intimidate you. All of this is not important to me, and I would have no trouble walking away from it for a more simple way of life."

"I can't imagine that."

"The only thing that you need to imagine is what our future will look like, Evan. I like you—a lot. Meeting all your friends and family tonight meant so much to me and gave me more insight into the kind of man you are. Maybe I could have any man out there, but it's *you* that I want. You make my heart excited. You make me laugh. I love the person you are, what you do, where you are in life. I adore your family and friends and you. You, Evan. Not some multimillion-dollar tycoon who only cares about his image or what I can give him, but you. A down-to-earth man who cares more about people than what is in his bank account or what street he lives on." I paused, searching his gaze. "Does that make sense?"

"What if I'm not enough for you? What if I can't give you what you want?"

I caressed his cheeks, staring deep into his eyes. "The only thing that I want you to give me is love. If you do that—if you love me unconditionally and with all your heart—then that is all I need. None of the rest matters. That is what I want more than anything. A man who will love me for me, not what I have or what I can give him."

"I couldn't give you more than that."

"That's all I want or need from you, Evan." I leaned forward and pressed my lips to his. He hesitated at first, but then he opened to me and, after a few seconds, wrapped his arms around me and shifted so he could bring my body closer.

The kiss quickly deepened and became more passionate, and I let all thoughts of money and property escape my mind as I focused on the feelings that Evan was bringing to life within me.

After a few minutes of kissing, I pulled back and stood, taking Evan's hand and pulling him off the chair and toward my favorite lounging sofa. On the way, I grabbed the remote control for the fairy lights, and as we reached the couch, the lights came to life, and the ones around the house dimmed.

Evan smiled as he lifted his face and looked around. "This really is incredible."

"I know, and just imagine how amazing it is going to be while we make love."

Evan drew me into his arms and stared into my eyes as he lowered his head. "Everything about you is amazing, Laney."

"I think the same about you, Evan."

Evan kissed me then, and his hands pulled the edges of my blouse up so he could run his hands over the skin on my back. I tugged the shirt he wore up, and he stopped kissing me long enough to yank it over his head and toss it away. My palms covered his chest and drifted down to his waistband at the same time that he began to slip my skirt off my hips.

A few moments later, the two of us were naked, and I took hold of his erection and stroked him a few times, eliciting a soft moan from his lips as his mouth drifted down my neck.

Evan began to shift over me, and eventually, we were lying down on the couch. I opened my eyes and sucked in a breath. With Evan's handsome face just above me haloed in the soft glow of the lights, it was like he was my guardian angel. Would he rescue my sad heart and help me with the true purpose of my life?

"Make love to me, Evan. I want to feel your love," I whispered to him, and he slowly descended over me.

Evan didn't hesitate. Whatever worries he had earlier about our differences were gone now, and we were just a man and a woman. There was no status quos here, no bank account numbers. Just two bodies meant to come together.

His hands skimmed tenderly over my flesh, his mouth following right behind them. He ran his lips down my arms, stopping to kiss each one of my fingertips, then rolled my arm over and kissed up the inside, making me giddy at the sensation.

He kneaded my breasts, lavishing kisses on each one, before taking a nipple into his mouth and savoring it like fine bourbon. Then he slowly drifted lower, brushing his lips gently over the skin of my belly, nipping at my hip bones, brushing his strong hands down my thighs before he lifted one leg and began to kiss the inside of my thigh.

So slowly that I thought I would scream, he moved his mouth down my leg to my knee and then over my calf. He leaned back on his heels, taking my foot in his hands, and I laughed. "Don't you dare suck on my toes."

He grinned. "Not tonight. I'll save that treat for another time."

Instead of kissing my feet, he gently rubbed the balls of my feet, then my arch and heel.

"Oh, good lord! The man knows how to massage. You're trying to kill me."

"Thank my nursing school for that," he said with a chuckle.

He started kissing up my leg again, and when he got to the top, I was ready for him to stop in the middle, but he moved right over to the other side, and I tried not to be disappointed. I enjoyed his touch and the incredible amount of attention he gave my body—my entire body. As much as my body wanted to jump on the wild ride and head for the sky, I chose to enjoy every touch from this man—no matter where it was.

Finally, Evan finished with my other leg, and his hands massaged over my thighs. I sighed at his touch, and the tips of his fingers brushed the sensitive flesh between my legs. Evan coaxed my legs apart and settled himself there as if he were planning on staying a while. By all means, I wanted to tell him, but words vaporized from my lips the moment I looked into his eyes.

"I love your body, Laney. Every single inch is absolutely incredible. Thank you for letting me cherish it. Now, it's your turn."

My turn? As if I hadn't been enjoying every touch he had already given me. Evan lowered his head and brushed his tongue over my heated flesh. I shivered when he moaned slightly, and then he added more pressure, and I was lost to the sensation, floating on a wave of desire.

I rode that wave for a long time, much longer than I had anticipated, but Evan seemed happy to keep me on just this side of hitting the stars. I would feel myself climbing, feel the rush of the wave coming for me, and then he would slow, lessen his pressure, and it would crumble, and then he would start it all over again. At first, I wondered if Evan couldn't tell I was so close. Perhaps I should give him a sign so that he didn't stop, but then I realized he was doing it on purpose. There was no way for him not to feel my body responding, for him not to know that I was ready to shatter into the dark abyss.

I was almost ready to scream with frustration when Evan once again increased pressure with his mouth and speed, and that heated wave filled me, lifting me toward the crest, but this time, he didn't stop. This time, he carried me over, and I gasped his name, my hands tangled in his soft hair, my body electrified as my muscles contracted, and my toes curled almost to the point of cramping.

It was intense, earth-shattering, and the most fantastic orgasm I had ever achieved. When I could finally open my eyelids, I found Evan staring up at me, a look of awe on his face.

"Wow," I breathed, unable to come up with a more intelligent word.

"Yeah, wow, is right. That was the single most beautiful thing I have ever witnessed."

I brushed my hand over his cheek. "Beautiful?"

"Yes, beautiful. The way your body arched and shivered. The way your head fell back and your neck elongated with your mouth open and your moans slipping out to fill the air. It was incredible."

"I have to admit that it felt very incredible." I took hold of his hand and pulled him up over my body. "That was, by far, the most amazing orgasm I have ever had. Thank you."

"Do you know how you can really thank me for that?"

"How?"

"Let me do that another thousand times." He nuzzled his nose against mine as I chuckled huskily.

"You got yourself a deal, Nurse Winston."

I kissed him, and he adjusted his body over mine, lining himself up as the kiss continued. Before he entered me, he lifted his face and stared down at me. "Before we go any further, do I need protection?"

I shook my head. "No, I have an implant," I said.

"And you don't want me to wear a condom? I will if you might be concerned that I'm not clean, or you've had recent partners we should worry about."

"Evan, I haven't been with anyone in three years."

"Three years?" he repeated, looking astounded at my answer.

"Yes. I want to feel you in me, and I want you to feel me. No barriers with us." I lifted my hips, taking him partially in, and with a thrust of his hips, he filled me. Both of us closed our eyes to take a moment to enjoy the feeling, and then he began to kiss me again as he moved slowly.

Even though there was still alcohol in my system, I didn't feel it. I did, however, feel drugged by his passion and his kisses. Those made me feel weighted and content to a level I had never experienced before.

We moved together for a while, and then I pushed at his shoulder, wanting him to move. "It's your turn to lie down. I want to ride you."

He grinned. "I'm not going to say no to that."

After he was situated, I climbed over his hips, kissing his chest and running my fingertips through the light splattering of hair. I sat up, and I didn't even need to adjust him to find the right spot. He was just there.

I sat back, taking him in, then grinding my hips against him. His hands moved between my breasts, alternating between pinching my nipples and squeezing the large mounds.

I picked up speed as the desire began to build deep in my groin again. Evan moved his hands to my hips, helping to guide me as we began to shift more urgently together. I hadn't wanted it to be so fast, but there was no stopping it. Neither of us was capable of putting on a brake just then, and the two of us raced up that mountain until we exploded off the top and into the stars above us.

As I collapsed onto his chest, the words fell from my lips without thought. "I'm falling for you, Evan."

He kissed the top of my head and lifted my hand to kiss my palm. "Take my hand, sweetheart, and we can fall together."

His words filtered through my mind, and I drifted off to sleep right there on top of him.

CHAPTER FIFTEEN

EVAN

*L*aney moved over my hips, and all I could see around her were the fairy lights glowing and changing in color, highlighting her features and her amazing eyes. It was magical as we came together—the most beautiful thing that I had ever experienced. Yes, it was explosive for sure, but there was something else there, something that I wasn't quite sure what to call it.

Was it love that I was feeling for Laney? Or merely lust? I honestly thought it was more than lust. That's why I told her to fall with me. I didn't want to be alone in what I was feeling.

I felt her drift away, each muscle in her body slowly relaxing and her body becoming heavier as she fell into slumber. Very slowly and carefully, I shifted her off me. I stood over her for a long time before I brushed a lock of hair from her brow. Then I collected the pale-peach lightweight blanket from the back of the couch and covered her. With my clothes in hand, I went to use the bathroom.

After cleaning myself up and dressing, I returned to the patio area and watched her sleep for a few more minutes. I wanted to curl up on the couch and join her in slumber with my arms wrapped tightly around her, but I couldn't. I was too amped up from the sugar and caffeine in the Coke that I had consumed earlier tonight and needed to calm down.

So I began to wander around her house. I strolled around the first floor, taking in the artwork, the furniture, the fancy dining room table, and the sparkling china cabinet with the elegant plates and crystal behind the glass. Did that pattern mean something to her, or did she pick it because she liked it?

After I had gone through the entire main floor, I took the stairs down to the basement. From there, I knew you could walk out to the patio. I had seen the glass doors, but Laney and I had always used the stairs up to the second-floor porch.

I flipped on a light switch at the bottom of the steps and went around the edge of the wall. "Holy—shit!" I murmured as my eyes about jumped out of my skull. In front of me was my dream family room. The flat-screen television must have been at least seventy-two inches, if not larger. The furniture was plush chocolate suede and comfy-looking and made me want to kick back in the recliner and flip on the TV. There were speakers in the ceiling and a bar off to the side of the room. I turned and found myself staring through the glass wall out to the patio. Laney was still sleeping where I had left her, and I continued looking around. Behind me, there was a large pool table and another seating area, along with a couple of closed doors.

They were probably storage and absolutely none of my business. I turned off the lights and retraced my steps to the main floor. Once there, I stood at the bottom of the other staircase and pondered what I was doing.

What would she say if she found me snooping around? It wasn't like I was going into her drawers. I was merely taking in the space and noting what she liked. I hadn't opened the doors in the basement, so I wasn't really snooping.

I started to climb the steps, pausing twice and almost

turning back around, but finally, I decided to at least see how many rooms were upstairs.

At the top of the stairs, you could go either way. The hallway to the right was shorter, so I went that way first and found three bedrooms. One had a private bath, and the other two rooms shared a bathroom. Both were beautifully decorated and looked like they were never used.

Back the other way, I came across another bedroom, along with another door that was closed. I tried the knob to see if it were a bathroom but found it locked. I stared at the handle and then the other handles of the doors in the hallway. This one had an actual key lock, while the others were traditional interior doorknobs. Huh, I wonder what was behind that.

I moved down the hallway, found another bathroom, and then stepped into the last door at the end of the hallway and came up short. This was obviously Laney's room, and it was larger than my living room, dining room, and kitchen combined. On the far wall was a four-poster bed, with a high mattress that she probably had to jump on to get onto it. There were several dressers, a seating area with an actual coffee table, and three doors on the opposite side of the room. One of those doors was open, and I headed toward it.

I stepped in, and my jaw hit the floor. Her bathroom was the most enormous bathroom I had ever seen, and the shower was probably the size of my kitchen. There were five jets from the ceiling hanging down and several more along the stone walls. Along the back wall of the shower was a stone bench, and on this side was a floor-to-ceiling glass wall to block the spray.

"You could fit a dozen people in this thing," I said to myself as I stood on the edge of it. "No wonder she likes it."

"You want to try it out?" A voice spoke from behind me, and I jumped as I spun around. My heart leaped into my throat for a moment.

"Jesus, Laney, you just scared the shit out of me. I never heard you coming."

She stepped into the room, holding the blanket I had left over her tightly around her body. "Sorry, I didn't mean to scare you. I woke up, and you were gone. I thought you went home, but I saw your car still in the driveway. I thought you might be up here someplace."

"Sorry," I said. "I wasn't really snooping, just checking your house out since I hadn't gotten a tour before."

"That's fine. I don't mind." She leaned back against the slate-gray marble counter. "Did you see my closet?"

I shook my head. "No. I didn't open any doors that were closed."

She nodded. "I'll have to show it to you later."

"You can show it to me now."

She cocked her head. "No, I have things I want to do with you now." She stood up straight and let the blanket fall to her feet. "I do believe you have too many clothes on, Evan Winston."

My gaze drank in her beautiful body as my libido licked right back into overdrive. "I can rectify that," I said as I kicked off my shoes.

She skirted me and entered the shower, turning on one of the ceiling jets, then another. She stood between them, the water falling on both sides of her as I got undressed. As I removed the last of my clothing, she pressed her hands against the glass wall, pushing her hips back, and my cock kicked hard at the thought of taking her from behind.

I was in the shower and taking her hips a few seconds later, the water raining down my arms on each side. Over her shoulder, I could see the large mirror, and Laney locked eyes with me, pressing her ass back against me. I didn't waste any time and lined myself up so I could push right into her.

I watched my cock disappear into her and come back out, and then I lifted my head to watch her face in the mirror. Her eyes almost glowed with brightness and desire, and then I'd repeat it, over and over again. I walked her body closer to the glass and pressed her against it, watching her breasts push against the glass. I had a deeper angle from here, and she gasped as I thrust forward each time. I reached around her and fingered her clit, determined that we would both come together again.

It didn't take us long before we did, and then we were both leaning against the glass as it fogged up with each of our exhalations.

I brushed a kiss over the shell of her ear and whispered, "I love your body, and I love this shower."

She snickered. "I had a feeling you might like this shower."

"How could I not? I can imagine having sex with you in here a million times."

She laughed. "Really, a million?"

"Or two," I said before I kissed her temple and then pulled away. I stepped back under the spray of the water and closed my eyes. A moment later, she joined me, and I held her to me as the water washed down our bodies.

"I thought you had left me," she said so softly I barely heard her.

"I was still here."

"Yeah, but when I woke up, I thought you had gone home."

I shook my head, then kissed the side of her wet head. "No. I had thought about it, but I got busy checking out your house. If I had left, I would have left a note."

"Don't leave," she said as she pulled back to look me in the face. "I want to fall asleep in your arms and wake up there tomorrow."

"I'll stay."

"You promise?"

"I promise."

She yawned as she nodded. "Okay, good, because I think I need to go back to sleep."

"Then let's get washed up and into bed." The two of us separated so we could wash up, and then I sat on the bench and watched her finish conditioning her hair. There was no awkwardness between us. No shyness, and I loved that. As I watched her finish up, my cock started to get hard again, and I wasn't the only one that noticed.

She arched her back, pushing her breasts out further as she rinsed her long brown hair. "You like watching, huh?"

I stroked myself. "Yeah, I do like watching you."

"Well…" She let her eyes drop to my hips. "I sure like watching you do that."

I couldn't help but smile and squeeze my cock a little harder. "Then I won't stop. I'd hate to disappoint you."

"No, we can't do that." She glanced behind her and then back at me. "Although, I think you should stand up and lean against the glass here."

"Why is that?"

"So I can sit on the bench and spread myself wide for you."

"Fuck," I growled and burst to my feet. She sidestepped me, a sexy-as-hell smile on her lips, and we traded places.

I leaned against the glass, hoping like hell I didn't fall through it, and she took a seat on the bench and bent one leg, putting her foot on the stone next to her to give me a beautiful view. She touched herself, and I about came on the spot. Somehow I didn't, but it didn't take long for either of us to orgasm almost simultaneously again.

After we cleaned up again, we dried off, and Laney pulled me by the hand to her bed. After peeling back the covers, she climbed in and slipped to the middle, then patted the bed. "Come here, baby."

I was right behind her, and she settled into my arms, her head on my shoulder. She kissed my chest, shoulder, and chin a few times, and then she was again drifting off.

This time, I closed my eyes and let myself join her.

When I opened my eyes, I felt extremely off-kilter. It was dark in the room, yet I felt very rested as if I had slept a solid eight hours. A sound caused me to turn my head, and I found light peeking through the crack of the bathroom door. I sat up and looked around, noting a clock on the side table that said it was ten after nine. Holy smokes! I had gotten a good night's sleep.

I heard the water running in the bathroom, and a few moments later, the light turned off and the door opened as Laney stepped out with a dark robe wrapped around her body.

"Hey, you. I can't believe it's after nine," I said huskily and then cleared my throat.

"Sorry if I woke you." She came around the bed and hopped up on the mattress.

"I slept long enough. Why is it so dark in here?"

"Ah, isn't that nice?" She reached over to the side table, messed with something, and then after a click, low whirling noises came from four areas of the room where the shades rolled up from the bottom of the windows.

Bright sunlight filled the room, and Laney started chuckling as she stared at me. Was my mouth hanging open? "You know, I knew they were available. I just haven't been anywhere they were used. That is a cool feature."

"Especially for someone who works shift work. Imagine how well you would sleep when you worked the night shift and had to sleep during the day."

"Yes, that would be very awesome. I guess I need to put those on my wishlist for my bedroom."

"Or you could just sleep here during the day," she said with a shrug. "It's not like I'm here most of the time."

I laughed. "Yeah, I can see that now. Hey, Laney, I'm coming over to use your bedroom while I'm on nights."

"Why not?" she asked seriously.

I frowned. "You're being serious?"

Her shoulders shrugged again. "Yeah, why not?" She crawled over the bed toward me. "I liked having you in my bed. I can imagine how nice it would be knowing you were here resting peacefully, while I'm at work."

I laughed. "Laney, we barely know each other. I'm not moving into your house."

"I didn't say move in. I said, sleep here when you are on nights. When do you start them?"

"I start my night rotation on Monday."

"So, there you go. You work Monday and Tuesday night, correct?"

"Yes."

"Then you can come here and sleep at least during the day on Tuesday. You will be amazed how well you sleep with all the shutters down."

"Laney—"

She put her fingers to my mouth, "Shh, don't. Just do it. I'm not asking for anything in return. You don't even have to sleep in this room. The second master on the far side of the house has the shutters also, so you could use that room if being in my room alone is odd."

"Let me think about it," I told her. I wasn't sure what I thought about staying at her house when she wasn't home. I liked the idea of getting a good sleep without having a pillow over my head to block out noise and light, but staying at Laney's house within a week of knowing her? I don't know about that.

CHAPTER SIXTEEN

LANEY

*O*kay, so maybe inviting Evan to sleep in my house during the day was a little forward, but Evan and I were progressing at a rapid pace. It was as if one hour with this man was equal to a month with anyone else. It was both exciting and slightly disturbing.

As I headed downstairs to make coffee and allow Evan privacy to get dressed, I thought about that.

Of course, falling in love with someone was the exciting part. What was disturbing was how quickly we were doing that. I had never been one to jump into anything. I thought long and hard over a decision, whether it was business, a relationship, or the flavor of coffee I was in the mood to drink in the afternoon.

Every decision was calculated against risk factors. Would an investment prosper, or was the chance of a return too much of a risk? Would the client balk at what was required of him, or would he sit back and wait for the return? Would the coffee bean I choose for my afternoon cup be flavorful or leave a bitter taste in my mouth?

When it came to relationships, I had always looked at them from what I would acquire to use in my life. I guess that was the same way I thought of a client relationship. What would I gain from helping this client? What would the relationship with this particular man give me?

I didn't need a man to be wealthy; I was financially independent. I didn't need a man to be romantic; most men didn't even understand the notion. I also didn't need a man to satisfy me sexually because I was pretty capable of doing that with any number of toys I owned. What other purpose was there for a man?

Bas had been more of a business transaction than a marriage built on some fable of love. I hadn't thought there would ever be a man that could give me something I didn't know I wanted. Not until I met Evan.

Evan made me want that love-at-first-sight, happily-ever-after fairy tale. It was something I never thought existed outside of movies and books, but I seemed to have it right here in front of me. Was I willing to reach forward and grab it? Embrace it and let it take me where it wanted to take me?

What was it about Evan that made me take that leap without even considering what he could do for me? There was no pro and con list with him. There was just this compassionate and strong man who could make me smile without a second thought. A man who made my heart beat faster when he looked at me and who loved to laugh and have fun. He was a man who took his job seriously and helped people. He didn't try to buy them or coerce them into doing something for him. He merely took care of them.

Had my career change also transformed the way I viewed everything else in my life? I had to wonder if it did. Had the death of my sister given me a new view of the world around me?

Of that, I sadly had no doubt.

What would the people I worked with before say about me now? Would they think I was soft? That I had lost my edge? If I had to go back and jump right back into my old position, could I?

Absolutely. Even though I had been away from the corporation for well over two years, I knew I could sit down behind my old desk and fall into work as if I'd only been off for a week. The makeshift office next to my bedroom here had boards covering all the walls that displayed the latest numbers, projections, and trends on the market. I kept the door closed and locked, more to keep me from wandering in there and losing track of time than to keep people out. I only allowed myself to venture in there once a week, maybe twice if I had extra time.

What had Evan thought when he found a locked door upstairs? If he asked what was behind the door, would I show him?

I frowned as I filled the coffeemaker with water. I didn't particularly want Evan to see what I used to do. It wasn't that I was ashamed of what I did. It was because Evan was already slightly on edge about the difference in our economic status. I had a feeling that if he saw what was behind that door, it would be somewhat overwhelming to him. I knew it could be daunting to anyone who didn't regularly deal in millions, sometimes billions of dollars.

I turned the coffee on and then moved to the fridge to pull out the eggs and package of Canadian bacon that I had in there. In my early years, Sunday morning had always been reserved for my father's favorite breakfast—eggs Benedict. Since he passed, I have kept that tradition going. I didn't have it every Sunday, but I would make it at least once a month. Today seemed like a great day to do that.

I had the eggs in the poacher and the bacon in the frying pan when Evan joined me in the kitchen.

Evan came up behind me and put his arms around my waist. "Are you making me breakfast?"

"I am."

"Is that going to be eggs Benedict?"

"It is. I hope you like that."

"Yes, ma'am, I sure do. In our house, we only had that on the holidays, but we all loved it." He paused and grew thoughtful for a moment. "Wow, I haven't had it since my mother passed."

"Funny you should say that," I said as he released me and stepped to the side to lean back against the counter. "I was just thinking about how this was my father's favorite, and we used to have it every Sunday. I try to make it at least once a month in memory of him."

"That's cool that you do that." He glanced around the kitchen. "Can I do anything to help?"

"Nope. You can have a seat and relax."

"I can do that." Evan took a seat on the other side of the counter at an area for bar seating, and while I cooked, we talked about other things that our families liked to eat when we were growing up.

I let him talk more than me because, quite frankly, his family life was a lot more interesting than mine had been. I wasn't very close to my mother, and when I wasn't away at school, my family rarely ate dinner together. My father was always too busy wining and dining clients, and my mother was too busy wining and dining herself.

Suzanne, never Susan or Sue, was the proverbial spoiled rich woman—dripping in diamonds and the latest fashions. Her social calendar was full of society functions not based on the causes she believed in but on the most important and influential people involved in the other charities. It was an image contest, and I had hated it.

She gossiped, and her tongue was many times tinged in venom. Early on, she had learned that I had no interest in being anything like her or attending her functions as the doting daughter. Larry had done better with the social aspect than I had, but even he hated it.

It was Lindsey that had followed our mother around and hung on her coattails. She was the beautiful, serene child who didn't mind our mother taking the spotlight and sometimes encouraged it.

Over breakfast, Evan talked more about his family, and we were laughing so hard that our food was getting cold. Halfway through, Evan's cellphone rang. "Sorry, gotta grab this. It's my father."

"Go right ahead." I took the time to focus on my food while he answered.

"Hey, Pop. Everything okay?"

He listened for a moment, smiled at me to let me know that all was well, and then nodded to himself. "Yeah, Laney is right here. I can ask her."

He grew quiet again, and I wondered what on earth his father might want to ask me. A moment later, he nodded again. "Okay, I'll let you know in a little while. We are finishing break-fast right now. Thanks for thinking about that, Pop."

He hung up with a massive smile on his face and set his phone beside his plate.

"What was that about?"

"Pop wanted to invite you to family dinner."

"Family dinner?" I echoed back. When was the last time I had any semblance of a family dinner? Seven or eight years ago before Lindsey married Matt?

"Yeah, every Sunday, whoever is around and not working heads over to my father's house for Sunday dinner. I only make it twice a month since I usually work every other Sunday. Ethan and Riley take turns going back and forth to her parents since they do the same thing."

"I love that. Once in a while, we used to do that with my family. I always loved those times." However, I could probably count them on my two hands without using my thumbs.

"I think sometimes we take them for granted. I know after

Cara left, things felt different without her there, but we have grown accustomed to the changes."

"Can I ask you something about Cara?"

He stiffened slightly. "What about her?"

"Well, I noticed that last night when Roxanne brought up her name in public, you all got tense. In fact, I've noticed that you guys get tense every time her name comes up. Many times you all look around to see who might be listening. What is the deal with that?"

He grew thoughtful, and I knew he was contemplating what to tell me as he cut another bite of his food. "Evan, whatever you tell me will stay between us. I would never share personal information about you or your family with anyone."

He chewed the food. "I know you wouldn't. That's not why I hesitate. The story isn't mine to tell."

"Well, wouldn't it be best to give me a summary of what is going on so I don't say anything that could cause an issue?"

"Yeah, I guess." He finished up the last couple bites of his food, set his cutlery down over his plate, and leaned back.

"Cara got herself involved with the local biker gang. It wasn't that she went looking for trouble; she didn't. She met one of the guys named Ryan at an accident scene. She connected with him. I guess similar to how we have. Before she knew it, she was in deep with him and the gang. He claimed her to protect her."

"Claimed her?"

"Yeah. It has to do with sex and announcing that Cara was off-limits to the club. I'm not sure of the particulars, but after Ryan claimed her, no one in the club could touch her or our family."

"But why would they want to?"

"Cara didn't know she was doing this, but she was transporting drugs over state lines. She did some part-time flying for a wealthy man nearby, and she would fly Ryan to New York, where he would pick up a shipment of heroin and bring it back.

She had no clue he was doing that. She thought he was just along for the ride."

"What did she do when she found out?"

He chuckled. "She lost her shit. Kicked him out of her life, but the thing was, he was doing it to protect her. The club had already set its sights on her. They were trying to find a way to use her, but Ryan was protecting her in his own way."

"So, she broke it off with him and left town? Is that what happened?"

"No, not quite. I mean, Cara did break it off with him, but Ryan was killed."

"Oh, god! How horrible for your sister."

"It was horrible, but then again, it wasn't. Cara was free then. The club couldn't touch her. She was still protected, but they couldn't force her to do anything." He paused and leaned forward, pushing his plate back slightly, and setting his forearms on the table. "Cara found out she was pregnant not long after that."

I gasped. "Oh, no! That's heartbreaking."

"Yeah, but it ends well. See, Ryan was working undercover for the FBI. I ironically knew who Ryan really was. That's another long story, but the FBI pulled him out and announced that Ryan Vigilante had died from his gunshot wound. The FBI transported him back to Texas where he lives happily with his wife and son, under his real name of Bryan Hemlock."

I stared at him, my eyes wide. "Oh, wow! So she's with him now, but the club thinks that he is dead."

"Yep, and he can never come back here. Which sucks because it makes it hard for Cara to visit us."

"Now I understand why you all don't want to talk about her in public. I get it. I promise I won't say a word to anyone."

"Thanks, we would all appreciate that."

"Does the biker club bother you at all? One of the men from the café was working at the tavern last night."

"Yeah, that's Bollard. He's probably one of the better ones. Bryan said that Bollard tried to keep his nose clean. He liked being in the club, but he wasn't into the drugs and violence that most clubs deal with. He's not a bad guy. I've talked to him a few times, and he seems honestly concerned with how Cara is faring."

"But he doesn't know?"

Evan shook his head. "Nope. None of them do."

"Well, okay then."

"Circling back to the original conversation, are you interested in joining us for dinner tonight?"

"I am interested, but I'm going to have to decline the invite and ask for a rain check. I have some work that I have to get done this afternoon, and I know it will take me quite a few hours."

"What kind of work?" he asked.

"Um, some additional training classes that I need to finish for the center. The state requires us to take these classes on our own time, and I've been putting it off. I promised myself and my boss that I would get them done this weekend."

"Okay, well, I understand that." He glanced at his watch. "I hate to do this, but I need to run. I told Carmen I would help her with something at her house."

"No, that's fine. I will get this cleaned up, get dressed, and start on my classes."

"If you get them finished early, give me a call. You are welcome to join us if you want to later." He stood and took his plate to the sink.

I joined him there. "I will let you know, but I think this will keep me busy all day and into the evening."

He turned to study me, a tender smile on his face. "I had a really great day yesterday. I can't believe it was just a day. It felt like we were together for a week."

I laughed. "You know, I was thinking earlier that spending

one hour with you is about equal to a month with someone else."

He laughed as he thought about that. "Well, I just hope that doesn't mean our relationship is going to run out of time faster than it should."

I wrapped my arms around his waist. "I doubt that, Evan."

He kissed me softly. "Me too. I'm crazy about you, Laney."

"The feeling is very mutual."

We stood in the kitchen and kissed for a few moments, and then I walked him to the door. "The offer still stands if you want to sleep here on Tuesday. I'll be working, so you would have the house to yourself. Just let me know, and I'll give you the codes to the door and alarm."

He chuckled. "I'll keep that in mind."

I was sure he would, but I also knew he probably wouldn't accept the offer. Not this soon.

I waved goodbye as he did a three-point turn in my driveway and then I watched his SUV drive slowly down my private lane to the main road.

As I closed the door, I wondered if he might be right, and our superspeed relationship might race to the finish line too fast.

CHAPTER SEVENTEEN

EVAN

*A*s soon as I left Laney's house, I dialed my sister's number and listened to it ring over the car speaker twice before Cara answered.

"Everything okay?"

I chuckled. "Yes, everything is okay. Why would you assume it wasn't?"

"Because you don't normally call me at ten in the morning. It's eight here, by the way, on a Sunday."

"There is that." I chuckled. "How are you guys doing?"

"We are all doing well. Bryan is out at the barn right now with Luke. He likes to bring him out there when he feeds the horses. Says it will teach him the proper way to grow up and be responsible."

I chuckled. "He's what, four months?"

"Three and a half, but close enough. I'm just happy that Bryan enjoys spending time with his son."

"Yeah, I am too."

"Not that I'm not happy to hear from you, but what's up? It always worries me when someone calls me at an odd time."

"Nothing is wrong. Relax. This isn't about the family. It's personal."

"Personal, huh?" Her voice lifted in excitement.

"I wanted to ask you a question."

"Does this have something to do with the beautiful woman you introduced to everyone last night?"

"It does."

"I have to admit that I was very jealous that I couldn't be there. Carmen and Candy both said that she was really nice, and you seemed so happy."

"Glad they liked her."

"Dad does too. I talked to him last night. He told me all about his day. He seemed in excellent spirits."

"Yeah, I saw him the other night, and he seemed oddly depressed. He called me to fix something, but when I got there, it wasn't broken. I think he was just lonely. We all need to make a better effort of spending time with him."

"That breaks my heart, Evan." She sighed. "I wish I could help with that."

"I know you do, but there are five of us here that should be doing it. Just because you are the oldest does not mean it's your job."

"I know, but you know how terrible I feel about not being there to help."

"Cara, you have your own life to live now. You know that Dad understands. We all do."

"I know." She sighed. "Okay, enough about me. What is your question?" I hesitated, and her laughter filled the interior of my vehicle. "Oh, this must be good. You're never leery about speaking your mind."

"Funny," I muttered, and my left hand squeezed the steering wheel. "How long did it take you to know that you were in love with Bryan?"

"Wow. I never expected a question like that, Ev. I thought you were going to ask me how to woo her or something."

"I know how to be romantic, Cara. That's not the issue."

She sighed. "I know you do. I was only joking." She paused as if thinking over her answer. "I don't know how long it took me to fall for him. Maybe I fell for him the first time I saw him. I remember not being able to forget him. I even dreamed about him a few times after I first met him. Or perhaps it was later after I'd slept with him. I don't know. I don't specifically remember when I thought, *I love this man*. It just happened, and I felt it. I do know that something attracted me to him from the first moment that I stared into his eyes. Something deep inside of him called to me, and as much as I wanted to resist it, I couldn't."

I heard beeps on her side as if she were punching buttons on a microwave. "At first, I assumed it was just lust and that eventually, it would fade, but it didn't. It grew stronger. With every moment that we spent together, I felt more and more like this was where I was meant to be—right by his side."

"You really felt that way?"

"I did. Even when I knew I shouldn't. Even after I found out that he used me and I told him to go away and never talk to me again, I felt like I had lost part of myself, and when I thought he had died." She paused as if to gather herself. "Evan, I wasn't sure at first how to keep going. There was this hollow part in my soul from what I had given of myself to him. A large piece of me wanted to die too, but then I found a reason to live. I found out I was pregnant, and that baby was his. I knew that eventually our child would fill in the gap that I had from his loss." She paused. "Thankfully, that worked out differently."

"I'm glad that it worked out for you, Cara."

"Me, too." She paused again. "So, how are you feeling? Or maybe a better question is, how does she make you feel? Tell me about how you met and what is going on."

So I did. I told Cara everything from when I met Laney until leaving her this morning. I told her how she filled my heart in a way I had never felt before. I also told her my conflicting thoughts on the differences in our financial status.

"Don't even put that in the mix, Evan. Money is just money. I have to agree with Laney on this. Yeah, she was lucky enough to have been born with it and knows how to invest it, but she sounds like a down-to-earth kind of woman. Having left a huge corporate job and moving on to social services is a huge change. It speaks mountains of what type of person she is."

"Do you think so?"

"Absolutely. If Laney was all about money, do you honestly think she would have moved here and started working for peanuts while trying to help victims of domestic violence? I mean, the woman probably makes half of what you make, so I don't think you should worry about that. She's doing what she feels she should be doing. Answering a calling of sorts."

"Yeah, I guess you are right."

"Evan, if you want my honest opinion."

"I do," I said quickly.

"Then stop second-guessing it, and go for it. Just leap. Let yourself fall in love and go for the ride. It might only last a little while, or it could be the longest and best journey you have ever been on, but you won't know until you do it."

"What if I'm all wrong? What if this is just lust?"

"Then enjoy it, Evan! Especially if the sex is good. Enjoy it. Don't look a gift horse in the mouth."

I pondered that for a moment. "Okay." I nodded to myself. "I'm going to jump in with both feet and just see where it takes me."

"I think that is the best idea. It might not work, and things might be over before they even begin. Or this could be the start of something beautiful that lasts for the rest of your life. I hope it's the latter for you, Evan."

"I do too, Cara. I really do."

After I hung up with Cara, I thought back over the conversation for the rest of the ride to Carmen's. By the time I got there, I had decided to take the chance with Laney. If that meant staying at her place on Tuesday to show her I was serious about us, then I would stay at her house as much as she wanted.

S unday evening, after dinner with my family, I sent Laney a text asking how her training was going. Instead of getting a text response, she called me.

"Great timing. I literally just finished my work a few minutes ago, and I'm pouring myself a glass of wine before I take a long hot bath."

"Hmm, hot bath, huh?"

She giggled. "You want to come over and join me?"

I laughed huskily. "I'd love to, but I think I'm going to stay home tonight and let you get a good night's rest for your week. Besides, I don't want to wear out my welcome too soon."

She laughed. "Evan, you know that's not going to happen."

"Maybe not, but still. I want you to get some sleep, and I have laundry and household chores to catch up on that I didn't get to on Saturday."

"That makes sense. How was dinner?"

"Dinner was great. Were your ears burning?"

She laughed loudly. "Oh, don't tell me that you guys were talking about me."

"Of course we were. Everyone was telling me how much they liked you and how wonderful you were—especially my father—but see, I already knew how awesome you were."

"Aw, I'm so glad that they like me. I'd hate to be an issue with your family."

"Pft, hardly! They might like you more than they like me."

"Oh, come on."

"Trust me, a few of them threatened me. Told me that if I messed this up, they would never let me live it down."

She laughed heartily. "That's funny." She paused. "I was thinking, and please tell me if this is way off base, but what would you say to me inviting your family over for a barbeque the next weekend you are off? That's in two weeks, right?"

"Two weeks, yes. I think that is really kind of you, but you don't need to do that. They already like you. You don't have to impress them with your house."

"What? That's not what I'm trying to do, Evan. I just wanted to do something nice for them. Plus, I know you aren't comfortable with my money, but I don't want it to be a big deal. So, I want your family to see it and know that just because I live in a fancy house doesn't mean that I'm any different than them. I work a regular job, pay my bills, argue with contractors, go grocery shopping, and do the same things that they do. I just have more money to use. Besides, I have wanted to entertain so badly since I bought this house, but since I don't have any friends, I haven't been able to do that. It would give me a chance."

I thought over what she said. It made sense. Her wealth was like the elephant in the room, and I needed to face that. "Your patio is pretty awesome."

"You haven't even seen the back part of the yard. I have a horseshoe pit and a flat area to put up a volleyball net. It would be so much fun. Please?"

"It sounds great. Do you want to do it in two weeks?"

"Yes! Oh, my god! Do you know how exciting this is for me?"

I chuckled. I loved hearing the excitement in her voice, and knowing it was all because of inviting my family over. "Alright, then I will ask everyone."

"How about you let me take care of that? I'd like to invite them personally."

"If that's what you want to do, certainly."

"Thank you, Evan. This is going to be great! I can't wait! You just gave me something to look forward to. I haven't had something to look forward to in a long time."

"And here I thought you might look forward to seeing me."

Her voice dropped lower. "Oh, I am."

"I was thinking over your offer today."

"What offer was that?"

"The one to stay at your place on Tuesday."

"Oh, really?" Her voice grew even more excited. "Of course, you are welcome to do that. Did you want to stay in the other master room or my room?"

"Whichever one would make you more comfortable. I don't want to put you out, but I would like to test out those sleep shutters."

"Absolutely. You are going to love the shutters, Evan."

"Too bad you won't be there with me."

"That is a shame, but I do have to work. Of course, when I am sleeping, you will be busy helping people."

"That is true. That's the hard part about working shift work when you are in a relationship."

"Absence makes the heart grow fonder," she commented in a singsong voice.

"If you say so. Would you be interested in having dinner on Wednesday?"

"I'd love that. Did you want to sleep here again on Wednesday? If you do, pack a change of clothes. Then when I get home, you'll be here and ready, but you have to promise me something."

"What's that?"

"That you will come back after dinner and tuck me in bed."

"Do I have to tuck you in? Or can I just undress you and lavish your body for a couple of hours."

"Oh, that sounds a lot better than tucking me in. I'll let you do that."

"Sounds like a plan."

"Perfect. Grab a pen, and I'll tell you the codes for the door and the alarm."

M onday night, I worked, and it was hectic as usual, but nothing out of the ordinary. I had spent most of my downtime thinking about Laney and telling Nicole everything that I knew about her. Nicole was blown away and admitted to being jealous of my story, but in a good way. On Tuesday morning, I drove to her house instead of my home. It felt a little weird to be going there, but I welcomed that different feeling. It meant that I was taking a chance.

I let myself in through the side garage door using the code she gave me. This time when I got inside the garage, I paused by the glossy black Maserati and then strolled around it, checking out every inch. At the back, I shook my head. It was a Quattroporte Trofeo—what a gorgeous machine.

I let myself into the house, keyed in the eight-digit alarm code, then went into the kitchen and glanced around. On the counter was a piece of paper, and I approached it.

Good Morning, Evan. I hope work went well for you. Send me a text to let me know you got in alright. There are eggs in the fridge if you are hungry or leftover chicken from last night if you'd rather have that. You are welcome to sleep in either room. The sheets are clean. If I had my choice, I'd have you sleep in my bed. It would make me feel closer to you tonight when I am sleeping, and you are working, but whatever makes you feel more comfortable. The shutters are already down in both rooms, and the controls are on the side table. Make yourself at home, and sleep well. Love, Laney.

I sent her a quick text message that I was in, and all was well.

I ended up making eggs and toast and then cleaned up the kitchen before I climbed the stairs with my overnight bag. At the top, I looked both ways and then smiled as I turned toward her room.

After a shower in her incredible bathroom and a few minutes of news, while lying in bed, I turned it off and rolled over—drifting into one of the best periods of sleep that I had ever had during the day.

When I woke up at three that afternoon, I made sure to write her a note before I left to go to the gym.

I am kind of in love with your window shutters, and your bed is not half bad either. Thank you, and I will take you up on the offer of sleeping here again tomorrow. You do know you are going to spoil me rotten. How about dinner at the Italian restaurant again? If not there, you pick. I'm up for anything. See you tomorrow. I missed you being next to me—especially in that shower of yours. Love, Evan.

I was grinning to myself as I punched in the alarm code and let myself out of the house.

CHAPTER EIGHTEEN

LANEY

*F*riday afternoon, I was sitting with Alice, one of our new clients, listening to her describe the abuse she had been dealing with for the last two years to the detective handling her case. I felt as if I was hearing what my sister had gone through, and I found it slightly overwhelming—although I didn't show it.

I was here to support her because that was my job. I was her liaison between the freedom she deserved and the legal system that would protect her. It was my job to help her every step of the way. Some clients didn't need extensive help. They needed someone to hold their hand, give them a little advice, and be a shoulder to lean on.

Then others needed a higher level of attention. That's what I did. I spent most of my time listening and not reacting to the horrible things that our clients had endured.

Sometimes it was once or twice before they left the abuser, but many times, it was years and years that they lived with the manipulation, total control, and violent abuse at the hands of someone who was supposed to love them.

I knew now that those people were not capable of loving

anyone but themselves, and I even had to wonder if they even did that. How could you like yourself after making someone feel so small? How could you live with yourself after striking someone and putting fear into them for the slightest wrong?

Alice explained as she rubbed the back of her hand that her husband had gotten angry once because she had given him a fork that didn't match the knife and spoon design. He had gotten so furious that he had held her hand down and then stabbed her through the hand with the mismatched fork.

I could not even comprehend the physical pain that would have caused, and it took everything in me not to vomit, although as hard as I tried not to, I cringed.

She shared how she had been to six different hospitals in eighteen months. One was even three hours away. He always took her to have the broken bones reset, and the lacerations stitched back up—wasn't that nice of him? Every time, he was the doting husband who pretended to be so worried over his clumsy wife. No one questioned it. No one paid much attention to it.

Why? Because he was an affluent white man. He drove luxurious cars, wore expensive suits, visited glamorous locations. He was a handsome man, someone that people instantly liked upon meeting. He could easily pull anyone into his spider web, and Alice had fallen for him hook, line, and sinker. Now she was in fear for her life.

Alice let it all out and talked for nearly ninety minutes. She went through two dozen tissues, three bottles of water, and two bathroom breaks before she sat back and looked between Detective Meyers and me. "That's it. That's everything that I remember him doing to me the last two years."

Besides the physical abuse, he had done degrading sexual things to her that she hadn't consented to. He had forced himself on her multiple times, even after he'd snapped a rib or broken her nose. He had forced her to please him before he would get her medical attention.

I was revolted, and I knew the detective sitting beside me was just as disgusted as I was.

"Alright, Alice," Detective Meyers spoke softly. He was one of the older detectives, and he could transition from being a compassionate listener to an intense detective in the blink of an eye. I had seen it. I had also seen the jovial man who loved to tell jokes and the man who was very intent on being the best that he could be at his job. "I appreciate you telling us all of that. I know that was extremely difficult. Before I turn the recorder off, is there anything else that you want to include in your statement?"

She shook her head, sniffing and staring at her lap. "No, I've told you everything that I can remember."

"Okay, well, if you recall anything else, you let me know." The detective turned off the recorder and then leaned back in his seat.

"What happens now?" Alice asked him.

"Well, I'm going to have you sign a couple of forms that will help get your medical files released so that we have the details of all the injuries that he inflicted and the treatment that you received. Once we have those, I will sit down with one of our assistant district attorneys to approve the charges. Then a warrant will be issued, and he will be arrested."

She nodded slowly. "I'll have to face him again in court, won't I?"

"Yes," the detective answered and glanced at me. "But Laney will be there with you, and so will I. You won't be alone, Alice, and he won't be able to hurt you."

"I'm sure he will find a way. He always does."

I leaned forward. "You won't even have to look at him, Alice. Except for about ten seconds when you identify him to the court."

"If you ladies will excuse me, I'm going to get the forms."

Detective Meyers slipped out of the room, and Alice watched him go before she shifted her weary eyes toward me.

"Do you think he's going to go to jail?"

"Tell me something, Alice. Would it bother you if he did? Would you feel guilty?"

"No!" she stated adamantly as her brown hair whipped back and forth. "I want Steve to go to jail! He deserves to be there. I'm sitting here listening to everything coming out of my mouth—everything I went through—everything that I put up with—and I can't believe I did that. I was never a weak person. I never let someone walk all over me. So why did I let him do that? How could I have let him treat me that way? It's not okay!"

"You're right. It's not okay." I inhaled deeply and then released it. "You remind me a lot of my sister. She never let anyone walk all over her either," I paused. "Until she did."

She blinked rapidly for a moment. "Your sister was abused?"

I nodded slowly. "My sister was abused, and not just abused, but she died because she never got the courage to say anything."

"And she didn't come to you for help?"

I shook my head. "At the time, I was working in a different field. We didn't see each other very often. Her husband kept her away from us, and I was so busy with my life that I didn't pay much attention. I wish I had. Maybe she would still be alive." I stared at my hands for a moment. "But that's why I do this now. I quit my job and moved across the country for a new start. I went back to school and got this job so that maybe, I could help someone out of a situation like the one Lindsey was in."

She leaned forward, reaching out and putting her hand on the table near me. "You have, Laney. You have made a difference. If you hadn't been on the phone that morning I called, I don't know what I would have done. If someone else had answered that phone, I might not be here either. You gave me the strength that encouraged me to walk away and leave it all behind. I will never be able to thank you enough for that."

I blinked back the tears that threatened to fill my eyes, and I put my hand over hers and squeezed. "Thank you for saying that, Alice. Sometimes I wonder if I make a difference."

"You do. Believe that you do. I would not be sitting here if it weren't for you. I know that if I had stayed, he would have killed me. God, if he knew I was here right now, he'd come after me in a heartbeat."

"I'm glad you think I make a difference, and I'm also grateful that you are sitting here too."

For the next few minutes, she asked questions about my sister, and I shared more about what I knew. I didn't typically talk about Lindsey with clients, but I had learned that sometimes I needed to share why I was doing this job. It helped them realize that they were not alone and that people did understand what they were going through.

After Detective Meyers returned, she signed the papers and asked a few more questions. Twenty minutes later, we walked through the lobby at the courthouse where the county detective's office was located toward the street.

As we stepped out of the building, I turned to Alice. "Would you be interested in a cup of coffee to celebrate your future of freedom?"

Alice smiled at me, then her gaze shifted, and I watched as her features shifted dramatically from relaxed and cheerful to frozen with terror. I started to turn to track what had concerned her when a loud popping noise filled the air, not once or twice, but three times, and then there was the squeal of tires.

I felt something hot on my left arm as I curled in on myself, and then a hand grabbed my right forearm, and as I turned, I found Alice slipping to the ground, blood already bubbling from her mouth as she tried to speak. Her eyes were wide and terror-filled, and I managed to catch her before she hit the ground.

I fell to my knees, cradling her. "Alice! Oh, my God! Help! I need help! Alice, hold on! Please, hold on!" I cried as I glanced at her chest and found it covered in blood. I held her, begging for her to hold on, but I knew it was no use. As I stared into her face, I saw her soul drift away.

Suddenly, there were people all around us, and someone was telling me to put her down, that I needed attention. I didn't need attention! Alice was the one that needed our attention. She couldn't be gone. This couldn't be the end of her story—it couldn't be. What had I done?

Suddenly, a hand clamped tightly over my arm. I started to yank it away, to fight against it, but the voice stopped me. "Laney, stop. You've been shot! I'm trying to stop the bleeding."

My frantic gaze jumped to the man. "Ethan, I'm fine! You have to help Alice."

Ethan cupped the side of my face with his other hand, making me look away from Alice. "Laney, she's gone. It's too late. You need to let her go so we can get you treated."

Someone else showed up at my side, and I saw a medical bag. Another person lifted Alice from my arms and laid her on the ground while I was coaxed from my knees and moved away. The road in front of us was now closed, traffic blocked off as the sheriff's deputies and other officers rushed out of the building to help or pursue the shooter. Other people stood around gawking at the poor woman who had finally dared to come forward.

"Her husband did this," I said weakly.

"Did you see him?"

I shook my head. "No, but I saw her face. When we came out the door, she was smiling, and then she looked over and saw him. Her face filled with terror, but before I could turn around to look at what she was afraid of, the bullets were flying. I know there is only one thing that could strike that much fear in her, and it was Steve."

"Okay, I'll let Cliff know, and we'll find him."

I stared at Alice while a deputy and another detective stood over her talking. "This was my fault."

"What? Why would this be your fault?"

I turned and looked into Ethan's concerned gaze. "Because I convinced her to get out and get help. I convinced her to file a police report and have her husband arrested."

Ethan took me by the shoulders, lowering his face closer to mine. "This was not your fault. You did exactly what you were supposed to do."

"But she's dead, Ethan! She's dead because of me." I couldn't help it; I started to cry. Ethan pulled me into his arms while an EMT bandaged my wrist.

They took me by ambulance to the hospital, and I stared unseeingly above me at the fluorescent lights as they wheeled me in. They had barely stopped the gurney and locked it in place before Evan appeared at my side, a look of concern on his features but a calmness about him that soothed me. "Hey, sweetheart, I heard you were shot."

"I'm okay," I told Evan, but one look into his eyes and I started crying all over again. Evan gathered me into his arms, whispering soothing words into my ear until I had calmed.

A nurse arrived and took my vitals while asking what had happened. My reply was short and sweet. "I got shot." It wasn't horrible. It was just a messy flesh wound that would leave a scar to remind me of my failure. I had failed Alice, just like I had failed my sister.

Evan stayed at my side for a while, and finally, my senses began to come back, and I looked at him. "I'm okay, Evan. How did you even hear about this?"

"Ethan called and woke me up to tell me what was going on."

"He didn't need to do that, and you don't need to stay here with me. I know you have to get ready for work."

Evan leaned forward, brushing a hand along my cheekbone. "I'm not going anywhere. I'm going to stay right by your side, and then I will take you home and make sure you are not alone. I already called my supervisor and told her I needed the night off."

"Evan, you didn't need to take the night off for me."

He smiled tenderly. "Maybe I took it off for me. Even though Ethan said it was minor, hearing that you got shot scared me, Laney. I need to stay by your side tonight for my sanity. Is that alright?"

I cupped his cheek with my good hand. "Yes, that is alright. That is very alright."

Two hours after I arrived at the hospital, Evan was driving away from the ER entrance with me seated beside him, feeling very woozy from the pain medication. I was a lightweight and never did well on narcotics.

I dozed on the way home, and then Evan helped me inside and up to bed. My arm was hurting now, not horrendously, but enough that I hissed and winced a few times when I bumped it. He tucked me in, kissed my forehead, and then said he would get me something to eat so I could take my next batch of medication on a full stomach.

I rolled to my side and drifted off to sleep almost instantly. It was dark in the room when I woke up, but not from the shutters. I could see a bit of light from the back patio area through the window. I slipped out of bed, wincing at my arm when I tried to move it, and used the bathroom.

I slipped quietly down the stairs and heard the television on in the kitchen. When I stepped in, I found Evan standing in front of it, watching the news as they talked about the incident at the courthouse. I froze as I watched the reporter talk about what witnesses described as a targeted attack. The suspect was believed to be the victim's husband, Steve Newman, and police were currently seeking his whereabouts.

They also mentioned that another person was injured, and they were treated and released from the hospital. Their name was being withheld for protection. Behind him, the camera focused on the spot where Alice had fallen, and a strangled sound left my throat.

Evan spun at the sound and was at my side before my knees could give out. In one fell swoop, he lifted me into his arms and carried me out of the room, and the tears started again.

CHAPTER NINETEEN

EVAN

My alarm was set for three, and while I had most of my notifications turned off, several people could still reach me. One of them was Ethan.

I fumbled with my phone for a moment and finally put it to my ear. "Yeah?"

"You're sleeping? Damn, I forgot what day it was. Sorry." I expected him to say he'd talk to me later, but he kept right on talking. "Are you awake enough to hear me?"

I sat up in bed as my heart rate began to accelerate. Had something happened to Dad? Cara? One of my other sisters? "Yeah, I'm awake. What's going on?"

"Okay, don't freak, it's not life-threatening, but Laney got shot today."

I threw the covers back and was on my feet in an instant. One hand clutched a handful of hair at the top of my head. "What?"

"I said don't freak. She's okay. It was a minor wound to her arm. She will probably only need a few stitches. I don't think she will need surgery or anything."

"What the hell happened? Where is she? Are you sure she's

going to be alright? You know that gunshot wounds can lead to other issues if not treated properly."

"Evan!" he growled into the phone. "Shut the hell up! I was there a minute after it happened, and I took care of Laney until EMS got there. I swear it is not serious. She's going to be more messed up by the fact that her client is dead than her getting hurt."

I closed my eyes, thankful that Laney wasn't seriously injured, but at the same time, my heart ached for the loss of her client.

My heart was pounding in my chest, and I took a calming breath before I asked, "Where did this happen?"

"At the courthouse. Laney was there with the client to talk to Cliff Meyers. He was working the case."

"Where is Laney now?"

"She's at the hospital. I thought you might want to check on her."

"I will. I appreciate the call. Was anyone else hurt?"

"No. Laney said it was her client's husband. We are looking for him."

"Is Laney in any danger?"

"I don't know. I don't think so, but I'd keep an eye on her."

"Yeah, I will. Thanks for calling, Ethan. I'm going to head to the hospital now."

"Alright. Let me know if you need anything."

"I will." I hung up and sank back against the bed, rubbing my hands over my face after tossing my phone to the mattress—my god, what was going through Laney's mind right now.

Ten minutes later, I was dressed and on my way to the hospital. As I drove, I called my supervisor, Deb, and told her what was going on. She relayed that Victoria had just asked if there were any extra shifts to pick up and knew she'd take it for me.

"You think she'd want the whole weekend?"

"Yeah, I think she might. She has college tuition due for her daughter soon. You know how she snaps up any and all shifts when it's tuition time."

"Alright, see if she wants it. If she can't, or if no one else is available to take a shift, let me know, but I am going to need tonight off."

"You got it, Evan. I'm glad it's not too serious. Do you want me to go down and check on her?"

"No, I'm about ten minutes away. Ethan said it wasn't serious."

"Well, she will be in good hands with you. Let us know if you need anything from us."

"I will, Deb. Thanks."

After I parked, I went straight into the ER and got waved in by a staff member behind the window. I checked the board as soon as I rounded the corner, found her room, and made a beeline for her. The moment she saw me, she fell to pieces, but I was there to comfort her.

I got her home and into bed without too much trouble, and I had gone down to make her something to eat, but when I returned, she was sound asleep. I figured it was better for her to sleep than think, so I let her be.

Several hours later, I was sitting on a stool in the kitchen when the ten o'clock news came on, and the lead story was about the shooting. Ethan had told me more when I spoke to him a few hours ago. Unfortunately, the husband was still on the loose, but he was glad that I had taken the night off to be home with her. I had made sure to turn the alarm on as soon as I got off the phone with him.

Now I stood, anger simmering under my skin to think that Laney had been so close to being killed. The memory of telling Cara that Ryan was dead was way too fresh in my mind, and it made me almost sick to think of what I had done to my sister with those words. If someone had told me that about Laney, I would have been devastated.

A strangled cry had me spinning around, and I caught Laney before she passed out on the floor. Her body was shaking as I lifted her in my arms and carried her from the room. We sat in the living room with her curled into my lap as I rocked her soothingly.

"You're okay, Laney. It's over now. I'm so sorry, sweetheart. I'm so sorry about your client."

She hiccupped on a sob and cried harder. I just kept holding her, stroking her back, her head, kissing her temple, and telling her she was alright. Eventually, she calmed down and stopped crying.

Her voice was a mere whisper, and I strained to hear all that she said. "I held her in my arms while she died. She was so scared when she saw him, so surprised to see him outside. I tried to look at what was scaring her, but then there were gunshots, and I started to cower. She grabbed my arm as she began to fall, and I caught her."

She was quiet for a few seconds, and I let her have her peace. "Then I begged her not to go, to hold on, but I watched the life leave her eyes, Evan. It was there one second and then gone—just gone. All I could imagine was Lindsey lying there, and that happening to her, and that she was all alone. No one that loved her was with her."

"What was her name?"

"Alice."

"Alice wasn't alone. You were there with her, and Alice is not Lindsey. Lindsey was surrounded by doctors and nurses who were trying to save her life. What happened today was different, and you need to remember that."

"Yeah, I guess, but she's dead, Evan." She lifted grief-stricken eyes to me. "Alice is dead, and it's my fault."

I pulled her chin back toward me as she tried to look away.

"This was not your fault, Laney. You didn't pull the trigger, and you didn't make that asshole pull it. He did it because of who he is. If Alice hadn't died today, she probably would have died in six months or a year. He was determined to kill her in any way that he could. Determined enough to do it right in front of the courthouse with all those witnesses and cameras."

A look of hope entered her eyes. "They got him on camera?"

I nodded. "Ethan told me that they have clear video of him waiting across the street and then firing toward the front door. It's only a matter of time before they catch him and he's behind bars."

"Good. Although he deserves worse than being put in jail."

"I agree." I kissed her brow. "How are you feeling?"

"My arm hurts, but otherwise, my body is fine. My heart is broken, though."

I hugged her tightly. "I am sure it is. If I could fix that, I would. What I can do is feed you something and get your medicine. Then we can curl up in bed and watch television. What do you think of that?"

"I think that's a great idea, although I don't want much to eat."

"I have a sandwich that I made you earlier, and my sister brought over your favorite chocolate tortes."

"Okay." She grinned. "Now I'm hungry."

I helped her get off my lap and took her hand. "Come on, let's get our food and have a picnic in bed."

She pulled my arm back when I started to walk away and lifted her chin. "Thank you for being here, Evan."

"I wouldn't want to be anyplace else, sweetheart."

I stayed by her side that night, holding her close, and in the morning found a text from Deb saying that Victoria was willing to take my weekend shifts. I was happy to hear that because I wasn't ready to leave Laney alone.

Not because I was worried about her injury, it was minor, but because I was concerned over her mental status. During the night, she'd had two nightmares, and while she never woke up, I could only assume they were about the incident—either the one with her client or the one with her sister.

Saturday morning, we had breakfast in the kitchen, and then Laney sat on the patio and spoke with her boss for a little while. I needed to run home and get some more clothes, so I had called Carmen to come stay with Laney so she wouldn't be alone.

I also figured that Carmen might have good advice for Laney on dealing with this stress since she was a psychiatrist. Laney was still on the patio when the doorbell rang, and I waved at Carmen through the window before turning the alarm off.

"Wow," Carmen said as she stepped inside. "What a house!" She hugged me tightly. "How is she?"

"She's alright. She's on the phone with her boss right now. Come on in. I have coffee if you want some."

"I can always use coffee." She followed me into the kitchen, her head twisting and turning to take it all in. When we got to the kitchen, she sighed. "Holy smokes. What I wouldn't do for a kitchen like this."

"Yeah, I know. I thought the same thing the first time I saw it."

"The cream walls and the peach accents with the black cabinets and black countertops are perfect! I'm going to have to remember this when I redo my kitchen next year."

I poured her coffee and collected the creamer from the fridge. Carmen was pouring some into her mug when Laney joined us. "Carmen! What are you doing here?"

"I came to check on you." She rushed to Laney and pulled her in tightly for a hug. "I thought maybe while Evan was running his errands, I could hang out with you, and we could talk some."

Laney smiled at my sister and then turned to me and said, "I'm okay, Evan. I don't need a babysitter."

Carmen laughed, putting her arm around Laney's shoulders and squeezing her. "I know you don't, but it would make Evan more comfortable knowing you weren't alone after yesterday."

"You aren't going to psychoanalyze me, are you?"

Carmen shook her head. "Not at all. If you want to talk about it, I can listen. If you don't, then we won't. Whatever you want to do, but you do have to promise me one thing."

"What's that?"

"You have to let me see the back garden that I have heard so much about."

Laney laughed, and I knew that she wasn't upset with me.

"I'm going to run home, and then I'll hit the grocery store on the way back. Is there anything special that you want?"

"You don't have to do that, Evan. I can have a service order food and deliver it."

I stepped in front of her. "Believe it or not, but sometimes I do like to go to the store. I enjoy picking out my food."

"Okay, if that's what you want to do, but let me give you my credit card."

She started to turn, and I stepped back and growled a little more harshly than I intended. "I don't need you to pay for it, Laney."

Laney stopped in mid-turn and glanced back at me. "I did not mean to offend you, Evan. I was offering to help since you are buying groceries for my house."

"To which I am also eating," I stated. I glanced at Carmen to find her observing the two of us, one brow arched. "I'm going to head out. I'll be back in a couple of hours. Thanks for hanging out with her, Carmen." I turned to Laney. "Turn the alarm back on after I leave, please."

I brushed my lips over her cheek and then marched to the mudroom. I pulled my SUV out of the garage, got out, and closed the door because even though I was parked inside, I didn't want a remote, and then I pulled down the driveway.

I didn't mean to snap at Laney, but I also didn't want or need her to pay for everything because I was staying at her house. I know Cara told me not to let it bother me, but her wealth *did* bother me. How was I supposed to get over that? Could I get over it? I guess only time would tell.

"The place looks great," I told Laney the following Saturday when I stood on the back balcony and stared down at the patio below. Laney curled into my side, smiling happily as she looked around, searching for anything she might have missed. "I think you got it all. It's going be a great time."

"And the weather is perfect," she commented.

I lifted her chin, staring into the eyes that I had come to love so much. "You are perfect."

She giggled. "Not even slightly."

I kissed the tip of her nose, then her mouth. "You are to me."

"Well, as long as you think I am, then I will take it. That's all that matters, right?"

"That's all that matters," I repeated and took the time to kiss her thoroughly for a few moments. We broke apart when the doorbell rang. She was all smiles, her eyes bright and excited.

"Okay, here we go! Our first barbeque!" She spun around and started to head toward the door, and I couldn't help but grin as I followed her. Even though this wasn't my house, I did appreciate that she included me in that statement. It was our first barbeque together.

This past week, I had forced myself not to think about Laney's money. Instead, I focused on our relationship and how she made me feel. It turns out she made me feel a lot—especially when I found out that she went down to Coral's Café and spoke to her about the barbeque. Coral had given her all my siblings' phone numbers and the Youngs', and she had called every one of them and invited them to come. My understanding was that they were all going to be here.

That in itself was a huge deal. It was rare when we were off work and could be in the same place simultaneously—the only people missing would be Cara, Bryan, their son, Luke, and of course, my mother.

Carmen came in with a covered dish, and right behind her was my father, with a small grocery bag. That was one thing that I had been able to get Laney to concede in—let everyone bring something to feel like they contributed.

She agreed with that, and it made both of us happy. We supplied the meat and drinks, and everyone else brought the salads, desserts, and other side dishes. As I studied Laney's face, I realized that making her happy was now the most essential thing in my life.

My father leaned toward me as he passed by. "I have something for you. Make sure we get a moment alone later."

"Okay, Pop, I'll make sure." What that was, I had no clue, but I'd take anything my father wanted to give me.

CHAPTER TWENTY

LANEY

*I*t took me a few days to get my feet back under me. I still dreamed about Alice at night, and sometimes her face would morph into Lindsey's, even though Lindsey hadn't died from a gunshot wound. Alice had passed quickly, whereas Lindsey had suffered after being kicked repeatedly and pushed down a stairwell.

Evan had been incredible. He had been nearby but didn't hover, and he didn't ask me a million times if I was okay or if I wanted to talk about it. I appreciated the space.

I also appreciated him asking Carmen to stay with me while running errands. I hadn't been all too excited about it at first, but it was nice to have someone else to speak with. She listened and even gave me a little advice about handling the flashbacks that were sure to come. She also told me repeatedly that it wasn't my fault.

In my heart, I knew it wasn't, but my mind wanted to play tricks on me. Joyce had told me the same thing. Steve would have killed Alice eventually. At least Alice had known peace for a few minutes before her death. I had given her that, and she would not want me to blame myself.

Joyce had even suggested that Alice had succumbed quickly to be at peace and away from him. Is that why Lindsey had finally stopped fighting? Did she realize as she lay on the hospital gurney that it would be better just to let go and be free of it all? Maybe.

On Friday, I had attended Alice's funeral, and Evan had accompanied me. We didn't stay for the luncheon, but we did want to pay our respects.

I had taken the week off from work to get my head on straight and had thrown myself into this picnic. I didn't have that much to plan, but I did spend time in my garden, pruning and cleaning things up.

I also bought new dishes, not paper plates, but heavy-duty reusable plastic ones with a floral design to go with the patio that would last for years to come.

Evan helped me when he wasn't working and slept at my house all week. I wasn't complaining. I liked having him here. It had only been a couple of weeks, and yet, it was almost like he had lived here for a while. I had even given him his own closet, and he had a few things hanging in there now. What would he say if I asked him to move in with me completely?

Was it too soon to even consider that? I didn't think so. I knew that I was in love with him, although I hadn't told him yet. Neither of us had spoken the words, but I was pretty sure he felt the same way that I did.

Perhaps after the picnic, I would broach the subject and see if Evan was receptive.

I stood beside Evan, feeling excitement bubbling deep inside of me. I had hosted many parties in my day, but none had ever made me feel this way. Most of the time, I had dreaded the thought of entertaining because the people were business associates or family friends. They weren't *my* friends, not people I truly cared to be around.

The people coming to my house today were people that I

liked. People who liked me and wanted to get to know me better, and hopefully, I would have them in my life for a long time to come.

I answered the door, practically bouncing on my toes, and welcomed Carmen and Rich with strong hugs and huge smiles. A few minutes later, more people arrived, and before I knew it, my home and patio were filled with laughter and talk.

There was juice and treats for the kids, and the older ones like Tonya and Tyler, who were Brad Young's kids, oversaw the younger ones who toddled around and tried to splash in the stream.

I frowned as I watched them. If we had kids, we would need to do something to keep them away from that. I laughed to myself as I turned and sought out Evan.

He was near the grill cooking with Wes, Huntley, and Cameron. My heart filled with love as I stared at him, and I could picture him there, holding a baby in his arms—our baby. I had never been one to dream of such things. In the past, the thought of children had always been pushed aside because work was more important.

Bas had once asked me if I would stop working once we had children, and I had laughed at him. I told him that I wasn't even sure I wanted kids. Would I be willing to stop working now if I had children? I just might, or perhaps go part-time. The thought was almost ludicrous to me, and I forced down the bubble of hysteria that was about to burst out. Me, the workaholic thinking about going part-time and having children? What a turn my life had taken since I arrived in Pennsylvania two and a half years ago.

That thought sobered me as I remembered what was coming soon—the anniversary of Lindsey's death. It will be officially three years soon.

"Laney, thank you so much for inviting us," Mrs. Young said

to me as she came to stand beside me on the balcony. "Your home is beautiful."

"Thank you, Mrs. Young."

"Please, call me Patricia," she said with a smile. "I can't imagine how much work went into that lovely garden."

"It was a lot. I had landscapers clean it up when I moved in, and I redirected it to fit my tastes."

"It's beautiful, and I know that Rich appreciates the fact that you came over and helped with his garden." She pointed down at him. "He's been walking that path over and over again since he arrived. He just can't get over how beautiful your flowers are."

"This is my favorite spot in the house," I told her.

"Oh, I believe it." She hesitated and then turned to me. "Evan is a fortunate man."

"Why do you say that?"

"I mean to have found you."

"Thank you, but I think I am the lucky one. When I came here, I was looking for something. I just didn't know what it was. I think I do now."

"And what is it that you were looking for?"

I put out my hand, indicating all that was below. "A family."

She looked sad for a moment. "Do you not have any family, Laney?"

"I have a brother, but we are not close. My sister died three years ago, my parents when I was in college."

"And no other family?"

I shook my head. "No, and I didn't realize how much I missed having one or how much I had missed out on from not having one until I saw Evan's family."

"They are a special group of people."

I chuckled. "Yes, they are, but your group is pretty special too."

She beamed at me. "Yes, that is true, and now that I know

they are all happy and married, I can relax a little bit and sit back and enjoy all the grandchildren they are giving me. We went from only having two to having nine in only a couple of years. Of course, some of those are from previous marriages or other circumstances, like Kayley's daughter Becky. No matter how we got them, we love them like they were our blood."

"That is pretty special."

"Do you want children?" she asked.

My gaze drifted back to Evan, and once again, my heart swelled in my chest. "I do. I didn't think I wanted them, but recently, I realized that I do."

She put her hand on my arm. "Perhaps you were waiting for the right man to come along. One that was worthy of you."

"Perhaps you are correct," I replied just as Tonya came rushing up to her grandmother and told her she had to come see something in the backyard. I watched as they headed down the stairs, and then I leaned on the balcony and watched everyone below.

This house was perfect for entertaining. My other house was too, but completely different types of people. The house I had in Santa Monica was glacial and modern. It was glass and chrome, white walls, carpets, décor with splashes of colors, and expensive artwork on the walls.

It had seven bedrooms and nine baths. Each bedroom was a master, and there were two full bathrooms on the main floor. The kitchen was over five hundred square feet and had two stoves and dishwashers, four sinks, and two extra-large fridges and freezers. When I lived there, I had a chef for dinners. I had company at least three times a week, and the rest of the time, he prepared meals for the staff or things for me to eat for breakfast or lunch. I also had three maids, a personal assistant, and two groundskeepers, plus a man who did my driving and was a bodyguard of sorts.

I had lived in the limelight, wearing the most beautiful

clothes and expensive jewels. My six-car garage had been packed, and two of those cars were here with me now. The other four sat in the garage back there, only coming out for monthly drives to ensure they stayed in perfect working order.

Only one maid continued at the house, and she made sure everything was kept tidy. One groundskeeper kept an eye on the gardens, home, and cars. The rest were let go.

I didn't miss any of it, not really. Okay, that's not true. I did miss some of Rachel's cooking. She was a fantastic chef, and luckily she found another full-time job with someone not far from where I lived.

The rest I didn't miss. I wasn't sure how I could have lived for four years in a house that was so starkly black and white. A pop of color here or there didn't really change things. That house was exactly like my life had been. It was either black or white. Straight and on point—focused and structured.

My life was nothing like that now. My gaze followed the winding path of the small stream as I realized that I liked the wiggle of my life now. No two days were the same. No clients were the same.

Someone stepped next to me, and I glanced over to find Daniella smiling at me. "This is such a fantastic place to have a barbeque. You do know that from now, you're going to have to host all these events."

I laughed. "I honestly don't mind."

"I don't think any of them would mind. I think I heard Henley say something about the only thing missing was a pool."

"Funny he should say that. I had been considering having one put in this winter for next summer. I might even have it constructed inside a building, like a sunroom, with a retractable ceiling so that it could be used year-round."

"That sounds incredible."

"Thank you."

Daniella glanced at me, nibbling on her bottom lip. "Does Evan know just how wealthy you are?"

I turned to study her profile. "Why do you ask me that?"

Daniella glanced around us and then shifted a bit closer as she lowered her voice. "I know you said that you have read several of my books, but did you ever by chance read *Wynter's Domain?*"

"No, I don't believe I have. Why?"

"I did a lot of research for that book. The main character was a very wealthy woman from an influential family. I wanted her to be strong, almost unbreakable, and powerful. I researched influential women, and I came across a woman named Alaina Buckworth." My smile faded as she continued. "She was the middle child in a very wealthy family, and I read a lot of articles about her. She became my inspiration for the character that I named Wynter."

I knew my mouth was hanging open, but I couldn't seem to close it. I immediately glanced toward Evan to find his back was to us. "When did you realize?"

She shifted to face me more directly. "I thought you looked familiar when we were at the tavern, but I couldn't place you. I was cleaning my office the other day and digging through a box to find information about something else, and I stumbled over your photograph and the notes I had made on you."

"Did you tell anyone else?"

She shook her head. "If anyone understands the need for privacy, it's me. Trust me. I would never share your secret, but" —she hesitated and turned to look at Evan—"I would make it a point to tell Evan the truth. I don't know if you know what happened with Cara or not."

I nodded. "I do."

"Okay, good. Well, after that, this family might not be quite so welcoming to someone if they found out another person was living incognito."

"It's not like it's against the law to change your name and start over," I stated in a rush.

"No." She shook her head. "It's not. I didn't want anyone to know that I was Veronica Raven when I moved here. I had a stalker who had attacked me in my last home, so I moved far away, and only a few people knew who I was, but my stalker found me. I know my situation isn't the same, but what Cara went through with Bryan is very similar. Hunt told me how furious Evan was about Bryan lying to his sister. I'd hate for him to get upset with you because he learns later on that you are someone else."

I sighed and leaned my elbows on the railing. "Daniella, to tell you the truth, I think that Alaina was someone else. The person I am today, Laney Marshall, is the real me."

"Perhaps they can coexist someplace, but I would suggest that you find a way to let Evan know. He's a simple, straightforward man. The whole family is. Not simple as in stupid, just as in they don't need much. They want love, family, a job to keep them happy and to be able to help others. Money doesn't mean anything to them. At least it doesn't matter to Hunt. When I told him I made six figures on my book sales, he told me that was my money, and he didn't want to know about it. I could save it for our kids or spend it on whatever, but he was taking care of me because that was how he was raised."

"I can see that in them—all of them."

"They are proud, and you need to let Evan know soon exactly what might be in his future. You might want to stay here and under the radar, but someday, something will happen, and you are going to be big news. Don't let the information blindside you two. I think you guys have what it takes to make a wonderful relationship."

"Thank you, Daniella. I appreciate that and what you said. I know that the few times money has come up, Evan has gotten tense about it, but I keep trying to assure him that money doesn't matter."

Daniella looked around. "Money does matter, and at your house, it is obvious that you have it. Maybe Carmen can help you with some ideas on how to cross that barrier if you reach it."

"I'll keep that in mind."

Daniella squeezed my arm and walked away, and I turned to look down at Evan. He was watching me, and I flipped on a smile as he waved me down. I would have to find a way to approach the subject and tell him the truth. Daniella was right. It wasn't fair to not explain everything to Evan, especially when I was thinking long-term relationship with the man.

I'd get it figured out and explain it all to him soon. For now, I would forget about it and enjoy the picnic.

CHAPTER TWENTY-ONE

EVAN

The barbeque was a hit, and everyone had a great time —especially Laney. She was happy and laughing the whole time, and I was pleased to see that after the last week. Perhaps this would help her move forward and put the incident behind her.

After everyone left, I helped Laney pick up the last of the trash and stack the final dishes to be washed the next day. Both of us were happily exhausted, and the only thing that I wanted to do was climb in her shower and then make love to her.

I made sure doors were locked and the alarm was on before we took the stairs hand in hand. "Did you have a nice day?"

"I did. I think everyone had a good time."

"Everyone had a great time, and who knew you were so good at volleyball." I squeezed her hand.

She laughed. "I'm not going to be able to move tomorrow, but it was fun."

When we reached the landing on the top floor, I let her go in front of me, and I wrapped my arms around her waist, leaning down to whisper in her ear, "I can give you a massage. Help ease those tight muscles."

"Oh, will your massage come with passionate sex and mind-blowing orgasms, too?"

"As much and as many as you want."

She laughed. "Then you are on."

"We can start the massage in the shower. Use that hot water to help ease those muscles." I kissed her neck, then nibbled on her ear as we headed straight to the bathroom.

Once inside, I spun her around and kissed her like I had wanted to do all afternoon. Our clothes were off in seconds, and we were in the shower shortly after that.

We stood under one of the rain faucets, letting it fall over us as we kissed and touched one another. Then I spun Laney around and put her against the glass like I had the first time we were in here together. I started rubbing her shoulders, then her shoulder blades, down her back. Her eyes were closed, and her mouth opened on a moan.

She arched her back as I got lower, pushing her ass out toward me, and I massaged each of her buttocks for a moment before I fisted myself and then lined my cock up to slide between her closed thighs. She leaned closer to the glass, sticking her ass back further, wanting it, almost begging for me to fill her, but I didn't. I teased her, lightly rubbing my head against her hot flesh as I continued to massage her ass cheeks. Then I rubbed my cock through the sweet crack of her ass, and she whimpered.

I was on my knees in a moment, spreading her cheeks wide and pulling her hips back so I could get to her better. I lapped at her desire and filled her as much as I could with my tongue. Then I licked her from front to back over and over again until she was practically begging me to give her more.

I used my fingers, pumping them into her, but she called out, "You, I need you in me."

Nothing like a fucking invitation. I practically shot to my feet, and ran the head of my cock through her folds again, then with one thrust, I filled her, and she gasped and moaned as I thrust forward again, hard.

"Yes!" she hissed as I did it again, and I pulled her back from the glass so I could palm her breasts, pinch her nipples, and still thrust deeply into her. One hand slipped between her legs and rubbed her clit. "Yes! Oh, god! Yes! Evan, please!"

I stopped instantly, spinning her around and pushing her to the glass wall. "No, you can't come the first time until my mouth is on you." I went back to my knees, lifting one of her legs and hooking it over my shoulder so I could fit perfectly between her thighs.

I feasted on her flesh, listening to her moans, her pleas, her explosion as I took her over the top, and then before she could come down, I stood again, turning her back to the glass and taking her from behind. She came again almost immediately as I rocked into her and rubbed her clit. She came so hard that she tried to get away from me, but I held her, making her accept all the pleasure that came with it as I exploded into her and then practically collapsed against her body, trapping her against the glass wall.

"Holy crap," I murmured.

She laughed. "You know, we could do that more often if you stayed here more."

I chuckled into her ear. "I might just have to do that."

As it turns out, staying at her place happened quite often. It had been a month since we met, and Laney and I spent every single moment together that we could. I hadn't slept at my place since the barbeque, and I began to wonder if I ever would again.

The day after the barbeque, we went by my place and packed two bags of my clothes. Laney helped me get them hung up and put them away in the closet's drawers that she officially labeled as mine. I had looked around at all the space and wondered if I'd even be able to fill half of it—I highly doubted it.

We had leftovers from the day before and snuggled on the patio, watching a movie in the evening, and that night, we made love again.

I had to work nights on Wednesday and Thursday, and when I woke up Wednesday afternoon, I came down to find that Laney had packed me several meals to take with me, plus a bag of cookies that she had picked up from Coral's Café.

When we were off work at the same time, we were inseparable. We talked about our jobs, wishes, and dreams, and we made love for hours. Sometimes in the bedroom, but we'd often end up having sex in random parts of the house. I think our favorite place was the back patio, but the stairs to the second floor, the kitchen counter, the basement couch, and even the pool table had seen some of our action.

There was no doubt in my mind that I was in love with Laney Marshall and that she felt the same way. While we hadn't spoken the words out loud, we had shown one another many times over the last few weeks. It wasn't even the lovemaking, but the little things we did for one another.

We'd leave each other notes. Cook each other a surprise meal. Pop into each other's place of work just to kiss the other or bring them a coffee. Sometimes, a gift would appear—a new pair of shoes for me, a leatherbound journal for her. I had learned early on that she liked to sit and write for a few minutes each day.

Those were the things that meant the most to me. The little things that we did and shared. I hoped that Laney felt the same way.

Tonight was our one-month anniversary of meeting, and both of us would be home. Since I was off today, I had decided to surprise Laney with a candlelight dinner.

As I prepared the dining room table, I decided to use the china from the expensive hutch. I even called Coral to make sure I had correctly set up the place settings, sending her pictures to approve.

In the center of the table were fresh flowers cut from my father's garden, and for dessert, I had two of her favorite chocolate tortes from my sister's café. Now all I needed was Laney.

She arrived a few minutes later, and I greeted her in the kitchen. She looked tired and weary. "I'm so glad you made something. I'm so exhausted. All I want to do is eat, then cuddle up on the sofa with you and fall asleep."

"We can do that."

"Let me put my stuff away, and I'll set the table."

"The table is already set," I told her as I stirred the pasta. I glanced back to see her frowning at the table, and I laughed. "No, I haven't lost my mind, and we are not eating on imaginary dishes. I set the dining room table."

She cocked her head, looking confused. "But why that table?"

I set down my spoon and came to her, taking her hands and kissing the knuckles on each one. "Because today is our one-month anniversary since we met one another. I thought I would do something special for you."

She blinked. "It's been a month?"

I nodded. "Yep."

She seemed to think that over for a moment, then grinned as she slipped her arms around my neck. "If it really has been a month, then I think I can finally say something to you."

"What is that?"

"I love you."

I stared down at her, feeling my heart ready to burst. "And I love you, too, Laney. I wanted to tell you that sooner, but I decided to hold it back. I didn't want you to think I was rushing anything."

"That is exactly why I didn't tell you. I didn't want you to think I was rushing anything."

"You and I are on the same wavelength here."

She grinned. "Yes, I do believe we are."

I kissed Laney slowly and then released her to get dinner ready to plate. Laney slipped into the dining room, and I heard her gasp. I rushed to her side to see what had happened. I expected to find the table had collapsed or the dishes were broken, but the table was as perfectly set as I had left it.

Laney stood, her fingers over her lips, and her eyes filled with moisture. "Laney, what's wrong?"

"You used the china."

"I did," I said slowly, glancing at the table and then looking back at her. "Should I have not done that? If you want me to put it all back, I can. I just thought it would be nice to use it for this special occasion."

Laney lifted her face to mine, tears streaking down her cheeks, and she shook her head.

"Laney, honey, I'm so sorry." I wrapped my arms around her. "I'll put it back."

"No!" she exclaimed, and I leaned back and wiped her cheeks.

"Okay, do you want to tell me why you are crying?"

"The dishes belonged to my sister. I bought her the twelve-place setting when she got married."

I winced. "I'm sorry. I'll put it back. I should have asked." I started to move toward the table, but she grabbed my arm.

"No!" she barked again, her eyes wide. "No! Today is the perfect day to use it—the perfect reason."

I wasn't sure I understood that, but I nodded.

She sighed and wiped the rest of the tears from her face. "Today is the anniversary of her death. It's officially been three years."

I winced. "Aw, Laney, I'm so sorry."

"I'm not. I'm sorry I got emotional, but I've been thinking about Lindsey all day. That's why I'm worn out. I didn't sleep all that well last night, and today I was distracted thinking about it. Lindsey would want me to use them, and I can't think of a better time to bring them out than for us to be celebrating a future."

"I like that. I love the sound of a future with you, Laney."

She curled herself against my chest and held me tightly. "I do too, Evan. I can't remember ever wanting to have someone else in my life this much. I can see a future for us—marriage, kids. I can see it all, and I want it. For the first time in my life, I want it all."

"You've really thought about marriage and kids?"

She nodded against my chest. "Yes. I know that might seem weird, but at the barbeque when all your family and friends were here, I could picture you holding one of our children or chasing another through the garden. I could see us having dinner at your father's, picnics at the park, with our kids running around the playground and sticking their hands and feet into the stream off the patio."

Even though she couldn't see me, I was grinning, for I, too, had been thinking about those things. I had spent quite a few minutes looking around at all the families, all the love, and knew that I was ready for it. "We might have to put a fence up around the stream for a while to keep them from drowning. You saw how attracted the little ones were to it."

"Yeah, that would probably be best," she said with a chuckle.

I leaned back and lifted her chin. "Laney, maybe this is crazy for us to even consider, and it's not something that I had planned for tonight, but now, I want to ask you something."

"What's that?"

I stepped farther back, then dropped to one knee. Laney's eyes brightened, but not from tears. I saw the joy on her face—excitement for what she knew was about to come.

I slipped my hand into my pocket and pulled out a ring. A very special ring that my father had given me at the picnic. He had pulled me aside and told me that my mother had wanted me to have her ring for my future bride. He told me that I would know when the time was right. I honestly believed that moment was now.

The ring wasn't big or flashy, but it was special to me, and hopefully, it would be just as special to Laney.

"Laney Marshall, I know we have only known each other for a month, but I love you, and I want everything with you. I want that family. I want you to be part of my family. I want those kids. I want it all with you. Laney, would you be my wife?"

Laney nodded, and then tears were once again racing down her cheeks as I slipped the ring over her finger. I was thankful that these were happy tears as she lifted the ring to look at it. Her mouth opened in surprise. "Evan, this is beautiful."

"I know it's not large or fancy, but"—I paused and swallowed the emotion that stuck in my throat—"it was my mom's. My father said she wanted me to have it."

"Oh, Evan! It's perfect. You are perfect. I love you so much." The two of us kissed for a few minutes, and then I had to rush away to get the food off the stove before dinner was ruined. While I did that, Laney went upstairs to freshen up.

I had just moved everything off the burners when the doorbell rang. I set the pot holders off to the side and went to find out who was at the door, a smile parked on my face and a spring in my step as I reached the foyer. A tall man with dark hair was outside, his back to the glass, and I frowned as a bad feeling began to slither down my spine. Who was this? Was this Alice's husband come to hurt Laney?

I opened the door. "Can I help you?"

The man turned, and his piercing, intense gaze slid down to my feet and then back up. His chin lifted higher as he looked me in the eye. "I'm here to see Alaina."

"I'm sorry, but there is no Alaina here."

He rolled his almost black eyes and shook his head. "I think she is using the name Laney Marshall."

I frowned and asked gruffly, "And who are you?"

His eyes bore into me so hard it was like he was pushing me back as he responded, "I'm Sebastian Garza, her fiancé."

CHAPTER TWENTY-TWO

LANEY

I could not have asked for life to have been better than it was. I was as happy as I could be with my job and content with my growing love life with Evan. I could easily see our future and wanted nothing more than to move forward and begin to create it.

The problem was that today was the anniversary of my sister's death, and everything was reminding me of it. Even our morning staff meeting had brought back memories when Joyce reported that one county over, a woman had been killed by her husband overnight.

I hadn't been able to avoid the avalanche of memories, and I had basically locked myself in my office to avoid speaking to anyone as I tried to deal with them. By the time I could leave for the day, all I wanted to do was crawl into Evan's arms and hide.

Seeing what Evan did for me lit the spark inside me that had almost diminished during the day. I was not going to hold back anymore. I was going to move forward, and loving Evan was the best way to do that.

That meant that I needed to have a serious conversation with him. I had thought over what Daniella had said many times these last two weeks and been looking for the right time. It seemed like tonight would have to be that time.

After telling him that I would marry him, I excused myself to clean up while he got dinner on the table. I was grinning wildly to myself as I disappeared into my closet to find something comfortable but nice for dinner.

Initially, I had planned on a frozen pizza or leftovers in leggings camped out in front of the television, but not tonight. Now, I wanted to look good for Evan, and I wanted to cozy up to him and enjoy the evening after a long day of hellish memories and plan a future—our future.

I heard the doorbell but didn't think much of it. For all I knew, Evan had a surprise being delivered. That was the kind of man that he was. His surprises were never elaborate or expensive, but they showed how much he cared.

One day after I told him how much my feet hurt from the high-heeled shoes I was wearing, he had my slippers waiting for me at the door and instructions to meet him on the back patio for a foot massage. That foot massage had turned into an elaborate lovemaking session and picnic of Chinese food under the fairy lights.

After I changed, I checked my image, brushed my hair, and wiped away a little stray mascara from under my eyes. There was no reason to put anything on my lips since we would be eating as soon as I came down.

I stared at the ring he had put on my finger. The elegant round diamond was in a traditional solitaire setting. It was both beautiful and timeless. The fact that it had once been his mother's meant so much to me. If I were to guess, it was close to a carat, but I didn't care how big or little it was. Evan had given me something to treasure—not just Evan, but his father, too. That told me just how important I was to this family, and I swore not to make them regret that.

I had just come down the stairs when I heard the man at the

door. My heart skidded to a stop, and my knees locked when the deep, slightly accented voice said, "I think she is using the name Laney Marshall."

"And who are you?" Evan asked.

There was a slight pause before the man answered, and I felt the blood rush to my feet. "I'm Sebastian Garza, her fiancé."

I was suddenly dizzy, and the temptation to turn and run up the stairs was there, but I had never run from anything. Instead, I started walking down the stairs again. This time, my hand clung to the railing so that I wouldn't fall down the stairs. Although falling to my death right then might have been preferable to what was about to happen.

"Her fiancé?" Evan's voice grew deep as if he were trying to control his anger.

"Yes, I assume she mentioned me," he stated as I began to round the corner.

"She most certainly has not," I stated roughly as my eyes landed on him outside the door. "What are you doing here, Bas?"

Evan shifted to the side, and I could feel him staring at me, but I didn't look his way. You never took your eyes off your opponent.

Bas let one of the sexy smiles that had first caught my attention slip over his face. It did nothing for me. "Alaina, you are looking well."

"Thank you. What are you doing here?"

He frowned slightly. "Where are your manners, Alaina? Did you lose them moving to this little Podunk town? Are you not going to invite me in?" He looked past me. "Much different than your other house."

I crossed my arms over my chest. "I'm not going to do anything until you tell me why the hell you are here, Bastion."

"Well, I believe we have some unfinished business to attend to."

"What business would that be?"

"The fact that we were to be married. Your brother promised me the connection to your company."

"I don't care what Larry promised you, Bas. He can go to hell for all I care."

Bastion's expression darkened, and I expected him to spring a heated retort toward me, but he didn't. He looked suddenly weary, and his voice was low as he next spoke. "Perhaps that is indeed where he is now."

I blinked and then blinked again. "What are you talking about, Bastion?"

He sighed and looked around. "May I come in, Alaina? I have news that would be better received inside and not on your front step."

Something terrible was happening here, and I wasn't sure I wanted to hear what it was, but I didn't have a choice. I nodded at Bastion and pushed the door open wider. Bastion gave me a curt nod, then peered at Evan as he walked past him.

I closed the door, and as I turned, Evan was glaring down at me. "Fiancé?"

I shook my head. "No, he's not, Evan. I'll explain it all later."

A muscle in his cheek began to tick, and after a moment, he said huskily, "I'll give you your space." I watched him walk away and down the hallway toward the kitchen. I sighed. Evan was going to have to wait. God! Just when I thought today was getting better. Could it get any worse?

I led Bastion to the formal living room, and he unbuttoned his suit jacket and took a seat. "Is he living here with you?"

"Evan is none of your business, Bas. Why are you here?"

He leaned forward and put his elbows on his knees. "I'm here to bring you home."

"I am home," I said as I leaned back in my chair, trying to appear calm. I fingered the ring that Evan had just given me, and Bas caught the movement.

He laughed and pointed at the ring. "Is that supposed to be an engagement ring?"

I covered my hand with the other one and faintly heard a door close in the back of the house. "You are aware that me leaving the ring that you gave me behind meant that we were no longer engaged."

He shrugged. "I figured you just needed a break."

"I needed a break from that life."

"Sorry, that can't happen." He pursed his lips and sighed. "Alaina, I'm sorry to tell you this, but Larry had a heart attack this morning. He didn't make it."

The words he spoke echoed through my head, and then again. My eyes locked on Sebastian's face.

"What?" I asked softly.

"Your brother is dead, Alaina. I'm sorry to be the one to tell you, but only your brother and I knew where you were."

"Maggie did too. Maggie could have called me."

"We didn't tell anyone yet. We had an early meeting over breakfast this morning, and Larry was rushed to the hospital from there. I called his office and told them that he had gone home not feeling well. I didn't want it in the news until I could tell you."

Thoughts of my brother spun around inside my mind. In the years before I left, Larry and I had not been close, but we had been civil to one another because of the corporation. Oh, my god! The company! If Larry were dead, his shares would revert to me. I now owned fifty-one percent of the company.

I closed my eyes, my mind running a million miles an hour, and I heard Bastion move, but I couldn't open my lids. I was dizzy and put my face into my hands. I was alone in this world now—no parents, no aunts or uncles or grandparents, and no siblings. It was just me.

Bastion squatted in front of me, and I finally opened my eyes when he laid a hand over mine. "I'm very sorry, Alaina."

Tears filled my eyes as I realized that not only had Lindsey died on this day, but Lawrence had too. Not to mention that Evan had proposed to me, and now I had no clue what he was thinking.

I stood, trying to get away from Bas, but he stood just as quickly and caught my arm, pulling me around to him. "Alaina, I know you were not close to your brother, especially these last few years, but he was your last living relative. I know that you must be hurting right now. I know what it is like to be alone."

Bas did. He had been an only child, and his parents had passed many years ago when he was just a teenager. An elderly aunt had raised him and then died just after he had turned eighteen.

He pulled me into his arms, and I accepted it, wrapping my arms around his waist and burying my face into his chest. He placed a kiss on the top of my head, and I began to cry quietly.

I cried for the brother I had once loved and for the sister brutally taken from me. I also found myself crying for the father I missed so much and the mother I never got along with. I sobbed for it all and for more.

I thought I heard a car in the back of my mind, but my memories were moving so fast through my mind that I wasn't sure what I was hearing or thinking.

After a few minutes, I pulled away from Bas and went to get a tissue, blowing my nose and turning to see the dining room table and the beautiful place setting. There was a vase of flowers in the center of the table, and I knew they must have come from his father's garden.

I strode past the table and into the kitchen. It was empty, and the dinner Evan made was still sitting in pots and pans around the kitchen. My feet took me quickly to the garage entrance, and I pulled it open and saw his SUV that he had started parking next to my Maserati was gone.

I wilted. Why had Evan left? Was it because Bas had told him that he was my fiancé? Did Evan think I had lied to him? I closed my eyes, sighed, and then closed the door. There was no doubt that Evan thought I had lied to him. Evan was probably wondering just who I was—especially after Bas had told him that my name was Alaina and not Laney. Thank god he hadn't told him my real last name. Buckworth was a household name, especially to those in the medical industry. We had an entire division focused on the latest technology for hospitals and operating rooms. Evan would have heard that and known that I was even more wealthy than I let on. Why had I put off that conversation for so long? Why hadn't Bas waited one day to show up?

"You need to pack your bags," Bas said from behind me as I stood in the kitchen and stared at the alfredo sauce that Evan had prepared.

"Why?"

"Because I have a plane waiting for us."

I laughed. "Did you think that you could just waltz in here, tell me that my brother was dead, and drag me home? I'm not going."

"Alaina, you have to. Buckworth Industries needs you back right now. If you don't come back now, the company will crumble. The stock is going to plummet, and people will start pulling contracts. We can't afford that."

Did I mention that Bas owned five percent of the company, while the final forty-four percent was split between many shareholders with smaller percentages?

"I just need a minute."

"You can have hours once you get on the plane, Alaina. I will throw this food away so that it doesn't spoil, but you need to go pack. You can return later and get the rest, or hire someone to pack it for you."

Did he honestly think I would go back to Santa Monica and never return? Ha! He was wrong in that thinking, but he was right in what he said. I did need to return—at least for now. This wasn't just about me. This was about the thousands of employees that worked for us. It was about the people world-wide that used our products, invested money with us, and owned other companies that we had our hands in. This situation was beyond me and way beyond Evan.

Slowly I climbed the steps and went to my bedroom. I didn't want to leave, but I didn't have a choice. I started packing and tried to ignore the evident traces of Evan in my room.

How was I going to explain all of this to him? Would he be able to accept it? How stupid was I to think that I could hide here in Pennsylvania and try to help victims of domestic violence when I had a billion-dollar company to oversee.

I had two bags packed, and then I unlocked my office, collected my laptop and quite a few documents that I had been working on, and was about to close and lock the door when I thought better of it. Instead, I left the door open.

Eventually, Evan would return—even if only to get his things —and he would see what was inside this room. Maybe if he had the time to absorb it all, it would make it easier to explain later —maybe.

I rolled the suitcases to the staircase, and Bas came up and retrieved them for me. I made sure to turn off all the lights, and for a long moment, I stood at the balcony to my garden patio, and I stared down. Of all the places here, I would miss that the most. I closed and locked the slider door.

I turned and followed Bas out of the house and into the waiting limo. As we started to pull away, I realized that I had left my cellphone sitting on the counter in the kitchen when I arrived home earlier tonight.

I glanced down at my hand and stared at the ring on my finger. I should have left this behind too. I doubted that Evan would want to have anything to do with me once he learned the truth this way.

CHAPTER TWENTY-THREE

EVAN

"*H*er fiancé?" I growled, feeling a little like the floor was about to open under me. What the fuck?

"Yes, I assume she mentioned me." The man stated, and I opened my mouth to speak, not that I knew what the hell to even say, but Laney's voice came loud and clear from behind me.

"She most certainly has not. What are you doing here, Bas?"

If I had thought for a moment that this guy had the wrong person, I was proved very wrong in two sentences. I watched her as she approached the door. Her eyes were focused and more intense than I had previously seen them on the man outside.

"Alaina, you are looking well."

Why the fuck was he calling her Alaina? Perhaps that was her full first name, and she shortened it and went by Laney. If that were the case, why had she not mentioned that?

"Thank you. What are you doing here?"

The man frowned at Laney and then spoke almost condescendingly toward her. "Where are your manners, Alaina? Did you lose them moving to this little Podunk town? Are you not going to invite me in? Much different than your other house."

Her other house? What?

I listened to them talk about business and her brother and that somehow this guy was promised her. You've got to be kidding me? Was she like part of a business transaction? I had officially fallen down the rabbit hole. What the hell was going on? None of this made sense.

"I don't care what Larry promised you, Bas. He can go to hell for all I care."

It grew tense for a moment, and then she allowed him to enter. When he did, I noticed the limo in the driveway. A man in black stood beside the car door, waiting patiently. I shook my head and turned to find Laney finally looking me in the eye. I could only utter one word. "Fiancé?"

She shook her head and responded, "No, he's not, Evan. I'll explain it all later."

I wasn't sure what to think of her response. The woman in front of me seemed like a completely different person than the one that I had proposed to ten minutes ago. "I'll give you your space," I finally replied and then turned and walked away, glaring at the man standing in the entryway as I did.

I went into the kitchen and paced back and forth. Part of me wanted to slip back into the room and listen, while another part wanted me to run for the hills.

Her name was Alaina, and this guy was—or used to be—her fiancé. She owned another house. Had she sold it? Or did she own two? Jesus, maybe she owned five. Who knew?

Anger began to simmer in my veins. Had she lied about who she was? What kind of life did she have before she came here? I felt suddenly trapped as if I were going to explode, and I grabbed my car keys and started toward the garage door. Only, I opened it and stopped, staring at the Maserati.

I had known she was very wealthy. People didn't have cars

like that unless they were. Deep inside, I knew there was more to her than she had previously told me. I had pushed back against her money, about learning more. Hell, I had even gotten angry when she had volunteered to pay for groceries.

Maybe she hadn't told me because she knew I was uncomfortable with it. Perhaps she was waiting until I had gotten used to her house and her cars before she explained it all to me.

I closed the door and stood there. That had to be it. She was waiting to tell me. Now that I had proposed, she would. She would explain it all, and it would be water under the bridge.

What I should be doing right now is sitting beside her. I should be in there listening to whatever this guy has to say to her. I turned and started heading back, slipping my keys into my pocket and bypassing the dining room.

I stopped a foot shy of the living room archway and paused. Was she crying? I stepped forward, preparing to kick that guy's ass for making her cry, except I came up short when I found him comforting her, his arms wrapped tightly around her, his head bent to rest on hers.

And that was enough for me.

I spun as quietly as I had entered and left. Right through the kitchen, right out the garage, and practically punched the button to lift the heavy door. I dug my keys out of my pocket, climbed into my SUV, and backed out, tempted to back right into the fucking limo. I didn't even pause to close the door. I just did a quick three-point turn and drove away. A fucking limo! Who drives in a limo these days?

Why had she left the guy? Was her story of moving here really because of her sister? Had that guy hurt her, and she had run from him? Was he abusive? The thought made me ill, and I almost turned around, but I didn't.

Something about that didn't sound right. If the story about her sister was true, and I did believe that it was, there was no way that Laney—Alaina, whatever she called herself—would be involved with an abusive or controlling man.

So what was the real story?

I ground my teeth as I drove home. Jesus, what was it with people keeping secrets? Why hadn't she mentioned that her real name was Alaina?

My phone began to ring, and my eyes quickly flashed to my console screen. I had expected to see her name there, but it was Huntley. I almost sent it to voicemail but decided that maybe having something else to focus on might be a good idea.

"Hey," I growled after answering the phone.

"Hey to you, too. What's going on? You busy?"

I squeezed my steering wheel. "No. What do you need?"

"Why do you sound so pissed off?"

"Because I am."

"You aren't at work, are you?"

"No, I'm not. Look, where are you?"

"I was going to ask if you wanted to grab a beer. Daniella is trying to get a chapter finished and keeps telling me to go away because I am making too much noise and affecting the vibe of the house."

I chuckled. "I'll meet you. Tavern?"

"That works. I'll see you there in a few."

After we hung up, I wondered how much to tell Hunt and realized I needed to spill it all since he was my best friend. If I couldn't talk to him, who could I? Cara? Nah, I wasn't going to speak to her about this—not yet.

I was at the tavern before Hunt and headed straight to the bar. Bollard was behind it and gave me a chin nod as he helped another customer. I took a seat and waited for him to approach me.

"What can I get you, Winston?"

"Whiskey shot and a beer to start."

He nodded, a hint of a smile on his lips before he collected my drinks. After he set them down, I tossed a twenty on the bar, and he took it and came back with cash. "How is Cara doing?"

"She's fine." I threw back the whiskey and then took a long guzzle off my bottle. "Why are you asking?"

He shrugged. "Just wondered. A lot has happened at the club since all that went down with Vigil."

"I'm sure. Didn't half of your gang get locked up?"

He nodded. "Yep, it did."

"How did you get so lucky to stay out of that mess?"

"Well, I guess because I always kept my nose clean. I might have wanted to be in an outlaw club, but I didn't necessarily want to be an outlaw."

"Should have joined another club then," I stated as I stared hard at him.

"Ironic that you say that. Those of us who are still active in this charter have been talking. We have the opportunity to either move to one of the other charters or officially step out without all the baggage. The new board has approved people to leave without being shunned or in a pine box."

"Too bad you didn't have that when Ryan was alive."

He eyed me carefully. "You think he would have left?"

"For Cara, I think he would have done anything."

He nodded. "Yeah, I do too. Those two had something special." He stared behind me as if lost in thought.

"You thinking of moving or getting out?"

He glanced around, then leaned forward. "Between you and me, I think I'm going to hang up the patch. It's not what it used to be, and I'm not as young as I once was."

I laughed. "You are hardly old, Bollard."

"I'm thirty-eight, old enough. My ass gets numb and then hurts for hours after being on the bike all day, and I don't want arthritis in my hands like some of those old-timers."

"Yeah, I can imagine that wouldn't be fun."

He glanced past me again and nodded at someone as he

stepped back, putting space between us. "Hunt, what can I get you?"

Hunt glanced at my empty shot glass and half-full beer. "I'll just take a beer, but you better get him another set. It looks like I'll be driving his ass home tonight."

"You just might," I told Hunt. After the drinks arrived, Hunt and I took them over to another table. It was a quiet night in the tavern, and only half the tables were full. There was no live music tonight, and the jukebox was playing an old 80s rock tune as we got seated.

"You and Bollard looked chummy."

I laughed. "Strangely enough, we were having a pleasant conversation."

"I'd ask what that was, but I'd rather hear why you are throwing back shots. What's up?"

Where did I start? I had no clue. The first words I could think of blurted from my mouth. "I proposed to Laney tonight."

Hunt jerked upright, his eyes going wide. "You did?" His shoulders slumped. "Oh, man, did she say no?"

"No, she said yes. I even put a ring on her finger—my mother's ring."

He looked confused. Join the club, I thought to myself.

"So, what's the problem? She didn't like the ring? I don't remember what it looked like, but maybe she wanted something fancier."

"She loved the ring," I stated defeatedly as I stared at my bottle.

"Alright, spill it," Hunt snapped. "I'm totally confused here."

"Five minutes after I proposed, a guy rings our doorbell, tells me he's her fiancé, and says her name is Alaina, not Laney."

"Alaina?" He looked constipated as he echoed her name.

"Yes, Alaina."

"Alright, what did she have to say?"

"Not much. I mean, Laney was focused on this guy who said

his name was Sebastian Garza. She called him Bas, and I was so confused with their conversation. She did tell me that he was not her fiancé, but they were talking about a company and that she had to marry him or some shit, and about her other house. It was all so fucking confusing, and the only thing that I kept thinking about was that she never told me her name was Alaina or that she had been engaged before. I left them alone, and then I decided to go back in, but then I found her in his arms, and she was crying, and he was consoling her. I got so pissed that I walked out. I just walked straight out the door. You called me like five minutes after I left."

"Whoa, okay. That was a lot. Let's start back at the beginning."

So I did. I went back to cooking dinner, and when Laney came home, how tired she was, how emotional she got at the table setting, and the proposal. Then I told him about the guy showing up and everything that I could remember of the conversation, leading up to the moment when Huntley called me.

He shook his head. "Dude, my head is spinning. I can't imagine what is going on in yours."

"Right now, I'm just trying to figure out who the guy was, and if anything that she told me was true."

Hunt took out his phone. "What did you say the guy's name was?"

"Sebastian Garza."

He typed on his phone screen and then pushed on a few things. "Is this the guy?" He turned the phone toward me, and I nodded.

"Yeah, that's the smug bastard."

He turned the phone back around and started messing with things. His expression remained neutral, except for once when his brows began to rise higher, then he was shifting his thumbs again, and it looked like he was reading something.

He whistled low. "Damn, the guy has some serious money."

"What does it say about him?"

"That he's a self-made billionaire."

My jaw dropped. "Billionaire?"

"Yeah, per this site that I'm looking on, it lists the top fifty richest men in the US. He's number twenty-three."

"He's a billionaire, and he's number twenty-three on the list? Jesus! How do these people make that kind of money?"

"I have no idea." He frowned and then clicked on something, his gaze popping up to mine and then back to his phone. "Um, you said he called her Alaina, right?"

"Yeah, why?"

He shook his head and turned the phone around to me. On the screen was a picture of Garza with Laney. The caption under the photograph read, *Billionaires Sebastian Garza and Alaina Buckworth to tie the knot.*

I lifted my stunned gaze to Hunt. "Am I reading this correctly? Is she a billionaire as well? That does say billionaires as in plural, right?"

"Yeah, it does."

"And her last name is Buckworth! She lied about her real name. Jesus, I thought maybe Laney was just a shortened version of Alaina. I had no idea her last name wasn't Marshall."

"It looks like her middle name is Marshall here. I found a profile on her." He turned the phone around to me again, and I started reading.

"Alaina Marshall Buckworth is the second child to the late William and Margaret Buckworth. She is currently the eleventh wealthiest woman in the United States and is a major stock-holder in Buckworth Industries with her older brother, Lawrence Buckworth. Their youngest sibling, Lindsey Buck-worth Martins, is currently married to Mathew Martins, the lead singer for the band, New Weather, and while she does have stock in the company, she does not actively work for it."

I closed my eyes, fighting the wave of fury that rushed through me before I continued. "Lawrence is said to be married to his job, but it looks like Alaina might be taking that matrimonial step with a close friend, business associate, and long-time boyfriend, Sebastian Garza. As of now, they do not have a date scheduled."

Without even asking, I started a new search on Alaina Buckworth and scrolled down the page, looking at all the hits. I shoved the phone back to Hunt. I did not want to see any more.

"She lied about everything."

"Everything?" he asked as he set his phone aside.

"Yeah! Did you see how rich she was! She lied about that, and her name, and Jesus, Hunt! She is part owner of Buckworth Industries! They build medical and testing equipment. You probably have some of their things in your medical rigs. God knows I have their machines all over the ICU."

He held his hand up. "Wait, did she lie about all of that, or did she neglect to tell you?"

"What's the difference?"

"The difference is that you asked her pointed questions, and she gave you false answers. Did you ever ask her if she owned a big company? Or if you did, did you ask what the name was? Did you ever ask her what she was really worth?"

"No! Of course, I didn't. That's none of my business."

"So, why is it such a big deal now? If it's none of your business, then why are you freaking out?"

"Because she should have told me, that's why."

"Did she ever mention anything about her money? I mean, you knew she was well off."

"Well off, yes. Crazy rich, no!" I thought about his question for a moment and sighed. "No, I never asked her about her wealth, and when she did say anything about her money, I told her it didn't matter to me, and I didn't want to know."

"So, you lied."

I jerked back. "The hell I did!"

"You just said it didn't matter, but you sure are making it out as if it does." He paused. "So I guess you need to figure out if being with a wealthy woman, and I mean, extremely wealthy woman, whom you care about is worth it or not."

"But she lied about who she was."

"Just like Bryan, she might have an excellent reason. Why don't you try asking her that?"

I slumped on the stool as Bollard came over to the table with another two beers and a shot for me. Hunt and I looked at each other nervously as we realized we'd just mentioned Bryan, but Bollard didn't appear interested in what we had been talking about. He set the drinks down. "By the looks on your faces, I'd say you all needed another round."

"Ha!" I threw the shot back and then slammed the glass on the table. "You don't know the half of it."

CHAPTER TWENTY-FOUR

LANEY

*W*e flew back to Santa Monica on Bas's private jet. I had been in it fifty times, but as I sat there now and stared at the polished mahogany, plush leather seating, and gold fixtures, it seemed unknown to me.

Yes, the house I bought in Millerstown was one of the most expensive around, and it had a lot of amenities, but it was nothing compared to this. The house had cost me around two million. I knew that Bas paid over thirty million for this plane. I had been there when he purchased it.

Since the moment Bas had stepped in my door, I had been pummeled with memories of my past—one right after the other. I felt off-kilter and slightly disassociated with what was happening.

My mind kept turning on the fact that today was the anniversary of Lindsey's death, and now, it would be that of my brother's. What were the odds? It was surreal.

While Bas had been attentive to me since we left my house, he had given me space and hadn't plied me with endless questions or bombarded me with business. He merely sat there and asked if I needed anything from time to time while he conducted business on his laptop as we flew across the country.

After settling back in my seat, I closed my eyes and wondered what Evan was doing. Where was he? Had he returned to the house yet? Had he called me? Was he wondering where I was? Or was he so angry with Bas showing up and calling me another name as he told him he was my fiancé that Evan didn't even want to talk to me?

I played back over earlier tonight when I had arrived home and how kind and concerned Evan had been when he realized how fragile my state of mind was. It seemed days ago, not mere hours.

It was as if the moment I stepped out of the house and into the limo, Laney Marshall receded into the darkness, and Alaina Buckworth returned. I didn't want that, but what choice did I have? With my brother dead, I needed to step up and take control. I had no choice. This was my grandfather's legacy. He was the one that built Buckworth Industries, and then my father came on, and the two of them made it legendary. I could not let it be destroyed because my heart was playing house in a small town.

Love had no place in my life. I knew that when I was here before. Hence the reason I decided to marry Bas. I cared about him and perhaps loved him in a way, but I wasn't in love with him—not like I was with Evan.

I also knew that since I had to return to my former life, what I dreamed of with Evan, would never come to be.

A single tear slipped down my cheek, and I let it drop off my chin and fall to my shirt. I couldn't afford to cry more—not now. I had to focus on who I once was and bring forth that strong, forthright persona that people knew of me.

What would they say when I returned? I hadn't told anyone that I was leaving, and here it had been two and a half years. Would people think that I couldn't do the job? That I wasn't up for it? That because I had been away, I wouldn't know what to do?

I was thankful for Maggie then and all the information she had sent me. Not only rundowns of financials and contracts, but on the big players of the company. People might think that I haven't been around, but that eight- to twelve-hour day that I spent in my office on Sunday kept me at least partially in the loop.

Maggie was getting a raise.

Somehow, I managed to drift off to sleep for a couple of hours, and when I woke, I found Bas watching me. Perhaps that is what woke me, or it could have been the change in altitude as the plane began to descend.

"We will be landing in about thirty minutes," Bas said.

I glanced at my watch to see it was almost four in the morning. Of course, in California, it was only one. Even though I had just slept, I was still tired—exhausted, really.

Maureen, his stewardess, brought me a cup of coffee and a Danish. I hadn't eaten dinner, and as much as I didn't feel hungry, I still ate it. It was okay, nothing as special as the treats from Coral's Café, which made me immensely miss Evan and the rest of his family.

"I guess I need to do a press release about my brother," I said after I finished the Danish. "Unless one is already prepared."

"Perhaps we should give it a few days. Maybe bring you back into the office, get you acquainted with what is going on, and then announce it in a couple of days."

"Why wait?"

"Well, I think you need to let everyone know that you are back before we tell people that the company is changing hands. We don't want people panicking because Larry is gone, and the sister who walked away from it all is back again."

"First of all, the company is not changing hands. I have

always been a major shareholder, and I didn't walk away from it all, Bas. I know what's been going on."

He laughed. "Do you?"

"Yes, I do."

"Do tell, sweetheart. I would love to hear you recite the nightly news reports."

I glared at him. "Don't call me sweetheart, Bas. We are not an item. Just because I am returning, it doesn't mean that we are engaged or an item or even dating. We aren't."

"You can't tell me that you care about that little nurse you left back there."

I lifted my chin higher. "Evan is more of a man than you could ever be."

He laughed. "Sure, darling, if that's what you think, but I promise you that we will be married. You and I are meant to be."

"No, we aren't, and I don't care what business arrangement you had with my brother. I will not marry you."

He shrugged a shoulder. "We'll see."

He turned his attention away from me and focused out the window. I was glad that he had forgotten about what he had asked just a moment ago. I didn't want anyone to know how much I knew about the company—not yet. Not until I got back and got my hands on everything.

A few minutes later, Bas turned to me again. "I took the liberty of hiring you a chef, along with having your maid bring in more help and get your house back up to standards for you."

Standards? I almost laughed out loud. What were my standards now? While I wasn't sure I wanted a whole house of employees again, I did know that I could not take care of it all and still focus on the business. "Thank you. I didn't even think about that."

"You'll stay at my house tonight, and then your driver will pick you up after work tomorrow from the office."

"No," I replied. "I will stay in my own house, Bas. Do not

think for one second that you will have any say or control over what I do. Not with me, not with my company."

He smiled, a soft chuckle coming from his lips. "You have gotten brazen in your time away. I wonder what made you that way."

"Nothing that you would understand," I replied cryptically and stared out the window as the lights of California came into view under the cloud cover. I didn't miss this. In fact, if I had never seen it again, I would have been happy.

Bas led me to his car, and a few minutes later, the luggage was loaded, and we were on the way. He made a phone call, and I assumed he was speaking to someone at my house because he told them to be ready for me. I wish he hadn't. I would have preferred to slip in unnoticed without any fanfare.

Twenty-five minutes later, we pulled through the gate of my property, and I stared at the mammoth building that came into view. Why did I have a house this large? Why was it all white? God, had I ever thought it was nice? Or even my taste? Come to think of it, my mother had sent me here to see it. It was her taste, not mine.

The minute the car stopped, the front door opened, and there stood Kate, my housekeeper. While she was neat in appearance, her eyes looked wild and stressed, and I shocked her by stepping forward and hugging her hello. "Sorry to wake you so late, Kate. You can go back to bed, and I will see you in the morning. Don't stress over what hasn't been done. As long as I have clean sheets and towels, I'll be fine."

Her eyes were wide as she stared back at me. "Yes, ma'am, they are."

"Okay, then good night, Kate."

"I'll take your luggage up and then retire for the night."

I was about to tell her no, but I had already thrown her for a loop when I hugged her. I might totally freak her out if I told her I'd do it myself. "I would appreciate that. Thank you."

I shifted around to Bas after she disappeared into the house, pulling my luggage behind her. "Thank you for the ride. I will see you at the office."

He leaned forward and brushed his lips over my cheek. "I'll see you soon. If you need anything, let me know, and welcome home, Alaina."

I watched him disappear into the back seat of his car, and then the driver closed his door, gave me a respectful nod, and left.

On a sigh, I stepped into my house and closed the door. Home. I would not describe this house as home—not by a long shot.

I wandered around the first floor, turning lights on and then off again as the stark white appearance grated my nerves. I missed the wood of my other house, the palate of colors I had chosen to warm each room. I stood at the glass wall at the back of my house and looked out over the city lights around me.

I missed my garden and the little fairy lights that changed color to make it magical. I closed my eyes, grabbing hold of the swirling memory of the last time I had been under them with Evan.

Oh, Evan, what are you thinking? What is going on inside your mind? If I had my phone, I would call you, or I would at least text you that I would explain soon. I didn't have my phone, and I had no clue what his phone number was. I had put it in and then never thought of it again. Memorizing a phone number was a lost art.

I would have to get a new phone and attach it to my line. Then hopefully, I could recover it and get in touch with him. What I would say, I had no clue, but I would figure it out—later.

A t six-thirty in the morning, I was pulling up to the building. I had driven myself. Hank might be upset, but I needed to be in control today. What better way than to show up unannounced, driving myself.

It had been a long time since I had pulled my car into the parking garage beside our building. It had been an even longer time since I had parked in my official spot—the one marked as Vice President of Buckworth Industries.

I inhaled a few times to calm the tension coursing through me and then climbed out of my Bentley, grabbed my laptop bag, and headed to the concourse that would take me to our building.

Inside the building, it was relatively quiet, but people were there. The early birds determined to climb the ranks—the ones who put their jobs above their families and even themselves. I had been one of those people.

As I passed, I nodded to a few people, smiled at a few more, and then stopped at security. "Ma'am, your badge."

"Badge? Since when did Larry approve badges to get into the building?"

"Excuse me, ma'am? It's been in place since I started here, eighteen months ago."

"I don't need one," I stated as I started to step around the gate, but the man bristled and jumped in front of me, putting his hand on my shoulder and holding me back.

"Sorry, ma'am, but without a badge, you can't come in. If you lost yours, you will need to see HR when the company opens at eight."

"Whoa, whoa, whoa, Johan! Get your hand off her and step back." A strong concerned voice came from behind me. "Ms. Buckworth, I'm so sorry. Johan is new since you were last here." Carl Avers, the head of security, rushed to my side, glaring at his employee. "It won't ever happen again."

Johan's eyes were wide as saucers, and his skin visibly paled.

"Hello, Carl. It's good to see you again. Please make sure that all your employees know I am back, and I will not use a badge to get into my own building. Thank you."

"Yes, ma'am. It's great to see you again too. Let me just, uh, let you onto the elevator. Without a badge, you can't get up to the tenth floor."

"Oh?" I sighed as we began to approach them. "Where else do I need one of those stupid things to access?"

"Just about everywhere, Ms. Buckworth."

"Please call me Alaina," I replied, and his eyes widened. "A lot is going to change here, Carl, but I guess, for now, you'll have to get me one of those stupid cards so I can at least move around my building."

"Yes, ma'am," he said as the elevator door opened. We stepped in, and he pressed his badge to the keypad, then punched in the tenth-floor button. "I'll ride up with you to make sure you can get into your office."

"I appreciate that." I stared at the numbers as we went up. "It's going to take me a little while to get used to everything again."

"Whatever you need, Ms.—um, Alaina, you just let me know."

"I appreciate that, Carl. I really do. I am sure I will need your assistance from time to time."

"I assume your brother knows you are back?"

I dropped my gaze to the floor momentarily, then lifted it. "Carl, I'm going to tell you something that no one else knows, and no one else can know. Can you keep this secret for me?"

He nodded. "Absolutely, ma'am."

"Larry is dead. He died yesterday."

He looked confused and shocked. "What? What happened?"

"He had a heart attack, and Sebastian came to get me yesterday. We don't want to announce it yet, but I thought that you should know."

"I'm so sorry, Alaina. I truly am."

"Thank you. I'm sorry too, but probably not for the reason you think."

The door opened, and I stepped out and turned toward the glass doors that I knew were there. They were different but similar. Obviously, Larry had redecorated.

I glanced at Carl. "If you could please keep that between us for just a short time. I'll make an announcement as soon as I get my feet under me."

"Absolutely, whatever you need, ma'am." He rubbed his badge against the panel near the door. "I'll have a badge brought up to you immediately. Full access."

"Thank you." I started to walk through the door and paused. "Um, you wouldn't happen to know if my office is in the same place or not."

He chuckled. "That's probably one of the few things that haven't changed, ma'am."

I nodded and turned away. I found my office and stood inside the door, looking around. It was tidy and looked like I hadn't been there in two and a half years. I dropped my laptop bag and stood at the window, staring out at the metal and stone city, my heart heavy as I whispered, "I miss my garden view."

CHAPTER TWENTY-FIVE

EVAN

I was half in the bag when Huntley took me home that night. I stood in my bedroom, staring at the queen-sized bed, and then as I fell over it, I groaned. It was so much harder than Laney's king-sized bed.

Even though I was pretty intoxicated, I was still very much aware of the situation that led me here.

Laney—where was she? Why hadn't she called me? She had to know that I was gone. Did she think that I would come back? Or did she not care because Mr. tall, dark, and handsome was here now?

I wrestled with that for a few moments, and then sleep claimed me.

Luckily, I didn't have to work the next day because I woke up around nine in the morning with one hell of a headache. I popped a couple of acetaminophens and then drank two large glasses of water before I even looked at my phone.

I had expected to see a message or a phone call from Laney,

but there was nothing. Hunt had sent me a message to check on me, and so had Cara. I had a feeling that someone had reached out to her because her message was, *Don't overreact until you know all the details—call me.*

Had Hunt called Cara? Or had he told Daniella, and she told Cara? I guess it didn't matter. By the end of today, everyone in the family and the Youngs would know that Laney was not who she said she was. Great—just fucking great.

I made breakfast and forced myself to eat. The whole time, I wondered if Laney and her other fiancé had enjoyed the dinner that I had cooked last night.

After I ate, I took a seat in my living room, kicked my feet up on the coffee table, and dialed my sister.

She answered on the third ring with a cheerful, "Welcome to the club."

I laughed despite how I felt. "Not a club I ever saw myself joining."

"Yeah, well, me either. At least she didn't have to die for you to learn the truth."

"But I don't know the truth," I responded. "I mean, this guy shows up calling her another name and telling me they are engaged, but the only thing she said to me was that he's not her fiancé. She said nothing else."

"Did you try to ask her?"

"I didn't get the chance. I left them alone to talk and then thought better of that. When I went back into the room, she was crying and he was holding her."

"Why?"

"I don't know! For all I fucking know he was apologizing, and she was forgiving him for something. That's when I left."

"You didn't stick around to ask her anything?"

"No, Cara. I saw red after that. I couldn't think straight, and I didn't want to see more or say something that I couldn't take back."

"I get that, Ev, I do. I'm sorry, but until you can speak with her and hear the truth, you can't believe what you saw."

"The truth? The truth is she is a billionaire who had been slumming it in our small town. I think *he* called it a Podunk town. He came in a freaking limo and laughed at the house she was living in. Said something about how different it was from her other one. How many houses does the woman own?"

"She could own a dozen, but what difference does it make, Evan? So, the woman has money. Who cares? You already knew that."

"I care, Cara. I care a lot. How can I care for someone when they make more money than God? I mean seriously!"

She laughed. "God doesn't need money, Ev. He relies on faith."

"Yeah, well, I'm even shorter on that these days."

"Oh, come on. What does your heart say? I mean really say?"

I was quiet for a moment as I thought that over. "It hurts. I love her, Cara. I don't want to lose her, and I don't want to care about her money, but I do."

"I know you do, but you have to learn to overlook it. If you love Laney, the person that she is, then the rest won't matter."

"The rest? You mean the fact that she lives in California, and her name is not Laney, but Alaina Buckworth?"

"If you love someone, Evan, it doesn't matter where they live or what their name is."

I thought about the fact that she had moved to Texas for Bryan. Would I be willing to move to California for Laney —Alaina?

The answer to that was more straightforward than I thought. No. I couldn't imagine doing that. Especially when my father needed me so much right now. Besides, I loved my job, loved this town. I had no interest in living in California.

"That is where you and I are different, Cara. I know you moved there to be with Bryan, but I have no interest in moving away from here. I love being in Millerstown and what I have here. I love being near Dad and Coral and everyone else. I understand why you left, but you're different than me. You have always been one for excitement and change, but I haven't. I'm more of a creature of habit."

"That you are, Evan, and I respect you so much for that. It's good that you know what's in your heart."

I nodded to the empty room.

"But you still need to speak with her and find out the truth. If you don't, then you will always wonder. I'm sure she is worried sick about you right now. Have you even texted her?"

"No, and she hasn't texted or called me either."

Cara was quiet for a moment. "She hasn't?"

"Nope. Zip, zero, zilch. What is that supposed to tell me?"

"Well, if you care about her, and I mean truly care about her, you need to go talk to her face-to-face. It might hurt, and she might tell you that's it's over, but at least you need to get an explanation."

"Yeah, I guess."

"I suggest you get dressed and head over to her house and talk to her."

"She won't be there. She'll be at work."

"Well, maybe she will be home, or she left you a note."

"Maybe."

"If you go over there and find her not home, then call her at work and plan a time to sit down and talk. If she is half the woman that you say she is, she will give you that."

"Alright, fine. I'll do that."

"Okay, go now. Right now, before you can talk yourself out of it, and then let me know how it goes."

I chuckled. "Damn, I sure do miss your pushiness."

"Good thing I can still be bossy over the phone, isn't it?"

"Yeah. I miss you, Cara. Let me go do this, and I'll call you later."

"Alright. I'll be rooting for you."

"Thanks."

After we hung up, I showered, dressed, and then made my way over to her house. I would be lying if I said I wasn't nervous, but I knew I had to face the truth now or drive myself crazy wondering.

The limo was gone, so that was a good sign. I went around the side of the garage and opened the door. Both of Laney's vehicles were inside, so she must be home. I let myself in, turned off the alarm, and walked hesitantly into the kitchen.

The light was on over the sink. The dishes from the night before were all piled on the counter haphazardly. I frowned as I approached them and then peered into the fridge to see if the leftovers had been saved. There were no leftovers. Something made me look in the trash, and I frowned when I saw the pasta and sauce congealed in the trash bag.

I walked toward the front of the house, afraid that I would find them sleeping on the sofa or in a compromising position. "Laney?" I called out and then rolled my eyes. "Alaina?" I called louder.

I looked everywhere downstairs and in the garden, but she wasn't there. Then I stared at the steps. Did I want to walk up there and find her in bed with the guy? No, but I couldn't leave until I knew.

"Alaina? Are you up there?" I called loudly but received only silence in return. I climbed the steps, peering down the hallway to the right and seeing all the doors open. I looked to the left and found them open as well—including the door that was always locked.

I went toward her room, glancing into the usually locked room and noting it was an office, but it was empty of people. I bypassed it and stepped into her room to find her bed thankfully empty. It was also still made, and her clothes for work yesterday were lying haphazardly over the quilt. She hadn't slept here.

Had she run off with Bas the minute I left? I went to her closet and found that the section that she usually pulled from daily was still pretty full, but the further down rod containing business suits was almost empty.

There was an enormous void where she kept her luggage in the back corner where the bigger ones had stood.

She was gone.

I returned to the bedroom and looked around. I entered the bathroom and found most of her stuff gone from around the sink and inside the medicine cabinet. I lifted my head, and my eyes fell on the shower behind me. Memories slammed into me as I turned to study it.

I left the room, pushing the memories away. I didn't want to think about them now. I was still reeling over the fact that Laney was gone—like literally gone.

I exited her room and stepped into her office. There were spreadsheets all over the walls and whiteboards with numbers that meant nothing to me. There were three monitors on the desk, but there was an empty place where a laptop would have been.

I stepped around the desk and sat in her seat, letting my eyes shift from one paper to the next. Bank statements, financial documents, contracts, proposals, stock statements, correspondence to many people littered the surface and made me slightly dizzy.

This was the real Laney. I mean, Alaina Buckworth, and I was somewhat awed by it.

I pulled back a drawer to her desk and saw folders with names of banks on them. I pulled out one of the folders and flipped it open to see more bank statements. This one had a balance of twelve point five million dollars. That was more than I would see in a lifetime.

I glanced at the drawer and scanned the tabs. There were at least eleven more banks in that drawer. The thought of how much money that represented made me ill. I shoved the folder back where I had gotten it and stood. I moved to the side and glanced over some of the papers there. Each one had a different corporation or large company printed at the top. Under that were percentages that went up and down. Large numbers shifted by the day, up ten thousand one day, down sixteen hundred the next. Were these stock numbers?

I spent about twenty minutes in the room, and my head was spinning. How did one person understand all of this? If this was what Alaina had done before she came here, it's no wonder that guy came looking for her. She didn't belong in a small town working with victims of domestic violence. She needed to be running the world.

I let myself out of her office and closed the door behind me. I didn't need to see any more. I returned to her bedroom and went into the closet she had given me. I packed all my things and then retrieved my other random items scattered around the room. There wasn't much. The last thing I stuck in my bag was my toothbrush.

I carried my things down the stairs, ensuring that the lights were off. I had no clue when Laney would be back. I stood on the balcony for a few moments, letting myself get lost in the dreams that I had stupidly let myself believe could come true. What an idiot I was to think that a woman like her could love a man like me.

It was not possible.

I locked the patio door and stopped in the kitchen. I set my stuff down, then went about cleaning it up. I had made the mess; I might as well clean it up. Not only did I clean the kitchen, but I went into the dining room and put the dishes away.

Before I left, I took the trash out, and it was as I picked up the last pot holder I saw her cellphone. She had left it here. Was that by accident, or had she not needed it?

I returned to the dining room, collected the flowers, and put them on the counter in the kitchen. They would probably be dead before she returned, but that would be fitting. Against the vase, I set her phone and then wrote a note. *I would appreciate it if you'd drop the ring off with my sister at the café when you have time.*

Then I collected my bags, turned the alarm on one last time, and walked out the door. I didn't look back. There was nothing there to see but a house with broken dreams.

CHAPTER TWENTY-SIX

LANEY

I was on my phone speaking with Thomas Croft, one of the board members that I trusted, when Maggie appeared at my door, eyes wide and excited to see me. She glanced over her shoulder, slipped in, and closed the door as I waved her in.

She waited patiently across from me at my steel and glass desk, and I shifted my chair around to stare out the window sightlessly.

I had called Thomas to let him know that I was back in town. I knew that he would get the word out to the other board members and the stockholders. Within a day or two, everyone would know that I had returned. Another couple of days to prove to them all that I was capable of taking care of everything, and then we would announce that my brother had passed.

In the perfect world, I would then take over as the CEO of Buckworth Industries. At one time, I had dreamed of that position. That dream seemed like a lifetime ago as I hung up the phone and turned to face Maggie.

"Boy, was I surprised to see your message when I woke up.

What is going on? What brought you back?" Maggie asked the moment she had my attention.

I glanced at the glass wall that led to the rest of the offices. Someone I didn't know was walking past, eyeing me curiously. I gave them a friendly smile and then shifted to Maggie.

"Mags, I came back because Bas showed up on my doorstep and dragged me back here."

"What?" she asked, surprised. Maggie was on the board of directors and was the head of our corporate marketing. She oversaw all marketing efforts for Buckworth Industries and those subsidiaries that we owned and controlled. Nothing went out without her approval or one of her trusted advisors.

"Larry is dead," I stated as I leaned back in my chair and crossed my legs. "He had a heart attack yesterday morning, and Bas came to tell me and bring me back."

Her jaw was hanging open. "How did I not hear of that?"

"Nobody knows—only Bas, Carl in security, and you. That's it. As far as everyone else knows, Larry is sick, and then he will be away on business or something for about a week while I get my feet back under me."

"Why not tell everyone?"

"Bas is worried that if other shareholders found out that Larry was gone, our stocks would plummet, and we might lose contracts. He's right. That would happen, so I need to show everyone that I have a solid grasp on the company."

"Jesus, Alaina. Man, am I glad I have been sending you those updates."

"Me, too."

She thought for a moment. "Do you think that will work?"

"I don't think we have much choice, and I'm sure we will still see a bit of a drop, but I think I can keep it from nose-diving, though. If we lost three to five percent of our contracts, I wouldn't be surprised, but I think that's better than ten to fifteen that we could lose. You know how scared people can be with change."

"Yeah, that is true." She paused. "I'm sorry about your brother."

"Thanks, but you know we weren't all that close."

"No, but he was your brother, and I know you respected the businessman in him."

"I did, and I'm sorry he is gone. For more than one reason."

"Yeah, I bet it is weird being back."

"Beyond weird. It doesn't seem real."

She laughed. "Honey, this is as real as it gets. What you were living in was a fantasy world."

I chuckled. "No, it was pretty damn real." I contemplated for a moment, then stood and turned to stare out the window again. "I met some incredible people, and learned some valuable lessons, Maggie. I saw things that I would never have the opportunity to see from this office. I think it made me a better person."

"Alaina, you are the best person that I know. I'm not sure anything could make you better."

"Evan could," I said without thinking.

"Who is Evan?" she asked, and I unconsciously looked down at my hand. I had removed the ring and put it in my safe at home. Eventually, I would have it sent back to Evan. Perhaps, I would have someone deliver it personally. It was far too valuable to get lost in the mail.

I turned and gave her a knowing smile. "A guy I was seeing."

She grinned. "Oh, do tell!"

There was a knock at the door, and I saw Bas standing outside, grinning. I waved him in while I responded to Maggie softly, "I will, but not now."

Maggie stood as Bas entered. "Well, welcome back again. I will talk to you later. I hope you get settled in quickly. Let me know if you need anything."

"Thanks, Maggie. Drinks later? You can fill me in on the scoop."

She chuckled because she knew I already knew the scoop. "Just let me know what time." She winked and nodded to Bas before she slipped around him.

"Good morning, Bas," I said. The humor and friendliness were now gone as I retook my seat and woke up my computer to see if Thomas Croft had sent over what I requested yet. I frowned as it wasn't in my inbox yet.

"What time did you get here?"

"Six-thirty."

"That's early even for you."

"You forget that I'm still on East Coast time. It was late for me."

"Ah, true, there is that. Was everything alright in your house?"

I leaned back in my chair, eyeing Bas carefully. "My house was fine. I appreciate you having it taken care of for me, and I appreciate you coming to get me and tell me in person about my brother. I don't need you to hold my hand, Bas, or watch over me. I am quite capable of taking care of business."

"I'm not watching over you, Alaina. You've been gone for two and a half years. You have no idea what is going on."

I laughed. "That is where you are wrong, Bas. Yeah, I didn't know that the office had been redecorated, or that I would need some stupid card to get me on the elevator and into my offices, but I am quite aware of what is going on here. I mean the real business. I know that the merger with Flint Manufacturing has stalled due to a contract issue with their union. We need to give them what they want and move forward. It's a waste of time and money at this point not to. I am also aware that we are looking to overhaul Mandall Plastics and Hoover Resources, but in my honest opinion, Hoover doesn't need it. They only need a new leader at the helm. He's the one that is killing the bottom line. I plan to rectify that immediately."

Bas looked surprised and confused as he slipped into a guest chair. "How do you know all this?"

"Because I had people who sent me regular updates, Bas. I might not have been here, but I am aware of almost everything that was going on. I kept tabs on contracts, sales, stocks, and procedures. I kept voting. Did you think that I was just casting a vote on a whim?"

"I figured you knew something; I just didn't know you were getting inside information."

"Inside information? You say that as if I were doing something illegal. I am part owner of this company, now with a fifty-one percent interest. Of course, I am going to follow what happens with it. Just because I moved away for a while doesn't mean that this company isn't important to me."

Bas began to smile. "And there is the woman that I know and love. Welcome back, Alaina."

"You don't know me, Bas, and I don't love you. I told you before that nothing will happen between us. Get that through your thick skull."

The smile vanished from his face, his voice even but stern as he spoke. "That is where you are wrong, Alaina. Your brother and I had a deal. For everything that I have done for him, and you, I deserve it!"

"I will not be controlled. Not by you, not by the board, and not by the death of my brother. If you aren't happy with that, I'd be more than willing to buy out your shares, and you can move on."

He burst from his seat. "The hell you will! I have given everything for this company, and you were promised to be part of my settlement."

I stood, glaring at him over the desk. "I am not a company to be acquired or a piece of property to own, Bas. I am a human being with a mind and a heart, and I control what I do and who I am with. No one else does that. Do you understand me, Sebastian?" He glared at me but didn't respond. "Do I need to call security up here and have you removed?"

He scoffed. "I'd like to see you try."

"Don't test me, Bas. I am not in the mood."

He shifted, rolling his shoulders and buttoning his suit jacket. "And don't test me, Alaina."

"Is that a threat, Bas?"

He blinked and then threw out a blazing smile. "Not at all, sweetheart. Everything that is happening is just a bit over-whelming. I'm sorry I snapped at you. Dinner tonight?"

I somehow kept my surprise to myself at his immediate change of mood. "Thank you, but not tonight. I am meeting Maggie to catch up, and then I need a good night's sleep."

"I could meet you at your house, help with that sleep."

"I am not sleeping with you, Bas. I told you that was over."

He shrugged and laughed. "You know I won't give up. I love you, Alaina. No one else knows you as I do."

He left without another word, and I sank back to my chair. My knees were shaking, but I don't think he realized. Luckily, I had been able to keep my voice at an even level.

I had known that Bas had a dark side but had always attributed that to being a hard-core businessman. Did it run deeper than that? He did tend to be somewhat narcissistic at times. Was Bas capable of being abusive? Would he raise a hand to someone? Would he control them?

Well, I knew the answer to the second one. He would control someone. I had seen it, and if I were honest with myself, he had been rather controlling with me. Luckily, I had woken up to that, and I would not allow someone to do that to me. Not now, and not with what I knew.

I stared at my computer screen, then turned and gazed out the window. I missed the peace of Pennsylvania, the green of the trees, the winding of the roads. I hadn't even been gone twenty-four hours, and I was already so homesick.

And I missed Evan something fierce. What must he be thinking of me? Before doing anything about that, I picked up the phone and called the domestic violence center where I worked. Mary Kate answered and transferred me back to Joyce immediately.

"Laney, are you alright?"

"I'm fine," I replied.

"Oh, thank god! I was so worried when you didn't show up, and I kept calling you, but there was no answer. I was worried that Alice's husband found you and did something to hurt you."

"No, I'm so sorry. I had to leave town in the middle of the night, and I forgot my phone."

"So, that's why you haven't answered." She sighed. "I called the police, had them send a car to your house, but they said that you weren't there. What happened?"

"Joyce, my brother passed, and I needed to come home."

"Laney, I am so very sorry to hear that."

"Thank you. I had to return to California to oversee the company."

"Company?"

"Yes, Joyce, I have a few things to explain to you." I took a few minutes to explain who I was and what I had done until a few years ago. She asked a few questions but mostly just listened.

"I'm sorry for not telling you who I was, but I needed to be away from that part of my life for a while. Working with you, with all of you, was what I needed. Unfortunately, I need to give my notice. I'm sorry."

"Well, I can understand," she said softly. "You did a wonderful job, Laney. If you ever want to change careers again, we would love to have you back." She chuckled.

"I appreciate that. We shall see what the future holds," I told her. "I appreciate all that you did for me and hope that you can find a replacement for me soon."

"Well, since we were looking to hire another full-time position, we already have resumes in, so hopefully, we can hire two from that list."

"I wish you the best," I told her, and shortly after, we hung up. Then I jotted down a note to myself to send them a substantial donation.

One call down, one more big one to go. I pulled up a search engine on my computer and typed in Coral's Café in Millerstown. A moment later, a link popped up, and I clicked the website to find the phone number.

It was the only way I could think of to get Evan's number. I had no idea if Coral knew or if she would even talk to me, but I had to try.

I dialed the number, and a moment later, it was answered with a hasty, "Coral's Café, can I help you?"

"Hi, I'm looking for Coral."

"Sure, can I tell her who is calling?"

"Tell her it's Laney Marshall."

"Okay, hold on." The phone went silent as she set it on hold, and I gnawed on my bottom lip for a moment. It was almost a full minute before the phone was picked back up.

"Laney, huh? Shouldn't I call you Alaina?"

I grimaced. "Hello, Coral, and you may call me either."

"Why are you calling me?"

"Because I need to speak with Evan."

"Then call him."

"I don't have his phone number. I rushed out of my house without my phone, and you were the only way I could think of to reach him."

"Why did you leave? Why did you lie to my brother? Why did you accept his proposal if you were already engaged?"

Her questions came fast and furious, and I sighed. "First, I'm not engaged. I broke it off with Bas when I left two and a half years ago. He's an arrogant man. He was being an ass. I love your brother, Coral, and I left because I found out that my brother died, and I had to come back."

She gasped. "I'm so sorry."

"Thank you, but I'd appreciate it if you didn't tell Evan that. I need to explain everything to him personally."

"Are you coming back?"

I turned my chair and stared out the window, my eyes slipping from one metal and cement building to another. "Unfortunately, not anytime soon."

"Oh," Coral said softly.

"I know Evan is hurt and angry with me, but I need to explain it to him. That was never my intention, Coral. I care very much for him. Can you please give me his phone number?"

There was silence over the line for a moment, and then she sighed. "Alright, I will. You broke his heart, Laney."

I closed my eyes as tears began to fill them. One tear slipped out and ran down my cheek. "I know, Coral, but know that mine is broken also."

CHAPTER TWENTY-SEVEN

EVAN

"Hey, do you know where Laney is?" Cameron Sexton asked after I answered my phone. I wasn't in the mood to talk to anyone, but I was worried something had happened when I saw Cam's number.

"No, why?"

"Well, her boss called in a well-being check for her. She's not answering her phone or her door, and no one knows where she is."

"She's not there. She left last night, and as far as I know, she's back home in California with her fiancé."

"Fiancé? What the hell are you talking about?"

Oh, man, I was not in the mood to get into it with him. "Look, she's fine. She's back where she belongs, and that's not here in Millerstown. If you want to know the rest, ask Hunt. I gotta go."

A few minutes later, my phone rang, and I saw it was Coral. I didn't answer, and five minutes later, Cara called. I didn't answer that one either. I received four other calls and at least a dozen text messages during the next hour. I ignored them all and focused on cleaning the basement closet that I had wanted to tackle for a while.

I had just sat down to eat lunch when my phone rang again. I did not recognize the number this time, and the area code was not from around here. My heart began to speed up, and I was tempted to ignore it, but something told me to pick it up.

"Hello?" I answered gruffly.

"Evan," her voice whispered through the line, and I closed my eyes, pretending she was right there with me.

"What do you want, Alaina?"

"Evan, don't be angry with me."

A bark of laughter jumped out of my mouth, and I burst to my feet to pace. "Don't be angry? I have every right to be angry! You lied to me about who you were. You lied to all of us! Did your sister really die? Or was that a lie too?"

"That was not a lie, Evan. How can you even question that?"

"How? Because you lied to me about who you were. I saw that office of yours. I did some research on you. You're one of the most wealthy women in the country."

"What does that have to do with anything?"

"Oh, come on, Laney. You know that I had enough trouble with the fact that I thought you had a couple of million in the bank, but we are talking billionaire here, and you're engaged to someone else."

"I most certainly am not, Evan. Listen to me. Bas and I are not engaged. I have no intention of ever marrying that man."

"Yeah, well, it sounds like your brother had other ideas."

"My brother is dead," she stated, and that stopped me in my tracks. "That's why Bas showed up. He came to tell me that Larry had a heart attack and died. I had to come back for the company. I wasn't thinking straight last night. I was exhausted, and when he told me about Larry, I just fell apart. I packed a couple of bags, and I flew back to Santa Monica, but I did that for the company. Not for Bas."

"So, when I walked in and saw him comforting you—"

"It was because he had just told me about Larry, and I realized that I had no family left. All of them were gone. I was alone. It hit me, and yes, I cried, and I let Bas comfort me, but it meant nothing to me. You have to believe me, Evan. I love you. I told you that I would marry you. My feelings have not changed."

"I'm sorry about your brother, Laney, but I don't know what to think or how I feel right now. You kept so much from me. How do I get past that?"

"I don't know." Her voice was barely more than a whisper.

"It is going to take me some time to digest this, but Laney, I know one thing. I know that I can't leave here. I'm not Cara. I can't pack up my life and move someplace else. Your life is there. Mine is here. How would it ever work, even if we wanted it to—and I'm not saying that I want it to."

"I know. I get that. Look, I have a lot that needs to be taken care of here to keep my company going. We need to talk face-to-face, but I know that I can't get away right now." She paused. "Evan, do you think there is any way that you could come here? You could see the real me. I will tell you everything. Answer every question that you had, and then you could decide if you even want to consider a future or not."

"You want me to come to California?"

"Yes. Just come out and see what I do. See who I am, and let us talk."

"I don't know, Laney. Let me think about it."

"I understand. I love you, Evan. Please believe that."

I wanted so badly to tell her I loved her, but I couldn't say the words right now. I was too hurt. "I'll talk to you soon. What number do I call?"

"I have to get a new phone today, but I'll have the same number. I'll text you once I have it set up. If you need to get ahold of me before that, you can call this number, and my assistant will put you through to me. It's my direct office line."

"Alright. Then I'll talk to you later."

"Evan, I'm sorry. I know I should have told you. Daniella and I talked about it at the picnic, and I was going to tell you all about it last night."

"Wait! Daniella knew? Why the hell did she know?"

"She recognized me from some research she did on a book."

"Jesus Christ," I muttered as I shook my head.

"Don't be upset with her. It wasn't her place to say anything, but I was going to tell you about everything last night. Know that I was, but then Bas showed up, and everything got out of control."

"I'll talk to you soon, Laney."

"Okay, bye, Evan."

"Bye." I hung up the phone and dropped it to the table, then I snatched it back up and called Hunt.

"What's up?" he said as he answered.

"Did you know that your wife was aware of who Laney was?"

"What?"

"She knew that Laney was really Alaina."

"How would she know that?"

"Something about researching a book."

"How did you hear about that?"

"Laney just called me."

"Oh, shit. What did she say?"

"A lot of things."

"Okay—" He waited. "You gonna fill me in or make me guess?"

"She said she's not engaged to that guy, and she was crying because he came here to tell her that her brother died."

"Oh, shit, man. I'm sorry to hear that."

"I was too, but that doesn't excuse her behavior and not telling me the truth about who she was."

"No, it doesn't. What else did she say?"

"She told me that she was going to explain it all to me last night before he showed up. Said that Daniella and her talked about it at the picnic, and she was just waiting for the right time."

"Okay, well, that's good."

"No, it's not, Hunt. Laney lives in California. I don't want to move there. My life is here."

"Okay, then it's just over? You're going to end it for good?"

"No, she wants me to come to California and talk. Because her brother died, she can't get away right now. She asked me to come there. She said she would tell me everything and let me see the real her."

"When are you leaving?"

"I don't know that I'm going, Hunt. She lied about everything. How can I trust her?"

"Evan, if you love her, then you need to give her the benefit of the doubt here. What is the harm in going out there and seeing her? When is the last time you had a vacation anyway?"

"I wouldn't exactly call it a vacation."

"Go. I think you should. If for nothing else than to get the ring back."

"That is true." I sighed and sank into my chair, pushing the plate with my half-eaten turkey sandwich away. "I'll think about it."

"I don't think there is anything to think about. I think you should go."

"I'll think about it. I'll talk to you later. Tell Daniella I have a bone to pick with her."

"You leave my wife out of this." He laughed, and we said goodbye.

I ended up finishing my sandwich and then wandered around my house for a few moments. Was it strange that I missed her house?

I grabbed my keys and jumped in my SUV. I knew one

person that I could talk to who would give me honest advice. He had never failed me.

When I got there, I went straight into the house and found him in the kitchen washing a plate, the coffee pot gurgling as it finished brewing. "Hey, Pop. How are you?"

He turned to look at me. "I was wondering how long it was going to take you to get here. Coffee is ready. Pour us a cup, and I'll get out some of Coral's homemade peanut butter cups. You can fill me in on all the details."

$\sim$

Two hours later, I left my father's house feeling better. I still wasn't sure if I was going to fly to California or not, but I felt a lot better about what was happening.

My father's advice was sound. I told him everything that had happened and repeated what Laney had told me earlier on the phone. He listened, asked questions, and then doled out his advice.

If I loved her, it was worth hearing her out and seeing who she was. The best way to do that would be to go to California and see her in her natural environment. He also told me to take him out of the equation, and if I felt that I would be happy out west, I should consider a move. My situation was much different than Cara's, and my father said he'd never been to California. He'd love to visit sometime.

I appreciated him saying that, but that didn't mean I wanted to move. There was one thing my father said that made me want to consider it.

If you love someone, location doesn't matter. All that matters is that you are together to build that relationship.

He was right, which is why I had gone to see him in the first place. Perhaps I had also needed to hear him say that he stood behind me no matter what I decided.

However, until I saw Laney again and talked at length, I wasn't making any decisions.

$\sim$

I didn't hear from Laney until the next day, and that was by text. *Evan, I have a phone again. Please let me know you received this.*

I texted her back. *I received your message.*

Have you thought about coming out here to see me?

Man, that was about all I had been thinking about. *I did.*

And?

Yes, I will come out so that we can discuss everything. You do owe me the truth, and I can retrieve the ring too. Maybe that last part was a dick move, but I didn't want her to think that I was running out there and everything would be hunky-dory. I wasn't sure that it would be.

Fair enough, she stated. A moment later, another reply came through. *Let me know when you would be available, and I will make the arrangements.*

I ground my teeth for a moment. I didn't need her paying for my ticket, but then again, the woman was a billionaire, and I was saving my pennies to pay off my home improvement loan.

I will let you know when I have a couple of days to get away.

Thank you. I'll talk to you later. I have to head into a meeting now. Bye, Evan.

Bye.

I set my phone down and thought over the conversation. I was a little excited to see her again if I were being honest with myself. Yes, I was still upset with her for not telling me the truth, but I was in love with the woman.

Well, in love with the woman that I knew from here. I wasn't sure what she would be like when I saw her out there.

Two days later, I texted Laney to tell her when I could come. She replied that she'd take care of everything, and less than an hour later, my flight information arrived in my email from a woman named Bridgett Long, who had the title of Assistant to the Vice President of Buckworth Industries.

Is that what Alaina was? The VP?

I looked at what Bridgett wrote and found I had a first-class round-trip ticket, and someone would meet me at the luggage area. I had a feeling it wouldn't be Laney.

I guess I was about to get a crash course in what it was like to be rich.

CHAPTER TWENTY-EIGHT

LANEY

*T*he last few days had been a whirlwind. I had been aware of much of what had been happening around the corporation, but not everything. There was a lot that I had to get reacquainted with.

I had focused most of my attention on acquisitions and investing in the past. Now, I had to spread my reach much further, and it made me appreciate what my father and brother had accomplished.

It was also under a lot of pressure from Bas. At least twice a day, we argued, and one of those arguments was always regarding the press release about my brother's death—the other most of the time, was about us.

People, and when I say people, I meant our board of directors, were becoming suspicious that they couldn't reach my brother. Larry had always been available to everyone, and now no one could understand why he wasn't checking in with them.

I told Bas we had to explain the truth because lying about him being sick was not cutting it, but Bas demanded that we didn't. Not yet.

If he didn't change his mind soon, I was going to take

matters into my own hands. I just needed to make sure that things were steady when I did.

So far, with the news that I was back in the office, the stock had risen slightly. Having all the major players on the board at the table was good business, but if something wasn't said about Larry soon, rumors were going to start, and that would be worse than just announcing he was deceased. Plus, I wanted to hold his funeral and allow myself to grieve for him.

I had yet to do that. I did, however, grieve daily for what I lost with Evan. I prayed that he would forgive me, and perhaps we could figure things out when he came out here to see me.

The thought that he would be here the following day both thrilled me and made me wonder if this was a good idea or not. What would Evan think when he saw all that I dealt with? What had he thought when he saw my office at home? Did he understand just how wealthy I was?

I didn't have the answers to those questions, and I didn't want to discuss any of these matters until he was here so I could see his face and I could make him listen.

He might come out here, see it all, and say, nope. None of this is for me, and no matter how I feel about you, this will not work for us. Or perhaps he would come here and see that he might be able to build a life. We had four hospitals in our area. I'm sure I could help him get a job at one of them. A big enough donation, and I could get anyone a job—not that I wanted to buy a position for him.

One of the things that I thought about often was his comment about collecting his ring. Would I give it back to him freely, or would he have to request for it back? I stared at my hand. I hadn't worn it in the seven days that I had been home, but only because I didn't know where our relationship stood, and I didn't want to answer questions that I might have to explain later.

Would he understand that? Would he take offense to me not wearing it? I hoped he would understand.

My speaker buzzed on my desk and my assistant, Bridgett, stated that they needed me in Acquisitions. I told her I was on my way, and with that, I put thoughts of Evan out of my head.

I got home late that night, kicking my shoes off at the door, and dragging myself into the kitchen to find something to eat. I was digging around inside the fridge when I heard someone step into the room.

"Ma'am, what can I get for you?" Kate asked as I peered around the door.

"Do we have any chocolate cake in here? I really want chocolate cake and a glass of red wine."

Kate chuckled. "We always have chocolate cake. I make sure of that. I know when you are overstressed, that's what you like."

As Kate opened the other fridge, I stepped back and watched her pull out a simple cake with cream cheese frosting.

"You are a godsend," I told her as she set it on the counter. I turned to collect a plate. "Would you join me for a slice?"

Kate was surprised by my question but smiled. "I would love to join you. I've had my eye on this cake since it was made yesterday."

I chuckled and allowed her to cut two pieces while I went to collect a bottle of wine from my rack. I had a wine vault in the basement that housed around three hundred bottles for entertaining and kept only a few bottles upstairs for my personal use.

I didn't ask if she wanted a glass. I just poured her one and then carried them to the small table on the side of the room that the help used for their meals. I had probably sat at this table no more than five times in the years that I owned this house. Usually, I sat at the formal dining table or my desk.

Kate brought the plates over to the table and took a seat across from me. "Oh, my god! It has cherries in it!"

"Yes. I told you it looked good."

I laughed. "There was a coffee café near where I lived, and they made the best pastries and cakes. I had to force myself not to go there every day, or I would have gained twenty pounds."

"Where was that?"

"Millerstown, Pennsylvania," I replied and took a bite of the cake, savoring the taste for a moment. "After Lindsey died, I kind of lost myself, Kate. None of this made sense to me." I lifted a hand to indicate the house. "What's the purpose of all of this if you can't protect the ones you love?"

It was a rhetorical question, and Kate knew that as I continued. "So I took off to visit Vinny and fell in love with the simple life. I went back to school and got a degree in social services, then started working for a domestic violence center."

Kate's eyes were wide with shock. "You did?"

I nodded and took another bite of the cake. "I did. I learned a lot about life doing that job. It's not very often that someone like me can become something else and live a different life. I understand people so much more now."

"That must have been very eye-opening."

"It was heartbreaking at times. A few weeks ago, a woman was killed coming out of the courthouse after being interviewed by detectives. She was going to have her husband arrested finally, but he somehow found out and shot her as she came out of the building." I twisted my arm and showed her my forearm. "I got shot too."

"Oh, my god!" Kate exclaimed as she examined my arm.

"It was nothing, just a graze, no stitches even. They used glue, but that small scar will always remind me of that."

The memory replayed through my mind, and I sat quietly, taking a few bites of my cake.

"Did you like it there?"

"I did." I smiled at her. "I bought this incredible house. It wasn't even half this size, but it was beautiful, and I didn't have any help either. Well, that's not true. I did have a cleaner who came in twice a week, but I did the shopping and the laundry, and I drove myself."

"I'm impressed," Kate said with a laugh. "But I always knew you had it in you."

I stared at Kate for a moment and then reached out and put my hand over hers. "I want to thank you."

"For what?"

"For doing everything for me. For always being here and watching over this place for the last few years without me. You have done an amazing job, you always did, and I never said thank you enough."

"You're welcome," she said, looking overwhelmed at my praise. "I must be honest; I almost left a few times. It got a little boring here without anyone around, but the job was easy, and the money was good." She looked sheepish as she finished.

"Please do not feel uncomfortable about saying that. You deserve a raise after all that you have done."

"Oh, no." She shook her head, waving her hand.

"I insist, Kate. I have taken so much for granted in the years that you have worked for me. I know next to nothing about you. Do you have a family?"

"I do. My husband has long since passed, and my children are grown now, but I have two beautiful grandchildren."

"Grandchildren! You do not look old enough to have grand-children."

She laughed. "But I am. I had my children when I was young, with my high school sweetheart. He died overseas serving our country, and his pension wasn't enough to support us, so I started doing housekeeping and worked my way up, but really, you don't want to hear this."

"On the contrary, I want to hear it very much."

"Well, okay, I have a grandson who is three and a grand-daughter who is four. They live on the East Coast, so I don't get to see them much. Luckily we can video chat."

"When is the last time you saw them?"

"For Christmas."

I leaned back. "That was months ago! You need to invite them here."

Her eyes nearly exploded from her head. "Here?"

"Yes, there is plenty of room. They would be my guests. This house is too quiet and way too stuffy. We need to make some changes here, and the first change is that you bring your family here for a vacation. Let the kids swim and play, and spend time with your family. It is so important, Kate."

Kate stared at me like I had lost my mind. "I'm sorry, but who are you, and where is my employer?"

I laughed. "Kate, if there is something that I learned while being away, it's that family, real family, needs to come first, and that family doesn't necessarily need to be blood-related. They can be friends, co-workers, neighbors, or people that we fall in love with."

Her gaze softened, and she leaned forward. "What is his name?"

"Who?" I asked, confused.

"The man you fell in love with?"

I sighed dreamily. "His name is Evan, Evan Winston. He is a nurse in the ICU at the hospital in Millerstown. I met him there when a client of mine was almost killed."

"Your job sounds very dangerous."

"Not for me, but for other people, the ones whom I was trying to help, it was perilous sometimes. But that is not the point, and while I bring up Evan, I guess I should tell you that he will be here tomorrow."

"He's coming to visit?" she asked excitedly.

"He is, but I don't know whether this is necessarily a good thing or bad."

"If you love him, then how could it be bad?"

I glanced at our wineglasses and lifted the bottle. "Do you

have plans tonight? This is kind of a long story and might require another bottle."

Kate chuckled and pushed her glass toward me. "I have nowhere to be."

"Don't say I didn't warn you," I told her as I filled her glass and mine and then began to share the entire story of where I worked, what I did, and the man that I fell in love with at first sight.

Ninety minutes later, and almost two bottles of wine, I finished my story, and Kate shook her head. "You need to be completely honest with him. If you love him, tell him the truth about it all. Don't hide anything. If he wants to know how much you have, tell him down to the last penny. If Evan is the type of man that you say he is, this will be very overwhelming to him, but if he has time to digest it, he will come to terms with it."

"He told me that he'd never move here."

"Then he doesn't move here, but you will be the President of Buckworth Industries. You can live wherever you want. You don't have to be in the office every day. Work from your other house, come here when you need to attend board meetings. Hire other people to oversee things here. CEOs and presidents do that sort of thing all the time. I mean, isn't that what Bas does for your brother sometimes?"

"Yes, he does," I replied, my mind spinning on the possibility. Could I work from there? Maybe not at first, but eventually, I could. I could buy a plane, fly back and forth, or even open a new corporate office there. No law said I had to keep the company in Santa Monica.

She laughed. "I see the wheels turning."

"You have given me something to think about," I told her. "But first, I need to see what Evan has to say."

"I assume you will want me to make a room available for him, in case he doesn't sleep in yours, right?"

"That might be a good idea. I don't want to push anything on him, but while he is here, please, make him feel as comfortable as you can."

"Absolutely, Alaina. I will do my best."

"And I was very serious about you inviting your family here. You have lived in this house for five years. This is your home too, and you are welcome to invite them here and use the house as if it were your own. The kitchen, the living room, the guest rooms, downstairs, and of course, the pool area."

She blinked rapidly for a few moments. "Alaina, don't mind me saying this, but I am so glad you left and came back. I see such a difference in you, and it is such a wonderful thing to see."

"I agree, Kate. I have made some fundamental changes in my life, and now I just need to figure out how to deal with the business side. Got any tips for that?"

"I'm afraid that is a little out of my league." The two of us laughed, and I felt like I had found something I hadn't expected to tonight. I had found a good friend in Kate.

CHAPTER TWENTY-NINE

EVAN

I sat in the second row of the plane with more legroom than I'd ever had before and enjoyed my second complimentary beer. So, traveling first class wasn't a horrible way to travel. I'd never thought much about it before, but it was a lot more comfortable.

That didn't keep me from being antsy in my seat, though. Luckily, the older woman beside me was good company and told me that her daughter was a nurse. We talked a lot about my job and hers. I didn't miss that she mentioned her daughter was single more than a few times. Had I not been traveling to find out what my future entailed, I might have paid more attention to those comments.

When I wasn't chatting with Clara, I was dwelling over what would happen once I arrived in Santa Monica. Would Laney sit down and spill all the beans, or would she wait to reveal things as I asked? How forthcoming would she be with me? Would she apologize for not telling me the truth? Would she tell me it was over? Or would she ask me to move my life there?

The crazy thing about it was that I had spent time the last

couple of days researching hospitals in the area. I'd even looked over employment opportunities, and while I didn't admit this to anyone else, I had updated my resume.

Not that I planned on doing anything with it, but just in case. There was nothing wrong with being prepared. Cara had told me to be open-minded, and that was what I was doing.

One of the things I had done while preparing was speak with Daniella. She revealed the entire conversation that she'd had with Laney at the picnic, and I trusted that she told me the truth. She explained that Laney wanted to tell me the truth, but she also knew that I was apprehensive about her money, and that's what had held her back.

The other thing I did, was return to her house and spend more time in her office. I read over a lot of stuff on her desk. Now that the shock was over, I understood more of what I was looking at. Perhaps she would be upset with me for doing that. I mean, these were personal and business documents, but if she hadn't wanted me to see it, she could have locked the door.

I had also searched more on the internet and absorbed everything that I could learn about her. Not that I believed it all to be accurate; the press walked a fine line sometimes, and I knew that.

I did find articles about her sister's death and the prosecution of her husband. At least Laney hadn't lied to me about that. I also found information on her parents' accident. I didn't find any mention of her brother's death—which seemed very odd.

If he was as all-powerful as the media made him out to be, wouldn't it be a big deal that he was dead? I would think so.

Until I arrived and had the chance to speak with her, I wouldn't know the answer to that question or many others.

While I was apprehensive about what was to come, I was also excited to see her again. We had texted a few times, but neither of us said much, other than how are you? Are you still coming? I look forward to seeing you.

I wasn't sure what kind of reception I expected to receive when I arrived. Would she hug me? Kiss me? Shake my hand? I didn't even know what I wanted her to do, but as the wheels touched the ground, I realized I would soon find out.

Before I had left, my sister Cara had called and told me not to hold back on anything or I'd always wonder. She also told me to call her if I needed someone to talk to. I appreciated my big sister more than ever right now.

After exiting the plane, I followed the signs to the luggage carousel. I had packed light as I was only here for three days and didn't need much, so I only had a carry-on, but since that is where my ride was picking me up, I followed along with the crowd.

As I came down the escalator to the bottom floor, I scanned over the twenty or so people standing at the bottom. Most of them wore suits and held a sign with names. A couple of women were interspersed, but it was primarily middle- to older-aged men. Geez, there were a lot of drivers here.

I found my name, and anxiety ran through me as I reached the bottom and approached the slightly overweight man in his forties with blond hair. "I'm Evan Winston."

"Mr. Winston, welcome to Santa Monica. My name is Hank. Do you have other luggage?"

I shook my head. "No, only this."

He reached for it, and I hesitated slightly, then held the handle out to him.

"If you'll follow me, the car is right outside." I followed behind him a few feet but felt weird as hell. I stepped next to him.

"Do you work for Alaina Buckworth?"

He smiled my way. "I do. I'm her personal driver."

Personal driver, huh? And so it begins. I was now officially in Wonderland. "Have you worked for her long?"

He considered that for a moment. "I have worked for Ms. Buckworth for around eight years."

"What did you do while she was away?" I asked as we exited the building. A gust of warm salty air hit me, reminding me that I was no longer in Pennsylvania, where the weather was getting warm but had not reached humid yet.

"I kept up with her home, gardens, and her other vehicles."

"How many vehicles does she have?"

He pointed toward a walkway that led to a parking area. "She has six normally, but two of them are not here, of course. They are at her other home in Pennsylvania."

I nodded, wondering what other cars she had. I remained quiet until we reached the parking area, and then Hank led me over to charcoal-gray town car. "This is it." He opened the trunk and set my luggage into the back. The case looked tiny compared to the size of the compartment. He shifted around the rear door and opened it. I hesitated.

"Um, would you mind if I sat in the front?" I paused. "So you could point things out to me. I've never been here, might as well get a little sightseeing in."

He chuckled and closed the door. "By all means, Mr. Winston. I much prefer to be up there myself." He went to the front passenger door and opened it for me. I slipped in and immediately put my seat belt on as he went around to the other door.

"You can call me Evan," I told him as he started to pull out of the parking space.

"Alright, if that is what you would like."

"I would prefer that. I still think of my father as Mr. Winston."

He chuckled. "Funny how that is, isn't it?"

"Yes, very much so."

As we drove, Hank pointed things out and told me stories about the town. From time to time, he also mentioned Aliana and things that she did around town. I listened with avid interest, and when we arrived at her office, he pulled up to the front door of a very tall building.

"I will have your luggage delivered to the house. Would you like Kate to have it unpacked for you?"

"Kate?"

"That's Ms. Buckworth's housekeeper."

"Oh, no. I can unpack it myself, but thank you."

"You are welcome," he said with a wide smile and went to put the car in park.

"You don't have to open my door, Hank. I'm quite capable. Thank you for picking me up." I glanced out the window. "Any idea where I should go in there?"

"Head to the security desk. They will be expecting you, and someone will take you up to her office."

I stared at the tall building. "Thank you again." I climbed out and stood on the sidewalk, staring up at reflective glass that just kept going up and up. A sign over the door read Buckworth Industries, and I sighed. "Here goes nothing."

I stepped into the lobby, my eyes drifting from one side to the other as I took in all the glass and chrome. People were coming and going, and it took only a moment to find the security desk.

"Hi, I'm Evan Winston. I'm here to see Alaina Buckworth."

The security guy nodded. "Just a moment, Mr. Winston. We have been expecting you. I have someone coming to take you up to her floor."

"Thank you." I stepped back and let my gaze scan around as I waited. She owns this building—this incredible building. My hands felt clammy, and I shoved my hands into my pockets and kind of wiped them off inside. A moment later, a man in a suit approached me.

"Mr. Winston, I'm Carl, head of security. If you follow me, I will take you to Ms. Buckworth's office."

He stepped around the metal detector, and I paused, getting ready to remove the items from my pockets, but he smiled. "That's okay, sir. You don't have to go through that."

I stepped around it and stopped at his side. He handed me a visitor badge. "If you could clip that on, I would appreciate it." I glanced down at my polo shirt, frowning. He chuckled. "You can clip it to your pants pocket. That's fine."

He swiped his card against the panel and pushed the number ten inside the elevator. The elevator began to climb a moment later and didn't stop until we reached the top floor.

I stepped out before him and glanced around at the elevator lobby. It was nicer than a four-star hotel lobby. "This way, Mr. Winston."

I continued to follow him through a set of glass doors and paused to look around. There were people everywhere, but it seemed unusually quiet. A few people smiled my way as they passed, and Carl led me down a hallway and stopped near the end at a desk.

"Bridgett, this is Mr. Winston."

Bridgett smiled widely at me. "Hello, Mr. Winston. I hope your flight went well."

"It did, thank you."

"Ms. Buckworth is in a meeting right now, but she should be done soon. She asked me to show you to her office."

I nodded and glanced around again.

Carl spoke, gathering my attention. "Mr. Winston, if you should need anything from us, please dial #88 from any phone."

"Thank you, Carl." He nodded and was gone.

"Where is Alaina?" I asked.

"In the conference room on the other side of the building."

"Can I see it?" I had this sudden need to get a peek at her.

"Sure, follow me." She wound through a few cubical halls and then came out on the other side. As we turned left, I was able to see the large room through the glass wall. The table was huge, and at the far end sat Laney. My heart sighed at the sight of her. She sat with her chin resting on her fist, listening to someone speak.

My god, she was even more beautiful than I remembered. She spoke for a moment, looking irritated, and then her gaze shifted out the glass and landed directly on mine. The irritated look immediately faded, and she smiled briefly. Then she sat up to the table and put her hands on it as she stood and spoke.

She started to head toward the door a moment later, and a few people seemed concerned that she was leaving. One man stood, and I heard his voice as the door opened. "Alaina, is that a yes or a no?"

She paused in the doorway and looked back at him. "I won't give you an answer until you get me more information. That is not enough. I want it by Monday morning at nine. If you don't have factual information to back that up, it will be a firm no."

She dismissed him immediately and strode purposely toward me. Was she as nervous as I was? She sure didn't look it.

"Thank you, Bridgett. I'll take Evan from here."

"Yes, Ms. Buckworth."

Bridgett disappeared immediately, and Laney and I stood three feet apart, staring at each other.

"Hello, Evan."

"Hi, Laney," I replied. Her name might be Alaina, but she would always be Laney to me.

She stepped forward and took my arm to turn me around. "Let's go back to my office."

I let her lead me back, and we went directly into her office, where she closed the door behind me. I glanced around, noting the fancy glass desk, the plush seating area, and a smaller conference table off to the side that only sat eight and not twenty like the other one. When I turned back, she reached for a button on the wall. She pushed it, and the glass wall to the hallway went from transparent to opaque.

"Nice trick," I said as she stepped forward.

She paused a few inches in front of me. "Can I give you a hug, Evan?"

I nodded, opening my arms, and she immediately stepped into them. It felt like she had come home, and I closed my eyes and savored the feeling. I had no clue if I'd ever feel this again when this visit was over. I breathed her in and kissed the top of her head.

She lifted her face to me, and the two of us stared at one another. "Can I kiss you, Evan?"

I lifted her chin with two fingers and brought my lips to hers. It was almost as magical as it had been the first time we'd kissed. It wasn't a passionate kiss, but it was enough to tell me that what I had felt for her before was still there, despite the information she had not revealed about herself.

She pulled back slightly, still keeping hold of me. "You have no idea how much I needed that."

"Me too," I replied.

"I know we have a lot to talk about, Evan, but you need to know that I never meant to hurt you. I was going to tell you the truth. I love you. Above all else, I love you."

I cupped her cheek. "I love you, too, but Laney, there are some huge things for us to consider here."

"I know. Trust me, I know."

She kissed me one more time and then stepped back, taking my hand and pulling me toward her desk. She brought me over to the window and stood beside me, putting an arm around my back. "I stare out this window and wish it was my garden every single time."

"Yeah, I would too. This is ugly compared to that view."

She shifted to look at me. "Evan, this is not the view that I want. I want that garden view. I want that garden view with you, with our children running around under the fairy lights."

I looked around her office. "But how can you have that when

you have all of this? How can you walk away from this kind of life for what I could give you in Millerstown?"

She stepped closer, lifting her face to mine, our lips just a breath apart. "Because you are more important to me than any of this. I would leave it all for you, Evan. I would give it all up to keep you."

CHAPTER THIRTY

LANEY

I had thought a lot about Evan during the last few days. After talking with Kate yesterday, I decided to contemplate my options, realizing I had quite a few.

I was so glad that he had come here to see me. So happy that he was willing to speak to me and allow me to explain everything. I hadn't intended to throw myself at him the moment he arrived, but I couldn't help it. Being in his arms again after this stressful period of return was like being back in my favorite place.

I stood with Evan at the window, trying to make him realize how important he was to me. "Because you are more important to me than any of this. I would leave it all for you, Evan. I would give it all up to keep you."

He frowned. "Laney, I know how important you are, how important your company is. I can't keep you from that."

"You wouldn't be." I sighed. "Look, there is a lot that we need to discuss, but unfortunately, I have to go into another meeting. It should take me about an hour, and then I will be all yours for the weekend."

"Alright, what do you want me to do in the meantime?"

"You could wait here in the office, but I thought you might want a tour of the building. Perhaps you'd like to see our R&D department that focuses on medical equipment. You could see what we are working on, although you would be sworn to secrecy," I joked. "I can't have you telling my competitors what we are working on."

He chuckled. "Yeah, I'm gonna run right out and do that."

I smiled, touching the side of his face just as the door burst open. The two of us turned to find Bas standing there, anger radiating from his eyes like laser beams. Behind him was Bridgett looking very apologetic.

"I tried to stop him," she said in a high-pitched voice.

"It's okay, Bridgett." I stepped away from Evan. "What do you want, Bas?"

"What the hell is he doing here?"

"That is none of your business."

He stalked farther into the room, smoke billowing from his ears. "It most certainly is my business," he snarled.

I approached him, my shoulders back, my chin held high. "Do you forget that I now own fifty-one percent of this company, Bastian? You own five. I can kick your ass out of here so fast that your head would spin. I suggest you remember who the hell you are talking to."

He compressed his lips, a muscle ticking in his jaw as he stared down at me. Then he inhaled sharply and visibly relaxed. "I'm sorry. I was surprised to hear that he was here. I thought it was over with him."

"I am far from being done with Evan, Bas. It would do you good to remember that."

He frowned. "You aren't going to marry him, are you?"

"That decision is between Evan and me and has absolutely nothing to do with you. Now, unless you have business to discuss, I suggest you turn around and leave."

He glared over my head at Evan for a couple of seconds, then smiled at me and stepped back. "My business can wait."

"Then goodbye, Bas."

He smiled again, glared one more time at Evan, and then stalked out of the room. The moment he was gone, Bridgett rushed in.

"I'm so sorry," she gushed.

"It's okay. Do you need something?"

She handed over a stack of messages. "They are ready for you in the conference room."

I glanced at the messages. There were eight of them. "Any of these important?"

She shook her head. "No, none of them said it was urgent."

"Alright, thank you. Can you call Tommy to give Evan a tour while I'm in the meeting? I already talked to him about it." I set the messages on my desk.

"Absolutely," she responded and hustled out of the room.

I sighed as I turned around to Evan. "I'm sorry about his bad attitude."

He shrugged. "It's not your fault." He paused. "Were you really going to marry him?"

"I was, but not because I loved him." I came to stand in front of Evan. "I was marrying him because I thought it made good business sense."

"And it doesn't make good business sense now?"

I shook my head. "Before I met you, I had no clue what I was missing in my life, Evan. I don't want a marriage for business. I want a marriage for love."

He glanced at my hand. "I see you aren't wearing your ring."

"It's at home in my safe. I wasn't prepared to answer questions about that right now, and I wasn't sure where your thoughts were."

He nodded. "I guess that makes sense."

"If you want me to put it on, if you still want me to marry

you, I will do it in a heartbeat and answer every question that comes my way."

He nodded but remained silent for a few seconds. "Let's figure things out first."

"Alright." I kissed him tenderly. "I have to go. Make yourself at home, and Tommy should be here soon. I'll be back as quickly as I can, and we can head home."

His brow furrowed for a moment. "How many homes do you have, Laney?"

I hesitated only a second. "I have four. The one here, and the one in Pennsylvania. I have another house in England and one in the Caribbean."

His eyes grew wide. "Wow, okay."

"I'll see you later." I rushed out the door before I could change my mind and decide to say the hell with the meeting so that I could start my weekend early.

The meeting lasted a lot longer than an hour, and I was antsy to be done, but I forced myself to keep my attention on what we were discussing and not on what Evan was doing somewhere in the building.

Evan was here. Every time I thought about that, I was tempted to giggle, but I held back. The other nine people at the table with me would have thought I had lost my mind.

The good thing was that since I returned and proved to everyone that I knew what was happening within the company, things had been running smooth. It was almost as if I had never left.

The moment I could excuse myself, I was out of my seat and rushing back to my office. I expected to see Evan sitting in there looking bored, but my office was empty. Anxiety filled me with the thought that he had left. "Where is he?" I asked Bridgett the moment she hung up her phone.

"Tommy took him on a tour, and then Maggie came by shortly after they returned. She took him on a different tour."

"Ah, okay. Any idea where they are?"

She grinned. "Yeah, Randolph's."

I laughed. "Of course, she would take him out for a drink. Can you call Hank and let him know that I'm ready?" After she said she would, I went into my office, collected the messages she had left on my desk, and sent Maggie a text that I would be there soon.

She replied that they were on their way back to the building, and they would wait in the lobby. I had just climbed inside the elevator when Bas joined me.

I sighed wearily. I didn't want to argue with him again. He stood in front of me, almost as if he were trying to intimidate me. I hiked a brow, waiting to see what he would say.

"He can't give you what I can."

"What is it that you think you can give me that Evan can't?"

"The world, Alaina."

"There might have been a time in my life that I wanted the world, Bas, but not now. What I want now, you can't give me."

"Pfft, what could that man possibly give you?"

"Love. A family. A future."

"I'm your future, Alaina. Me! This company!"

I shook my head. "No, Bas, you're not. This company might be important, and it will always be important, but it's a company. It's not my life—not anymore."

"What did that place do to you? Where is that fierce woman who wanted to control the world?"

"She realized that controlling the world was not important. She concluded that life was more important, and she wants to live it to the fullest."

"You are going to run this company into the ground. When your bro—" He stopped, and I observed him.

"What were you going to say about Larry?"

"If he saw what you were doing, he would be fit to be tied."

"Then it's good that he's not here," I replied as the door opened. "Now, if you will excuse me, I'm going home to spend time with my fiancé."

I stepped around him, and he grabbed my arm. "You cannot marry that guy."

I stared at his hand, then lifted my chin and glared at him. "Take your hand off me, Bas." He let go. "If you ever touch me like that again, I will have you arrested for assault. Do you hear me? And as for marrying Evan, there is nothing that you or anyone else can do about it." I leaned forward and hissed into his face, "So back the fuck off!"

With that, I stalked past him and started toward the security desk. Standing off to the side were Maggie and Evan, watching me. Ugh, they had to have seen that.

"Hi," I called cheerfully as I reached them. "Did you two have fun?"

Maggie was grinning as she hooked her arm with his. "If you don't want him, I'll take him from you. This guy is a gem."

"Not on your life, Maggie," I growled playfully as Evan winked.

Evan spoke up. "We had a nice chat, and Tom gave me a great tour."

"Good, I'm glad you weren't bored," I told him. "Hank should be here. Maggie, thanks for keeping him company."

"Anytime," she said and then kissed Evan on the cheek. "You really are a gem, Evan. I'm sure I will see you later. Enjoy your visit."

After Maggie left us, I hooked my hand in his arm. "You ready to see my house?"

"You mean house two of four?" he asked.

I chuckled, trying to make light of it. "Yes, house two of four, but this was my main house. My house in England isn't that large, only about two thousand square feet. My Caribbean house is awesome, though."

"Yeah, where is that?"

"On a little island called Jumby Bay in Antigua."

"Always wanted to visit Antigua."

We stepped out of the building, and I saw Hank and the car at the curb. I smiled up at Evan. "Stick with me, kid, and you'll get to see it."

Once we were inside the car, Evan turned to me. "How often do you go there?"

"To be honest, I haven't been in about four years."

"You haven't visited it in four years, but you still own it?"

I nodded. "Yep, although right now, I rent it out so that it's not sitting empty."

He nodded. "Wow, nice. How much does it go for a night?"

I chuckled. "People rent it for the week or month generally. For a week, it would be twenty-five thousand. More if they want my chef." I shrugged as his lips parted in surprise. "It helps pay for the upkeep of it and the staff."

He eyed me carefully. "How much does a place like that cost to purchase?"

I thought about that for a moment. "I think I paid thirteen million for it eight years ago. Now, it would probably be worth more than twenty million."

"Twenty million, as in US dollars?"

I nodded. "Evan, I don't know if you are aware or not, but I am a billionaire. Twenty million is a drop in the bucket for me."

He shook his head, staring at the passenger side window for a moment. Finally, he turned to face me again. "Yes, I was aware of that. I have done a lot of research on you, and I'm going to admit that I went through your office to find out more. I hope you aren't upset about that."

"I purposely left that door open so that you could see it. I wanted you to take your time and understand what I do. Who I am."

"Who are you?"

I took his hand. "I'm Laney Marshall. The woman you fell in love with. The woman who fell in love with you."

"But your name is Alaina Buckworth."

"It is, but I don't want you to call me Alaina. My father was the only one that ever called me Laney, and I much prefer that—especially from you. Marshall is my middle name."

"Yes, I do know that."

"Then you know I didn't completely lie about who I was. I didn't want everyone to know that I was a Buckworth, not that I'm not proud to be one, but I needed to step away from it all."

"Now that you're back, how is it? Do you want to be here? Does it make you happier than what you were doing?"

I contemplated that for a moment. "I will admit that I missed some of it. Not all the stupid meetings and overseeing every aspect of the company, but I did miss the acquisition side. When I left, I couldn't function in the company. I do miss working with the DV center, but to be honest, that was starting to affect me, and not in a good way."

"So, you wouldn't go back?"

I shook my head. "Not to the position that I had, no. Perhaps to volunteer, but not to work."

"You are considering going back to PA?"

I tugged my bottom lip under my teeth for a moment. "I can't say that I'm not, but I would have quite a few things to figure out if I did consider that. I'm not saying no, but I'm not saying that I can right now either."

"Okay, I guess that is better than a flat-out no."

I shifted so that I was facing him more. "Evan, I love you, and I want us to figure out how to make this work. Do you think there might be a chance?"

He studied me, and I stared into his warm brown eyes. "I want to say yes, Laney, I really do, but I'm not sure I can be part of all this."

"Why not? I mean, I know it's a lot, but it's just stuff, Evan."

He laughed. "Just stuff. See, here is the difference between us. You have never in your life had to count your pennies to make sure you had enough food to eat or wondered how you'd pay your mortgage because your heating system broke and needed to be replaced."

"No, you're right. I haven't, but that doesn't mean that I haven't had my own struggles."

He chuckled. "What? Deciding what car or house to buy next?"

I frowned at him. "Now, that's not nice. I can't help it that I'm wealthy, Evan."

"You're right. I'm sorry. I just don't see how your struggles can compare to people like me."

"Okay, try thinking about this. I spend a lot of time thinking about companies I want to take over. Not because I want to ruin a company or just get wealthier. I try to figure out how I can rebuild a company so that the people like you don't lose their jobs, health care, and homes. I don't just have one home to worry about; I have thousands. I have to find the best way to either build them or tear them down and find other places for those people to go. That weighs heavily on me."

He pondered that for a moment. "Okay, I never thought of that."

"I'm sure you didn't. You would have no reason to. I want you to understand that I get it. There is a huge difference in our bank accounts. I probably earn more interest in one month than your annual salary, but that doesn't bother me. It might bother you, Evan. I get that. You need to figure out if you could learn to live with it. Can you accept it and embrace it? Yes, being with me would change your life and that of your family's, but only you can decide if you love me enough to do that."

CHAPTER THIRTY-ONE

EVAN

*D*id I love her enough to overlook the vast difference in our lifestyles and economic status?

She squeezed my hand and smiled tenderly. "You don't have to answer me now. I want you to see it all, and then you can go home and think it over."

"I appreciate the fact that you aren't pressuring me to decide now."

"I would never do that, Evan. I know that my world is a lot."

As we drove the rest of the way to her house, she asked me questions about what I thought of the R&D department, and I told her it was incredible. I had enjoyed my tour with Tom and had asked him many questions. He, in turn, had answered them all and even asked my opinion on some new things they were working on. Having someone who worked firsthand with these devices was helpful. At least, that's what he told me.

As we drove, my mind drifted back to the next part of my afternoon.

After my tour with Tom, I had gone back to Laney's office, hoping she would be there, but another woman entered the office shortly after I sat down.

"You must be Evan." She held her hand out. "I'm Maggie, a good friend of Alaina's."

"It's nice to meet you," I replied.

"Alaina told me all about you and her life in Pennsylvania. Are you feeling overwhelmed yet?"

I laughed. "Does it show?"

"You do have that deer in the headlights look about you." She chuckled. "How about I give you a tour of the bar on the corner. I can keep you company until she's done. The meeting is going longer than she expected."

"I'd love that."

She grinned. "Come on. I can give you a little dirt on Alaina that you might not know."

"Oh." I chuckled. "Now that sounds good."

Maggie was very friendly and helped me to relax. She told me more about the company and what Laney was responsible for overseeing without making it sound overwhelming. The more I heard, though, the more I wondered how this could work out for us.

This company was above and beyond anything I could imagine. It was so different than small-town America, and I had a hard time picturing Laney in her house back in Millerstown after seeing her seated at the conference table, with all the people around her.

This business was not a language I spoke. Talk to me about any medical care, and I was on board, but taking over companies, building, selling, creating, stocks, takeovers, that was all foreign to me. I didn't want to be depressed over that, but I was.

Maggie had looked at me carefully. "Evan, that overwhelmed look is back in your eyes. What are you thinking?"

I took a few seconds and tried to put my thoughts into words. "I'm wondering how someone like her and someone like me could possibly ever work. She's this powerful woman who controls a huge corporation. I'm only a nurse who administers medication to sick people."

"Don't sell yourself short, Evan. If Alaina didn't think you were special, she wouldn't have invited you here. She is one of the most down-to-earth people that I know." She swirled her glass for a moment. "After her sister died, she changed. I worried about her, and I was glad that she stepped away from the company. She needed to do that for her sanity. I think she found herself while she was gone. I could tell it in her emails when she told me what she was doing. She never forgot about what was going on here or her responsibilities, but it also didn't consume her anymore."

"Does it now?"

She shook her head. "No. She's still incredible at what she does, but I can see in her face how much she wishes she wasn't here. Would she leave? I don't know, but I know that she will find a balance between work and life now, no matter what. I know that she wants you in her life. I think she needs you in her life."

"Needs me?" I laughed. "I hardly see that."

"You ground her, Evan. I have never seen her so happy. The other day, she was staring off into space and I asked her where her mind was. Once upon a time she would have recited stock quotes or told me about contract issues with the latest acquisition. Instead, she laughed and said, 'Oh, with Evan under the fairy lights.'

"The old Alaina would have never made such a comment. She smiles more now—laughs, even. Alaina never did that before. She was always so professional, but she's changed. She has conversations with people she would have dismissed immediately previously, and I'm not the only one who notices."

"I think that has more to do with the job she was doing in Pennsylvania than me."

"Perhaps, but you are part of that. Just give Alaina a chance to figure things out. If anyone can find a way to blend corporate life with family life, it's Alaina."

We talked for a few more minutes and then returned to the building. As we waited, we witnessed another incident with Bas. "That guy doesn't like me."

"He doesn't like anyone," Maggie replied dryly. "Don't worry about him. Alaina has no interest in him."

"*Were they really engaged?*"

"*Yes, but trust me, she is well past that. She wouldn't marry Bas if her life depended on it.*" *Just as she stepped away from him, Maggie leaned closer to me.* "*You own her heart, Evan. Give her a chance.*"

Could I give her that chance?

Laney squeezed my hand and turned to me. "Okay, so before we get there, I want to tell you something."

"Okay?"

"I hate this house." She laughed. "I didn't realize how much I hated this house until I came back. It is nothing like the one in Millerstown, and I don't want you to pass any judgments on me over it, okay?"

I laughed. "Okay, I won't."

"Alright, you promised." She gave me a stern but playful look, and the car turned into a driveway.

Twenty feet in, it stopped as a large black gate opened. The car passed through and then down a winding lane. A few moments later, the house came into view.

"Holy crap!" I said in a low voice.

"No judgment!" she reminded me.

"That place is huge, Laney!"

"It's just a house."

"Yeah, a house that my entire family could live in, and we'd never even see one another."

She laughed. "It's not that big, although there would be enough bedrooms for them all to have their own room." I turned to her, shocked at what she said. She shrugged. "Well, it does."

The car stopped, and Hank was opening our door a moment later. The front door to the house opened, and an older woman stepped out to the front stone porch, smiling.

Laney took my hand and pulled me toward the house. "Kate, this is Evan. Evan, this is Kate, my housekeeper. If you need anything, you just ask her, and she will get it for you."

Kate smiled brightly at me, and as her eyes fell on Laney, I saw adoration in them. It made me think of my mother, and I instantly missed her.

"Welcome, Evan. I have heard so much about you. Please, come in."

"Nice to meet you too," I said and followed Laney into the house. My jaw was hanging on the floor. I knew it was as I stood in the foyer that was probably at least two-thirds the size of my house.

Laney pushed my chin closed. "It's just a house, Evan."

"Yeah, if you say so."

"Evan, I put your things in the room beside Alaina's. If you'd like me to move them to her room, you just let me know."

"Thank you, but that's fine for now." As much as I wanted to have Laney back in my arms and under me, I wasn't rushing to get her in bed. We had other things to discuss before that happened.

"What time is dinner, Kate?"

"Would six-thirty be alright?"

"Perfect, on the terrace, please."

"Absolutely." She nodded and was gone. At least she wasn't wearing a maid uniform.

"She seems like a nice lady."

"She is. Do you want a tour?"

"How about a shot of whiskey and then a tour?" I said around a laugh.

"Deal." She winked, and I followed her down the hallway through a grand arch into a room that was all white.

"You have something against color?" I asked her as I waited near the bar and let my eyes skim the expensively furnished room.

"A lot different than back in Millerstown, huh?"

"I don't think it could be more different."

After she handed me the glass, she came around and told me

to follow her. Even though I knew the house was enormous, every turn, every room, every view out the window had my jaw dropping again.

Once we had finished the bottom floor, she turned to me near a staircase. "Do you want to see the bedrooms?" She lifted a brow playfully.

I stepped closer to her, running my knuckles over her cheek. "I want to see your bedroom, but not right now. I'm afraid if you showed me that, we'd miss dinner, and I'm kinda starving."

"Oh, yes." She shook her head. "I forgot about the time difference. My body has finally adjusted, but you are three hours ahead."

"Yes, I am."

"I'll have Kate bring out a snack." She started to step past me, but I took hold of her arm.

"It's okay. I won't starve to death. I don't want to bother anyone who is working."

"Evan, the people in this house are here to serve us. I do not doubt that they have a snack tray ready for us, and within two minutes of asking for it, it will appear. Come on. I didn't show you the kitchen."

"I can't even imagine what that looks like after seeing the rest of this house."

She gave me a shy smile. "It might be a bit more impressive than my other one."

I laughed and took her hand as she led the way back toward the kitchen. We found two people working there when we stepped in, both wearing aprons.

"Alaina, do you need something?" the younger of the two males asked.

"I wanted to show Evan the kitchen. We don't want to get in the way, but he did want to see it."

I felt like I was in some fancy restaurant with all the equipment and counters.

"What do you think?" she asked.

"I think I want to cook something in here."

The older chef grinned at him. "You are welcome to help."

"No." I put my hand up. "But thank you so much. I do enjoy cooking, but I don't want to get in your way."

"You wouldn't be in the way, but if you change your mind, you're welcome to come back."

Alaina asked them to prepare a snack tray, and the younger man that she called Tim pulled open the fridge and pulled one out. "We have one ready. I'll have Kate bring it out to you. Where do you want it?"

"On the terrace, please," Alaina said and pulled me from the room.

While I had seen the backyard from the windows, I hadn't been outside yet. I followed Laney out and stared at the pool. "And I thought your backyard was nice at the other house."

"It's a nice pool, huh?"

"Nice? It's fantastic." It was huge, like forty feet long and twenty wide, with a waterfall at the far end and elegant seating areas around the sides. On the far side was a dedicated grilling area with a fancy bar. I whistled. "I bet this place has stories to tell."

"Probably not as many as you think."

"Do you use the pool? Please, tell me you use this pool."

She laughed, the sound so warm as her eyes sparkled at me, and I felt myself falling in love with her all over again. "Yes, I use the pool, but not as often as I should."

"You're going to get in there with me, right?"

"Of course, but would you be offended if I didn't wear a suit?" she asked playfully.

I growled at her, taking two steps toward her and wrapping my arm around her waist. To hell with waiting. I wanted this woman right now. "No suit," I growled before I captured her lips with mine. It was the first passionate kiss we had shared all afternoon, and I didn't want to stop.

However, I heard something behind us and pulled back to see Kate walking in the opposite direction. On the table not far from us was a bottle of wine and a tray of snacks. "Whoops," I said with a chuckle.

"Oh, please. You need to learn about the staff. They are very discreet. They see and hear all kinds of things, and good staff never reveals any of it."

"I am sure they do." I let her go so we could go to the table. Laney poured us each a glass of wine as I reached for a piece of sushi. It practically melted on my tongue. "Holy crap, that is good."

"Glad you like it," she said and collected a piece for herself as she took the seat beside me on the love seat. "What did you think of the house?"

"It's impressive," I replied. "I can't imagine you living here alone, though. It doesn't seem to fit the personality of the woman I know—or maybe that should be the woman I knew."

She took my hand. "Evan, I'm still the same person." She sighed. "I'm sorry for not telling you everything before, but if I had, what would you have done? I have a feeling you would have run away as fast as you could because you wouldn't have thought you were enough."

"I still don't think that," I told her.

"But Evan, you are. To me, you are enough. You are more than enough. I told you before that I can't help that I am rich, like crazy rich, but I don't want it to scare you off. Yes, if things worked out with us, you'd have to accept that life would be different, but if you open yourself up, you might find you like it. You might come to enjoy the lifestyle."

"Who wouldn't enjoy being able to have anything they wanted?"

"Right, but remember that I didn't get all of this because I sat around spending money. I have worked hard my whole life, and I earned this."

"I know. I can see how hard you work, and Maggie told me more about what you do."

She shifted to the side, curling her feet under her and taking hold of my hand. "Evan, do you think that you could learn to come to terms with all of this? Do you think you could find a way to meet me in the middle, and we could bridge our two lives? I want that, and I know that we can find a way, but you have to want it too."

I glanced around, taking in her backyard, feeling the weight of her questions sitting heavily on my shoulders. As much as I wanted to tell her, yes, I could, I wasn't sure. "Laney, I honestly don't know. Yes, I love you, and in a perfect world, none of this would mean anything to me, but I can't see myself living here."

"We could buy a new house. One that makes you feel more at home. I would prefer it."

I sighed. "It's so easy for you to say that. We'll just buy a new house. You know that most people think over decisions like that for years, not seconds."

Her sigh was loud, and I saw her stare out over her backyard for a moment. "What can I do to prove to you that you mean enough to me to do anything for you?"

"I'm not sure there is, Laney. I'm not sure there is."

CHAPTER THIRTY-TWO

LANEY

I didn't want to hear that. Did Evan want me to give it all up? Walk away from everything that I had done or accomplished? Would he expect me to give away my money and go back to work for forty grand a year?

Was I willing to do that for him? Maybe not all of that. I had lived thirty-two years in this lifestyle. Even though my home in Millerstown had been minimalist compared to this, I still knew that I could spend money on a whim. I could redecorate my house every month if I wanted to or buy every house on Phillips Street and not blink an eye.

"I'm not saying that I won't be able to adjust; I'm just not sure that I should have to, or you should have to adjust to changes with me."

"But I am willing to change, Evan."

He stared at me. "Would you give it all away? Would you give up everything and leave?"

"No," I told him. "And if you loved me, you would never ask me to do that. My money, my corporation, is me. It is who I have been since I was born. It's my legacy, and one day, I will leave it to my children and then their children. I will not give that up for anyone."

We continued staring at one another, and I lowered my voice. "But I would be willing to make sacrifices. I would be willing to adjust my life so that it is not so in your face. I would do that for you—for us—for our future."

"I don't know if that's enough, Laney. I still have moments where I am so angry with you for lying about who you are. I asked you just how wealthy you were several times, and you didn't tell me the truth. How do I know you are telling me now?"

"You don't, but you can trust me, Evan."

"That's hard to ask of me when you haven't been honest yourself."

"Look, I didn't tell you about the money in the bank or that I owned a successful business, but I never lied to you about how I felt or what I wanted."

"What would have happened if we'd gotten married, had a child. Would you have told me before that? If your brother died then, would you have left us and come back here on your own?" He paused. "Speaking of your brother, how come he hasn't been in the news. I couldn't find anything about his death."

"Because we haven't announced it yet. I wanted to, but Bas wanted to keep it quiet until everyone knew I was back. He didn't want people to freak out and cancel contracts because they thought the company would go belly up. Trust me. I have been on Bas for a while to let me do the press release."

"Then why don't you?"

"Because he keeps telling me to hold off."

"You own fifty-one percent of Buckworth Industries, right?"

"Yes, or I will once we announce his death and go through the paperwork."

"Then who cares what the hell he says. It's your company,

Laney. Fuck that guy. He wants to have control over you. That's so obvious."

"I know, I know." I put my hands over my face and rubbed it for a moment. "Trust me, I know. I will do the press release on Monday. It needs to be done, and I don't care what Bas thinks or says."

"Good. That guy is a spoiled child. That is what I think when I think of a man who has too much money."

"I'm not like him, Evan."

He touched my cheek, and I pressed into his hand. "I know you aren't, Laney. I wasn't saying that you were like him."

I pulled his hand from my cheek and kissed his palm as he liked to do to mine so often. "I want nothing to do with the man, and when I can find a way to ban him from the building, I will. Trust me. I will."

"Good. You should."

I shifted closer to him. "Can we not talk about him or my brother? How is your family? Your father, how is he doing?"

For a few minutes, he talked about everyone back home. He even told me that he'd had a long conversation with Daniella about our talk at the picnic.

"Why did you leave that night?"

"What night?" he asked.

"The night Bas showed up, why did you leave?"

"Well, at first, I went into the kitchen to give you space to talk. Then I got flustered and started to get angry, so I decided to leave, but I didn't. I came back, intent on coming to sit in the room with you to hear what was going on. I wanted you to know I was there for you. That we were going to be a team."

"Then why didn't you?"

"Because when I came back, you were in his arms crying softly, and I honestly thought that maybe you two were making up."

"Never!" I snapped. "I swear, Evan, I have no feelings for that man—or at least no good ones."

"I believe you, but my head was reeling that night, and I didn't know which way was up. I met up with Huntley, and between the two of us, we figured out who you were."

"When did you go back to the house?"

"The next day. Cara talked me into going back to talk to you, but you weren't there. I packed my things and looked around your office. Then I left."

"You know you can always sleep there on your night shifts."

"Yeah, that might be weird without you there."

"Then move in," I told him, and he shifted back, his face contorted.

"Why would I do that?"

"Because it's a nice house, and someone has to enjoy the garden." I smiled as I said it.

"I don't think I could enjoy being in that house without you." He paused. "I went back a few days later and spent more time in your office. I read over a lot of what you had in there, and some of it made sense. I felt like I understood you a little more."

"You did?"

"Yeah." I nodded. "I realized that you are a lot more important than I ever thought you were."

"Evan, I'm not any more important than you. In fact, I might be less. I buy and sell things. I direct people to run things, attend meetings, and make sure someone takes the fall when something goes wrong. You save people's lives. You watch over them and comfort them. You are there in their darkest moments, and when someone dies, you have to tell their family they are gone. I might have to tell a CEO that I'm taking over his company, but I don't have to tell someone that their loved one is gone forever. I could never do that, but you can. That takes an incredible person. You are an incredible person. Every single one of your family members is incredible."

I paused and thought for a moment. "I envy you all. You can choose where you want to go and when you want to do it. You can change jobs, go back to school, take a vacation, have a baby. In my life, the way it was, I couldn't do any of that. I was always tied to the phone, email, and my assistant. There was never any real vacation. I might get a few hours to lie in the sun, but the calls still came; the contracts still needed to be gone over.

"When I left here two and a half years ago, I hated all of that. I was done with it. I didn't want anything else to do with it, and I had the opportunity to live a life and make decisions. I could set my phone down and forget it when I was off work. I didn't have to check my emails or rush from one dinner to another after spending all day staring at contracts and stocks. I could curl up on the sofa with a book or watch a movie, and no one bothered me. I liked that."

"You could do that again if you left it behind."

"And who would run this? Who would take care of it?"

He shrugged. "I don't know."

"There isn't any single person who can oversee all of this. Not like Larry and I could. Bas might think he could, but his vision is different than ours is—or was. I have no clue what my brother was thinking at the end. It doesn't matter, though." I paused, contemplating my following words. "I guess what I'm saying is that as much as I'd like to leave all this behind, I can't—not one hundred percent. I would, however, like to find a balance between life and work. You could help me with that."

"Perhaps," he replied and grew quiet. I didn't say anything and let him think over what I had said. As we sat there, I shifted closer to him and put my head on his shoulder. He curled his arm around my shoulders and pulled me closer. "I missed holding you."

"I missed being held," I whispered back.

He kissed the top of my head and rested his cheek on it. For a long time, neither of us moved, and I wondered if this was the last time I would get this opportunity. I ran my fingers over his chest lightly, and he squeezed me.

He lifted my chin with a finger, and I stared at him. I felt as if something important was going to be said, but as he opened his mouth, Kate announced it was dinnertime.

I put my finger over his lips. "Save that for after dinner."

The meal was incredible, and Evan appeared to enjoy it immensely. He even popped his head into the kitchen to tell the chef. After we ate, we returned to the terrace, and we were heading toward the chair we had been sitting on earlier, but I started to take a detour toward the pool.

"You up for a swim?"

"Now?" I nodded. "I have to go change."

I ran my hands up his chest. "No, you don't."

He chuckled. "I'm not going to swim in my clothes."

"That is not what I was suggesting." I stepped back, starting to unbutton my blouse. Evan stared at me, and his tongue slipped out over his bottom lip. I finished unbuttoning it and let it fall to the ground. Evan was staring at my chest, his hands fisted at his sides as I began to unbutton my slacks.

"Better hurry up. The last one has to suck the other's toes," I told him, and he barked out a laugh and whipped his shirt over his head. The two of us rushed to beat the other, but I did have the advantage here. I wasn't wearing shoes or socks. I slipped my panties down my thighs and shifted my hips from side to side as I watched him. His pants were now around his ankles, and he was stepping out of them. As he stood tall, I saw the evidence of his desire, and he hooked his thumbs into his boxers. Before he pulled them down, he glanced back toward the house to make sure no one was there, and I stepped to the side of the pool, preparing to jump in.

I waited for him to start pushing them down before I stepped off the edge and fell into the water. There was a large splash a few feet away when I popped back up, and then I was pulled roughly under by the ankle. I came up just as fast, laughing, but Evan had other thoughts. The moment I turned toward him, he crushed my body to his, capturing my mouth and devouring it as if he were a starving man, and I was his next meal.

I clung to him, and there was no preamble as he automatically lined himself up and thrust forward. I threw my head back as he rained kisses over my neck and moved us toward the slightly shallower water. I ground against him, and he gave back just as hard. It didn't take us long before we were both panting from the orgasm, and I continued to cling to him as we kissed slowly.

"God, I missed that," I said to him in between kisses.

"Yeah, I did too," he replied as he cupped my face. "More than I want to admit."

"Why would you not want to admit it?"

"Honestly, I was hoping I would come here and see you again and not feel what I thought I felt."

"You didn't want to be with me?"

"It's not that. I think it was more like I wanted to come out here and that the two of us would see how different we were, and we'd part as friends."

I frowned and shifted off his lap, dislodging him from my body as I moved back. "You came here to end it?"

"Wait, Laney." He grabbed my arm and pulled me back. "No, I did not come here to end it, but I did think that it might be easier if, when I got here, we realized that we didn't feel the way we thought we did."

I could understand that. "It would have made things easier."

"Yes, it would have." He cupped my cheek and kissed me again. "But then I came here and saw you, and in the space of a few hours, I found myself in love with you all over again."

I sighed happily as I climbed back into his arms and wrapped my legs back around him. "I love you, Evan."

"I love you, too, Laney." He kissed me and then furrowed his brow. "But that doesn't change that your life is here, and mine is in Pennsylvania. I don't want to move. I love my job, love where I live, and I can't imagine being that far away from my father or my siblings."

"Then I will move the company," I announced matter-of-factly.

"What?"

I shrugged. "I'll move the headquarters of the company. Just imagine how many people I could hire in that area if I did that."

"What about all the people here that you fire?"

"I wouldn't fire them, Evan. They would get the opportunity to move with me or stay here. I wouldn't be able to close this office down—not entirely, but I could open a second head-quarters."

He studied me. "You could do that?"

I laughed. "I could, and for you, I would."

CHAPTER THIRTY-THREE

EVAN

"Jesus," I muttered and gently pushed Laney back from me in the water.

"What?" she asked, confused.

"You have an answer for everything. I'll just move the company. Just like that. I'll move the company," I said somewhat sarcastically.

She bobbed a foot away from me. "You do know that a lot of companies have more than one office, Evan. We have to keep things here, but this would not be the first time it came up for discussion. About four years ago, we almost opened an office in New York."

"Yeah, well, that's New York, not the middle of the sticks in Pennsylvania."

"What difference does it make where it is?"

"Shouldn't a company like yours be in a major metropolitan area?"

"No, not really." She sighed and swam to the side of the pool. "There are advantages of having a corporate office in a less populated area, like taxes and land prices. If we looked at setting up another office, we could bring many jobs to the area." She explained details that would affect such a decision for a few moments, and I listened attentively.

"You make it sound easy."

"Oh, it's not easy, but it can be done." She sighed. "Can we not talk about this anymore tonight? I'd much rather relax and enjoy one another for a little while."

I glanced around, wondering if there was a way to avoid these conversations, and then I looked at Laney. I saw brightness in her beautiful eyes, but they lacked the usual sparkle they had. I also noticed circles under them and wondered if she was getting enough sleep.

I swam closer to her and wrapped my arm around her waist before pulling her to my body. Her legs locked around my hips as my lips landed on hers. We made love in the pool again, and then we drank wine while sitting on her terrace, wrapped in fluffy robes that had magically appeared.

I told her more stories about what was going on back home, and she told me about her other two houses. The conversation was light as it could be, and finally, we retired for the night after she yawned.

We walked hand in hand up the stairs and past several open doors. I peered into each one to check out the other bedrooms until we got to the end of the hallway. Laney paused and took my other hand as she stood before me.

"I'd like you to stay with me tonight, but I won't force you to."

I cupped her cheek. "I want to stay with you, Laney."

She nodded and opened her bedroom door. I noticed my suitcase sitting to the side near the seating area inside her room. At least this room wasn't all white. It still wasn't as vibrant as her other house. I chuckled. "I guess Kate figured out I would be in here tonight after all."

"She's pretty good like that."

"Do you ever feel like you are being watched?"

She shook her head. "I grew up with it, so it's been all I've known."

I couldn't imagine having people there, always slightly behind the scenes, waiting to be there to help you.

Laney stepped backward toward her bed, peeling back the edges of her robe. "The only person I care about watching is you." She let the robe drop to the floor, and all thoughts of employees landed with it.

That was pretty much how the rest of the weekend went. Laney took me to her favorite places, and we spent a few hours at the beach. When we were at her house, we were either in the pool, the hot tub, or her bedroom.

I put the last of my things into my suitcase on Monday morning while Laney was out of the room doing something. As I zipped it closed, I thought about how we had yet to decide on what our future might hold. We had skirted the issue several times, but I honestly could not imagine Laney leaving this world and coming back to Millerstown now that I had seen it firsthand.

I set the bag on the floor and glanced around. I couldn't give Laney any of this. Not that I needed to, because she could give it to both of us, but I couldn't ask her to uproot everything just because I loved her.

I sighed because I realized that even though we hadn't spoken about it, I had made my decision. I pulled my carry-on behind me as I left the room, knowing that once I left Laney's home, it would be over. My heart ached because I loved her so much, but it would never work for us.

I found Laney coming into the foyer. Her eyes were as glorious as ever but sad.

I set my luggage by the door and turned to her as she approached. "I'm glad that you came, Evan."

"I am too."

She inhaled sharply and let it loose slowly before she picked up my hand and held hers over it. When she opened her fist, I felt it drop into my palm.

I nodded. "I wish that things could be different."

"Maybe one day they will be."

"Maybe," I replied before I cupped her cheek, but I knew they never would be. "I love you, Laney. I always will, but this is your home."

She didn't say anything, just nodded as she blinked rapidly. I leaned forward and kissed her tenderly one last time. When I pulled back, I wiped a tear from her cheek. "Take care of yourself, Laney."

"You, too, Evan," she replied as another tear drifted over her smooth skin. I hated seeing the sadness in her eyes, but there was nothing I could do to fix that.

I stepped back and let my hand drop as I felt the urge to cry myself. I turned and collected my suitcase, and without a look back, I walked out the door.

I was in the car before I glanced back at the house, and Laney and Kate stood on the porch. They both waved, and Hank pulled away. I let the tears drop then, and for a few minutes, I wondered if I had made the right decision.

In my heart, I knew I had. Cara might have been able to uproot her life for the man she loved, but I couldn't leave Pennsylvania, not right now when Dad needed me.

Maybe one day, I would come to regret that decision. For now, I would cherish the memories that we made and move on with my life back home.

"You did what?" Cara shrieked into the phone three days later.

I laughed. "Calm your jets, Cara. It was the best for both of us."

"Why? Did you go out there and realize that you didn't love her?"

"No, just the opposite. I realized how much I loved Laney, but you don't know her life. It's crazy, Cara. I don't see myself living that kind of life."

"Because you never had the chance, bonehead! Anyone can get used to having money."

"I am happy with my life now. I am."

She made a gurgling sound. "I still think you are an idiot."

"Yeah, well, when I got out there, and I saw how important she was, how much she had, I couldn't picture her here, with me. I couldn't imagine her giving up that world."

"You do know it was her choice to make, right?"

"I do, and in the end, she made it. She gave me Mom's ring back and wished me well. We both might have wanted it to work, but even she knew that it wouldn't. She knew that her life was there, and they needed her."

"I'm so sorry, Evan."

"Me too, but I have some great memories, and now I know what true love feels like. I won't settle for less."

"I hope you don't. I love you, Evan."

"I love you, too, Cara."

A week after I returned, Laney asked me to go by the house and check on it for her. She also asked me if I could box up the contents of her office and get them ready to send. If I got them ready, Laney would have someone pick them up from the garage. She told me that she'd deal with the rest of the house later.

I had spent a lot of time at her house that day. The memories were bittersweet, and before I left, I grabbed a beer out of her fridge and went to sit in the garden. I thought over every moment of our time together. I also thought about what could have been and what I had dreamed of the day she had the picnic.

She had called it our first barbeque, and I was confident that day that there would be many more to come. How quickly life can change.

I sat for a long time there, listening to the sounds of the water and noticing that her garden looked overgrown. I was tempted to start cleaning it up slightly, but that wasn't my place.

In the end, I sat there until it got dark, and then I turned on the fairy lights and thought of what could have been. When I started to feel sorry for myself, I turned off the lights, locked up the house, and stood in her garage, staring at her Maserati. I had secretly wished I could have driven that at least once, but that would never happen.

I let myself out of the garage and walked away, knowing that I would never come back.

It had been nine weeks since I had seen Laney. I kept myself from stalking her via the news. Once in a while, I'd get a text from her. We'd chat briefly, but eventually, even that began to lessen. The last time I'd spoken to her was six days ago, and she said she was working eighty-hour weeks and life was crazy. She promised to talk soon, but I wasn't holding out any hope.

I came to realize that I might have dodged a bullet. If working eighty-hour weeks was typical for her, what time would I have gotten? A few minutes here, a few there? That wasn't the kind of relationship that I wanted.

My family had been supportive, and I'd made sure to spend more time with my father. My other siblings were too, and even Cara came home for a visit for a couple of days two weeks ago. Of course, she left Bryan home, but we were glad to see her and Luke at least.

On Sunday evening, I pulled up to my father's house for our family dinner. I was looking forward to a relaxing evening before I started back on day shift the following day.

Inside, I found the usual hustle and bustle in the kitchen, and I kissed my sister's cheeks, chucked Corey's chin as she sat in the high chair, banging the tray with a spoon, and grabbed a beer to sit with Ethan and my father on the front porch.

Ethan was sharing a story about something that happened at work, and my father was laughing. This was what family was about—sharing stories, laughter, being together. If I had moved out west, I would have lost all of this. Yes, I might have had Laney, but I would have lost this.

Candy came out to the porch, peering at me, then quickly looking away. "Dinner is ready. We are just waiting on two more people."

"Who else is coming to dinner?" I asked.

Candy lifted her chin. "Kayley."

I frowned. "Why is Kayley coming?"

"Because she wanted to talk to me about something, and I told her to just come by. She should be here soon. She got held up in traffic."

I frowned. What traffic? Traffic in Millerstown lasted five minutes during rush hour at the two traffic lights in town. She must be coming from Plattsville or Summersville if she got stuck in traffic.

We were all inside the house getting ready to sit down when Carmen said Kayley had arrived. Ethan slapped me on the back as he chuckled and took his seat. I had no clue what I had missed that was funny, so I ignored him. Coral stood across the room, grinning like a fool, and I frowned at her.

A moment later, Kayley walked into the room, smiling, and then she stepped aside, and I did a double take. I had expected Cam to be with her, but it wasn't Cam. Laney stood here with sun-kissed skin and bright eyes.

"Sorry we are late," Kayley stated, but I couldn't tear my eyes away from Laney.

"What are you doing here?" I blurted the question.

She looked at the table. "Well, I was in town, and I was invited over for dinner. I hope that's not a problem."

"No, but why didn't you tell me you were going to be here?" I had yet to approach her. I was still reeling that she was even in the room. She came to me.

"Because I wanted to surprise you." She grinned up at me.

"Okay, you two can talk later. Can we eat now?" my father asked. "I'm starving, and the food is getting cold."

Laney winked at me and waited to be directed to a chair. She sat across from me, and I couldn't keep myself from staring. The feelings that I had thought I had put aside had successfully rushed back.

While we ate, I wanted to ask her a million questions, but other conversations were racing around the table so fast that I couldn't find a place to jump in. Finally, halfway through the meal, I put my hand up.

"Okay, enough!" Everyone looked at me like I'd lost my mind. "What the hell is going on?" I directed my question to Laney.

She glanced around the table. "Sorry, perhaps Evan and I should excuse ourselves for a few minutes and talk."

I pushed my chair back. "Sounds like a great idea!"

She wiped her lips, excused herself politely, and stood. I walked out of the room, and I wasn't too far before I heard laughter around the table. It made me angry, and I didn't stop walking until I was on the front porch. A few seconds later she joined me.

I spun on her. "Why are you here?"

"I'm sorry, Evan. I thought you would be happy to see me."

"Oh, don't get me wrong, Laney. I am happy to see you, probably way more than I should be, which is why I'm asking you why the hell you are here."

"Well, Kayley was showing me some real estate."

I laughed. "What, four houses aren't enough for you?"

She shook her head. "I am looking for commercial property for the medical division."

"Excuse me?"

She stepped forward. "Evan, I have been busting my ass the last few weeks to finalize everything, but I decided to move the medical equipment division here. I will one hundred percent oversee that, but I can do that from here. I don't have to live in California."

I stared at her. "What about the rest of the company?"

She cupped my cheeks. Those damn eyes that haunted my dreams were staring up at me, and I was afraid that it was all a joke. "Don't worry about the rest of the company. I promise I will explain it all later. All you need to know now is that I'm moving back here, Evan, and I hope that you will give me another chance."

CHAPTER THIRTY-FOUR

LANEY

*W*atching Evan leave was more difficult than I had imagined. I knew I had to let him go. If I had pushed him to stay, things would have torn us apart. That didn't mean that I would give up on him. There was no way. I knew that Evan would be my future in the deepest parts of my heart.

He made me a better person, made me want to do more, and enjoy more out of life. I would find a way.

That way arrived an hour later. I was sitting on the terrace thinking over my visit with Evan when I heard voices in the house. One of them was Sebastian's, and I sighed as I stood. When I turned, I froze. Walking a few steps in front of Bas was my brother.

The shock of seeing him rocked through me so hard, I stumbled and grabbed on to a chair beside me as I croaked, "Larry?"

"Hi, Alaina," he said as he approached. I stared into his face as he stopped in front of me, and before I could think any further, I slapped him. A moment later, I threw my arms around him as tears began to flood my eyes. Larry held me to him, tighter than he ever had.

"You're alive!" I said, and then suddenly realized what this meant. I jerked back from him. "You're alive! You lied about this?" I growled toward him, and then my gaze flew to Bas. "And you were in on it? How dare you do that!"

"Wait, Alaina, it was the only way I could think of to get you back."

"Back? Back!" I screamed. "So you pretended to die! After everything that we have gone through! After losing Mom and Dad, and Lindsey, you pretend to die! How dare you, Larry! I can't believe you would even think that was something to be done."

"Alaina, relax!" He put his hands up, and I saw red.

"I will not relax! Do you have any idea what this has done to me! Do you?" I shouted at him. "Not only did I think I was alone, but you ruined the first good relationship that I have had in my entire life!"

He compressed his lips and had the decency to look ashamed as his head dropped. My eyes skittered over to Bas. Of course, he didn't look that way.

"You lying son of a bitch! Get out of my house! You are never welcome here again!"

He had the audacity to roll his eyes. "Stop being so dramatic. We did this for your own good."

If my brother hadn't been there, I would have launched myself at Bas. "Get the hell out of my house!" I shouted as Larry held me back.

"Go wait by the car," my brother told him, and Bas shook his smug head and walked away, muttering about how I'd thank him one day.

I jerked away from Larry. "If you think for one second that I am going to marry that man, you are wrong. Dead wrong!"

"I get it, Alaina. I get it."

I walked away from him on shaking legs and grabbed my wineglass off the table, throwing back almost a full glass in a couple of gulps. I set the glass down, glaring at him before I wiped at my cheeks.

"How could you do that, Larry? How could you pretend to be dead? Was that your idea?"

"No, it was his."

"And you went along with it? You're both nuts!"

He sighed and came over to sit in a chair near me, looking defeated. "I'm sorry. I could probably say that a million times, and it will never be enough, I know that. But I am sorry, Alaina. I had thought it was a good idea at first, but my conscience got the better of me."

"Larry." I sank into a chair. "You have pretended to be dead for almost two weeks."

"I know, and it was so damn hard not to contact you."

"Why did you do it? Was it just for Bas? Is there another problem I'm not aware of?"

He shook his head and then leaned his elbows on his knees, hanging his head. "Honestly, I missed you."

"You missed me? You did this because you missed me?" My voice began to rise again. I had never been a hysterical female, but I was feeling that way right now.

He lifted tired eyes my way. "Yes, I missed you. You refused to take my calls. I missed having family. You might not think that I miss Lindsey, but I do. Not a day goes by that I don't realize that I am to blame for her death."

I rocked back. "What?"

"If I hadn't pushed her and tried to get her to break it off, she never would have married him. I know she did it to spite me. I felt so guilty after she died. I still do."

Okay, so I felt a little sorry for him, but that did not excuse him from what he had done to me. I sat there watching my brother, glad that he was alive, but at the same time, still furious.

He sat back. "I missed working with you—missed what we

used to have. They called us the dynamic duo, and I missed that."

"I will admit that being back has been nice in a way, but you had no right to upturn my life the way you did, Larry. I was happy. I was building a life. I had dreams of a family with a man that I loved very much."

He nodded. "I know, and I know that he was here this weekend."

"How do you know?"

"Hank."

"Hank knew you were alive?"

"Yes, but don't be angry with him."

I pursed my lips. As much as I wanted to be angry at Hank, my brother was the more appropriate recipient.

"Hank told me that Evan is a really nice guy and that you looked happier than he had ever seen you."

"Evan is a fantastic man. You could only wish to be like him, and he did make me happy. Very happy until you ruined that."

"Is there a way that you could fix that? That you might be able to be with him again?"

I sighed. "I don't know, Larry. I can't think of that right now."

"If you think of an idea, you let me know. I'll help you get Evan back. No matter what it takes. Just promise me one thing."

"What?" I asked skeptically.

"You won't run away again. That we can find a way to be a family again."

A week later, I walked into my brother's office and sat down. "I know how I can get Evan back and still be part of this company."

He set down the pen he had in his hand and leaned back in his chair. "How is that?"

Over the last week, Larry and I had spent a lot of time together. In doing so, we began to build a new relationship. We even laughed together and had meals—not ones where we were entertaining clients, but just the two of us around my pool or his. I hadn't realized just how much I had missed him until then.

"I want to move the medical division to Pennsylvania and oversee it."

"Why?"

"You know as well as I do that we have talked about building a new facility. One to house the R&D, and also manufacturing of those devices."

"Yes." He nodded. "That has come up."

"Well, I did some projections. Most of the parts that we purchase are from Virginia. The shipping alone would save us a lot of money, plus we have only tapped into thirty-five percent of the market on the East Coast. We could build our customer base by making it easier to get the equipment. The property taxes are much lower, and land is cheap there. It's in an area that we could help grow. We could bring in more jobs, more business."

He grinned. "And it would bring you closer to Evan, right?"

I nodded. "Yes. It would."

"Have you spoken to him about this?"

"No. I want to get it all figured out and make the cost projections to ensure it is viable. I don't want to get his hopes up."

"What about your hopes?"

"I hope that I'm going to get this figured out." I grinned at him, and he studied me for a minute.

"I like it, but if you left here, what would we do without you?"

I laughed. "What did you do the last two and a half years?"

"True."

I pointed at him. "Just don't let Bas do it."

"No." He laughed. "Bas won't be doing anything for us. I am buying out his shares."

My jaw dropped. "He's going to sell to you?"

"I didn't say that." He grinned, and the two of us laughed.

Now weeks later, I was back in Pennsylvania and had spent the day with Kayley Young, who had hooked me up with a commercial real estate agent to help me look for either a building or property. We had seen some tremendous potential, and now I needed to figure out the particulars.

But before I did that, I needed to know if this was all for nothing. Would Evan want me back in his life? Would he accept me and my money back in his life? I prayed he did.

I was a nervous wreck as we pulled up to the Winstons' house, and Kayley laughed at me. "He is going to be speechless when he sees you."

"I hope so."

He was, and I was kind of delighted with the fact that he couldn't take his eyes off me. I saw how he wanted to bombard me with questions, and I pretended not to notice. Once dinner was over, the two of us would have plenty of time to talk.

Only Evan blew up at dinner, and the two of us excused ourselves. Everyone had been aware that I was coming. I had called Coral and asked her what she thought of the idea, and she had spoken to her father, who was thrilled to have me join them for dinner.

Now I stepped out on the front porch with Evan. I wanted to throw my arms around him and proclaim my love all over again. However, he had other ideas.

He spun toward me. "Why are you here?"

"I'm sorry, Evan. I thought you would be happy to see me."

"Oh, don't get me wrong, Laney. I am happy to see you, probably way more than I should be, which is why I'm asking you why the hell you are here."

"Well, Kayley was showing me some real estate."

His laugh was slightly strangled. "What, four houses aren't enough for you?"

"I am looking for commercial property for the medical division."

"Excuse me?"

I approached him. "Evan, I have been busting my ass the last few weeks to finalize everything, but I decided to move the medical equipment division here. I will one hundred percent oversee that, but I can do that from here. I don't have to live in California."

"What about the rest of the company?"

I couldn't help myself. I had to touch him. "Don't worry about the rest of the company. I promise I will explain it all later. All you need to know now is that I'm moving back here, Evan, and I hope that you will give me another chance."

He blinked. "Did you walk away from it all, Laney? I can't let you do that."

"No, Evan. I didn't walk away from it all. My brother helped me figure out how to do this so I could be with you."

He blinked at me. "I thought your brother was dead."

"So did I, until he miraculously walked into my house an hour after you left."

"What?"

"Bas and Larry lied to get me back. It's a long story, but you will be happy to know that Bas is entirely out of the picture now."

"Your brother pretended to be dead?"

I nodded. "Yes, and trust me. I gave Larry a piece of my mind after I slapped him and then hugged him. My brother and I have come to an understanding."

"What is that?"

"That I want my own life, my own family. I want you. I still want to be part of the business, but I want more. I want a family with you. I want all of those crazy people in this house to be part of my family too."

He swallowed, shuffling his feet forward slightly. "And your brother is okay with that?"

"Yes, he is. He helped me get this all figured out. He will be here tomorrow. I would love for you to meet him."

"I'm not sure about that. I might punch the guy."

I laughed. "He would probably be expecting you to."

"Why did he do that? Was he trying to get you back with Bas?"

I shook my head. "No, he was trying to get me back for him. Come to find out I'm not the only one who missed having a family." I paused. "I was kind of hoping that once he met you, that you two might get along, and your family might kind of be part of his too."

"Yeah, well, we'll see about that," he said, but it wasn't said with malice.

I stepped closer to him, touching his chest. "What do you think, Evan? Would you be willing to give it a chance? See if you can learn to live in my world, one that is slightly diluted?"

He gave me a lopsided grin. "I might be able to learn to live with it, but on one condition."

"Anything. Just name it."

He put his arms around my waist, pulling me close. "If we do get married, we honeymoon at your house in the Caribbean."

I grinned as I slipped my arms around his neck and leaned forward until my lips were only a breath away. "See, you do understand business better than you think. It's a deal."

EPILOUGE

EVAN

*T*en weeks later, I stretched out on the chaise lounge beside Laney and let my gaze slip over the beautiful ocean before me. She reached over and took my hand, and I kissed the back of hers, checking out her engagement ring again.

While we had used my mother's diamond, we had it set into another setting that had a bit more bling to it. I was worried that it would offend my father, but he got all teary-eyed as he looked at it and said it was perfect.

Peels of laughter caught my attention, and I turned to see Hunt running toward the ocean with Daniella over his shoulder. On the beach not far from us was the rest of the family. Not just mine, but the Youngs too. Laney had decided that since she had no family, she was adopting them too.

Our wedding, while planned by Roxanne, wasn't back in Millerstown. Laney had hired a private jet to bring all of us here for the week. We would stay an extra week to enjoy our honeymoon, and I couldn't wait for it to be just the two of us.

Not that I didn't enjoy having all the family and kids around us, we both did, but I wanted to enjoy Laney alone. I wanted to make love to her anyplace my heart desired.

I was slowly getting used to the money. Cara had been right. Who wouldn't want to be rich, but I was hoping it didn't go to my head. Although, Laney had given me a very extravagant present. She gifted me her Maserati. Maybe I should have said no, but I was married to a billionaire now, so why not.

Speaking of Cara, I turned to watch her and Bryan sitting on towels with Luke between them as he dug his shovel into the sand, happy as a clam.

One of the reasons we had gotten married here was so they could attend. It had been Laney's idea, and I had almost cried when she told me she had already called Cara to ask if it would be alright.

The only person missing was my mother. I tipped my head back, closing my eyes to the sun as I thought about her. She was shining down on us. She would have loved Laney, and as much as I wish she had been here physically, I knew she had been in the soft breeze around us.

"Are you happy, Mr. Winston?" Laney asked me, and I turned and smiled at her.

"I am Mrs. Alaina Marshall Buckworth-Winston." Her burst of laughter made my smile wider.

"Talk about a mouthful," she said.

"It is, but what a mouthful."

She peered around the beach. "I can think of some other things I'd like to have in my mouth."

"You can, huh?"

She sat up and quickly got off her chair. "And if we hurry, maybe we can get away without any of them noticing."

I was right behind her, but we weren't five feet from our chairs before her brother laughed and pointed us out. "Look, they are trying to disappear again."

"Get a room!" Riley yelled, and I turned around, walking backward.

"That's what we're trying to do!" I called out, and then Laney grabbed my hand, giggling, and yanked me around before I fell on my ass.

We raced back to the house and up the stairs to our room. I had to admit that I loved this house. I made Laney promise that we could come back at least twice a year to stay for two weeks.

Inside our room, I could see straight out to the ocean. A few laughs from the beach filtered back on the breeze through the open doors. I lifted Laney in my arms and carried her to the bed.

After laying her down, I smiled. "Now what was it you wanted in your mouth? My toes?"

She blurted out a laugh. "No!"

I kissed her and then leaned back and brushed the hair from her face. I could not believe how much I loved this woman. It made my heart want to explode at moments. "I love you, wife."

She brushed her hand along my beard. "I love you, husband." She grew quiet for a moment. "How long do you want to wait before we start working on our own family?"

I glanced at my watch. "Would about ten minutes work?" I had the woman I loved, and I didn't want to waste a moment before we started a family.

She grinned. "Ten minutes? Is it going to take you that long to get ready?"

I winked at her. "No, that's how long I'm going to tease you before I take you, wife."

She sighed as I pulled her bikini bottoms over her hips. "Then maybe we should wait fifteen."

I chuckled and bent forward to kiss the soft skin above her pubic bone. "Let's make it twenty."

"Deal," she said on a sigh as I dropped down to love her.

THE END

SNEAK PEEK: CANDY

Enjoy Chapter One of Candy, Loving a Winston, Book 3

<u>Candy</u>

" *H*i, Dad." I brushed a kiss over his weathered cheek as I breezed by the kitchen table where he was reading a newspaper. He was one of the few people I knew who still read a physical copy and didn't get his daily reports from the internet. "How are you?"

I pulled open the fridge and put away a few groceries I had purchased for him. My father had been a widower for over a year and a half. For the most part, he had done very well adjusting. He could cook, clean up, and do laundry, but grocery shopping was not an activity that he enjoyed, and he had no problem asking one of us to swing by the store for things as he needed them. I think he also asked us to do it so he'd see us more often.

It was always a quart of milk here, a jar of peanut butter there, and if you think about it, can you grab me a bag of those chocolates I enjoy after dinner? That's what I was delivering, along with other things like fresh broccoli, a rotisserie chicken, and mashed potatoes that he could pop into the microwave tonight.

"I'm doing well, but I didn't expect you so early. I thought you said you'd be here this afternoon." He glanced at his watch as he spoke next. "Unless I lost track of time again."

I spun around. "Wait! You lose track of time? How long has that been happening?"

He gave me an annoyed look. "All my life. It's normal to get busy doing something and lose track of time."

I set the bag on the counter and studied my father. Since Evan told us that we needed to spend more time with our father because he was lonely, we had all been better about ensuring we checked in with him. Even my oldest sister, Cara, who lived in Texas, did video chats with him at least twice a week so he could see his grandson.

I was glad that I was from a big family. I couldn't imagine having to keep an eye on my father on my own with my crazy work schedule. "Oh, that is true, I guess, and I am early. A few minutes after we spoke, I got a notification for a local last-minute inspection. Did you know the tavern was up for sale?"

"What? No, I did not. I hope they don't sell it to some city slicker who wants to change everything."

"I have to agree with you. The tavern might be old and weary-looking, but it has charm."

"That it does," my father agreed. "By the way, how did your date go Friday night?"

I pursed my lips and frowned. "Who told you I had a date on Friday?"

"Evan did."

"Yeah, well, Evan needs to stay out of my business."

"He was just watching out for his sister."

"I'm a year older than Evan. I should be watching out for

him." I growled slightly, then balled up the plastic bag and shoved it into the recycling container under the sink.

"It doesn't matter who is older. You all watch out for each other. Evan said you looked bored."

I winced. "He thought I looked bored?" My father nodded, and I sighed. "I *was* bored. I was bored out of my skull. Tammy set us up," I lied, "and the guy only wanted to talk about video games. He's thirty-five years old, and the only thing he likes to do when he's not working is play games. I don't get that."

"What did he do for a living?"

I frowned as my head cocked to the side. What did the guy do? "I don't even remember, Dad. That's how memorable that part of our conversation was. Honestly, I couldn't wait for dinner to be over."

I sat in the chair next to him and crossed my arms on the table. "Everyone I know is finding someone to fall in love with, and I can't even find one decent guy to date, much less build a relationship. Aren't there any men out there who can hold an intelligent conversation with a woman?"

My father chuckled and patted my arm. "You will find one. Give it time, Candy."

"Dad, I'm almost thirty-three. I don't have much time left. I want to get married, have kids, train a dog, and go on vacations. Is that too much to ask?"

"No, it's not too much to ask. You know you can go on vacation and own a dog alone, right?"

I sighed. "I know, but it's not the same."

"Maybe you aren't looking in the right spot?"

"What do you mean?"

"I mean, where are you meeting these men?"

I clamped my lips shut, embarrassed to admit that I was using a dating app. "Just around."

"Well, maybe you should look in different places than your

phone." He looked at me pointedly, and I knew he knew I was using a dating app.

"I don't have time to look for someone, Dad. I'm lucky I have enough time to swipe left or right."

He shook his head. "I don't understand young people. Back in my day, we met people while we were doing things. We weren't attached to our phones and waiting for some computer program to determine that we were compatible."

I rolled my eyes. "Dad, times have changed."

He went to the fridge and inspected what I had brought him. "Guess I'm having chicken for dinner. Did you bring anything for lunch?"

"Yes, I bought you the salami and cheese that you like. You still have bread."

"Do you want something before you go?" he asked, glancing back before he closed the door.

"Nope, sorry, I don't have time." I held up my phone. "That was my reminder that I need to be at the tavern in fifteen minutes."

"Hope it goes well," he commented as I smacked a loud kiss on his cheek.

"I'll be interested to see who is buying it. I'll give you a call later. Love you, Dad!" I called over my shoulder.

"Love you too, Hershey Kiss."

I snickered as I made my way to my vehicle. My parents had a sense of humor when they named me Candy. People had commented on it my entire life. Many of them had said that I looked as sweet as the food, and the name was fitting. My father constantly called me a different kind when he saw me. Hershey Kiss was one of my favorites.

From him, it was cute. From anyone else, it was annoying as hell. My entire life, I had been the sweet sibling. The one who would bend over backward to help someone. I always kept my mouth shut and never complained. I volunteered to work with charitable organizations and got involved in many clubs at school.

Everyone in the family would tell you that I was the smartest of the bunch. It wasn't that I was smarter. I just applied myself better.

Cara hated school and would have preferred to run around chasing boys and partying all the time. Ethan and Evan put all their energy into sports, girls, and studies came low on their list.

Carmen was intelligent, but in her sophomore year, she met Tim Kohl. If something didn't revolve around Tim, then it wasn't necessary. At least, not until they broke up the day after graduation, and then college became her focus to hide her broken heart.

That left Coral, the social butterfly of the high school. She didn't care to do it unless her schoolwork could get her something from someone. However, she did achieve decent grades. If she had applied herself, she could have rocked her grades out of the park and gotten an academic scholarship as I had.

I had received offers from nine colleges, and three had full rides because of my academic excellence. I attended the University of Michigan because they had one of the best civil engineering programs available. Some were better, but I wasn't crazy about what they had to offer outside their classes. It didn't hurt that U of M had offered a four-year, almost full scholarship. I paid for my books and meals, which was about it.

After six years, I was lucky to step out of college with a master's in civil engineering and very little debt. I came back to Millerstown and found a great job. By the time I was twenty-six, I had paid off my last student loan and, a year later, bought my house.

I was employed by two companies, one that did home inspections for mortgages and loans and the other that did structural assessments on buildings in need of repair.

I loved what I did, and there were very few women in my

field, especially in my county. I was only aware of two, a woman named Rhonda Brickwater and me. Most women got snapped up as minorities in large city firms, but I had no interest in leaving my small town. Ann Arbor, Michigan, had been plenty enough for me.

I pulled up to the tavern, parked, and collected my briefcase from the passenger seat floor. As I got out of my SUV, I glanced at my phone to see that I was right on time. Two cars were in the side lot, but the front door was locked when I tried to open it. I banged on the door and waited—then knocked again with no answer.

It was two hours before opening, per the sign on the door. They were probably in the kitchen working, so I made my way around. There was a door open at the back, and I was just stepping in front of it to call out when a box flew through the entry and smacked me right in the face.

"Oh, my God!" I screamed as my arms flew up to bat the offending cardboard away, but it was too late. The rough edge of the box had scratched my cheek, but when I reached up to check, there was no blood.

"Aw, shit! Did I just hit you?" A deep, rough voice spoke from the doorway, and I looked up to find Bollard standing there.

While I barely knew the man, I knew he had a checkered past. He ran with an outlaw motorcycle gang and worked behind the bar here at the tavern. I'd never said more than fifty words to the man; they consisted of drink names and thank you.

"Yes, you just hit me! Square in the face, I might add." I brushed my hand over my cheek to ensure it wasn't bleeding.

"Oh, man, I didn't see you. Come on in. Let's get you some ice." While his voice appeared concerned, the look about him said he was anything but. If I had guessed, I would have said he looked pissed.

Bollard had brown eyes and brown hair that was down to his ears with light streaks of blond and one of those beards that looks like it is just growing in, but he purposely leaves it that way. I was not too fond of those kinds of beards. They were distracting.

I stepped in through the back door, my hand pressed to my cheek, and stopped as I watched Bollard kick a few boxes out of his way. "Who pissed in your Cheerios this morning?"

He glanced back. "What?"

"Nothing," I mumbled, shaking my head as I followed him further into the kitchen.

"Go through that door and have a seat. I'll get you some ice." He turned away from me without another word, and I glared at him—what a grump. The guy hadn't even said he was sorry.

I went through the door and came out on the opposite side of the bar. For a moment, I glanced around. I'd been in the tavern many times but never behind the bar. What a different view you got from here. I went to stand behind the soda fountain and turned until I was facing the liquor shelves. My gaze jumped to the mirror behind it, and my eyes went wide as I saw a bright-red spot on my cheek. "Ouch!" I leaned forward and inspected it closer.

I frowned and started heading toward the tables when the door from the back swung open, and I threw my hands out to stop it before it smashed my face. "Holy crap! Can you be more careful?"

"Jesus Christ, Candy! What the hell are you doing back there? I thought you'd be sitting at a table."

"I was looking in the mirror at the damage you did," I replied, slightly surprised that he knew my name.

"I didn't do that. The box did." He walked away.

"Oh, so the box just magically flew through the air. Now I get it. I didn't know you knew magic, Bollard."

He sighed as he set the small first aid kit down on a table as I followed him. "Yes, I kicked the box, but I was angry about something. I wasn't trying to hit you."

He turned quickly, and his elbow almost collided with my chest. I jumped back. "What is your problem?" I snapped at him.

"What?"

"You almost hit me again!" I replied. He closed his eyes, shaking his head slightly as if annoyed. "Don't be angry with me because someone upset you."

He scoffed, "You don't know the half of it."

Nope, I didn't, but little ole me who always wanted to help suddenly wanted him to tell me what was wrong—maybe I should have been the psychologist and not my sister. "Why are you upset? Did someone do something to you?"

"The owner told me today that he's selling the tavern." He frowned at me, his brow lining all the way across.

"I'm sure the new owners will keep you on if that's what you are worried about."

"No, I wanted to buy the place. I asked Howard to give me three years, and I would be better able to purchase it, but no, he had to go behind my back and sell it to some city creep. Now some stuffy asswad is coming here to inspect the property, and I have to show them around. It's the last thing I want to do." I blinked and then blinked again, and he huffed a sigh and lifted his hand like he was going to check my cheek. "What are you doing here anyway? You know we aren't open."

I stuck my hand out to him. "Hi, I'm the stuffy asswad that will inspect the property."

His eyes went wide, making the brown a lighter color, almost like cinnamon, and he dropped his face down and muttered, "Well, fuck!"

Candy, Book 3

What happens when your lustful heart wins over your intellectual mind?

When Candy's sister, Cara, was dating outlaw biker member Ryan Vigilante, Candy paid little attention to Ryan's club buddy, Bollard. Sure, Bollard, who works behind the bar at the local tavern, was pleasing on the eyes and made a mean chocolate martini, but he was an outlaw, and that's not the kind of person Candy associates with.

Michael Bollard is out of the club now, and he hopes to purchase the tavern. He had never wanted anything more than his bikes and the club, but now, Mike has hopes of building a future, a future that is colliding with sexy and intelligent Candy Winston in ways he could have never imagined.

Just when he thinks he might have his future figured out, a stranger enters the bar with a surprise he never saw coming. Will that surprise send Candy running for higher ground, or will it cement her future in the tavern with Mike?

Candy, Book 3

What happens when your lustful heart wins over your intellectual mind?

When Candy's sister, Cara, was dating outlaw biker member Ryan Vigilante, Candy paid little attention to Ryan's club buddy, Bollard. Sure, Bollard, who works behind the bar at the local tavern, was pleasing on the eyes and made a mean chocolate martini, but he was an outlaw, and that's not the kind of person Candy associates with.

Michael Bollard is out of the club now, and he hopes to purchase the tavern. He had never wanted anything more than his bikes and the club, but now, Mike has hopes of building a future, a future that is colliding with sexy and intelligent Candy Winston in ways he could have never imagined.

Just when he thinks he might have his future figured out, a stranger enters the bar with a surprise he never saw coming. Will that surprise send Candy running for higher ground, or will it cement her future in the tavern with Mike?

LOVING A WINSTON SERIES

The *Loving a Winston Series* is a five-book steamy romance series that spins off of the *Loving a Young Series*. Characters from both series will appear from book to book. Each book is a standalone romance with suspense and spicy romance scenes.

Cara, Book 1

What happens when the man you fall for is all wrong for you?

Cara Winston has always been a bit of a rebel and an adrenaline junkie. As a helicopter pilot and paramedic, she relies on that to do her job.

When Cara and her team respond to a multi-vehicle accident involving motorcycles, she's expecting the worst. What she's not expecting is to find herself intrigued by the blue eyes of a man wearing motorcycle gang colors.

Ryan Vigilante rides the road, mostly on two wheels, not

four. When several of his club end up in an accident on the highway, Ryan never expects to see a future in the eyes of the intense female paramedic. The only problem is, she's way out of his league, and he knows that getting involved with her could only put her in jeopardy.

With Cara's family trying to keep them apart and Ryan's club breaking the law, Cara finds herself more of a rebel than usual. Will things work out for Cara and Ryan, or will Cara's law enforcement brother, Ethan, find a way to put a stop to it for good?

Evan, Book 2

What happens when she's not really who you think she is?

Evan Winston is dedicated to his job as a registered nurse in the ICU department of the local hospital. He's one hundred percent focused on the needs of his patients and his family, or at least he usually is. That all changes the day a woman visits one of his patients and turns his world upside down.

Laney Marshall wants nothing more than to help people who struggle. Especially those women and children who are fighting to survive domestic violence situations. After losing someone close to her to an abusive man, she is determined to do everything in her power to help.

Unfortunately, Laney has people that don't want her to do that. In fact, they don't even want her in this town or even the state of Pennsylvania. They prefer her on the other side of the country, where they think she belongs, living the life planned for her.

Can Laney and Evan find a way to build a relationship while

keeping others from getting involved, or will the revealed secrets be enough to end any chance of a future before it begins?

Candy, Book 3

What happens when your lustful heart wins over your intellectual mind?

When Candy's sister, Cara, was dating outlaw biker member Ryan Vigilante, Candy paid little attention to Ryan's club buddy, Bollard. Sure, Bollard, who works behind the bar at the local tavern, was pleasing on the eyes and made a mean chocolate martini, but he was an outlaw, and that's not the kind of person Candy associates with.

Michael Bollard is out of the club now, and he hopes to purchase the tavern. He had never wanted anything more than his bikes and the club, but now, Mike has hopes of building a future, a future that is colliding with sexy and intelligent Candy Winston in ways he could have never imagined.

Just when he thinks he might have his future figured out, a stranger enters the bar with a surprise he never saw coming. Will that surprise send Candy running for higher ground, or will it cement her future in the tavern with Mike?

Carmen, Book 4

What happens when your first love returns to town—twenty years later?

C hild Psychologist, Carmen Winston, spends a lot of time at the schools, and when she come across a man and the name of a new student, she is thrown back to a time of young love and dreamy hopes of the perfect future.

Tim Kohl lived in Millerstown for six years before his parents moved him across the country. He never expected to return, and when he does, it's with three kids in tow. The last thing he expects to find in town is his high school sweetheart still beautiful as ever and single.

When sparks fly, can these two put the past behind them and plan a future, or will the years apart separate them before they can figure it out.

Coral, Book 5

What happens you overhear your family talking to the man you've fallen for?

C oral Winston has felt out of touch with her family since her mother passed away and throws everything she has into her coffee café. When her family forces her to take a vacation, they all decide to come along for the fun.

Landan Lancaster is the oldest of the eight Lancaster children, and he's still trying to deal with walking away from his cheating bride the night before their wedding many months prior. When a large family comes to stay in the Lancaster guest house on the lake, he finds himself intrigued by the woman standing at the water's edge.

On the slopes, Landan realizes he has met his match in more ways than one, and Coral begins to feel as if she has finally found where she belongs. When a conversation is overheard,

Coral gets the wrong idea and flees, only to find a mountain of trouble waiting for her back home.

Can Coral overcome the issues facing her and find her way back to the beautiful mountains and water of Lake Tahoe, or will Landan lose her before he can ever call her his own?

COMING IN 2025
Loving the Lancasters! Another 8 book Spin-off to keep the reading pleasure coming!

LOVING A YOUNG SERIES

Wesley, Book 1

Traumatized by events of her past, Charlotte Bennett is not a fan of strangers. When she sees a man touching her daughter at the park, she reacts without listening. It's only later when her daughter is rushed to the hospital that she realizes how wrong she had been.

Doctor Wesley Young only wanted to help the tender-aged girl he witnessed fall, but when her mother attacks him at the park, he's left stunned. When the little girl arrives later in the emergency department, he comes face to face with the mother who makes more of an impression on him than the cut she left on his face.

Things heat up quick when Marisol is no longer his patient, but when things from the past are revealed, Wes isn't sure that Charlotte is the woman for him. Can Charlotte find a way to explain it all so that Wes will accept both her and her daughter before it's too late?

Henley, Book 2

Being a wedding planner is hard, especially when someone is

always trying to steal your business, and your family doesn't support you. However, Roxanne Novak is determined to keep her business afloat.

When Roxy's in a car accident hurrying to meet a potential bride, she's injured and scared, but paramedic Henley Young takes good care of her.

Henley loves his job and thrives on the adrenaline of helping people in need. Maybe that's why when he meets Roxy, he's inclined to help her with more than just medical care. Hooking her up with his older brother Wesley and his bride-to-be could be just what she needs. It might also be the start of something between Lee and the spunky little wedding planner.

When a position at a country club is offered to Roxy, she finds herself rethinking her entire business plan. Excited to start someplace new, Roxy and Henley begin making plans for the future. Just after she starts her new job, Roxy learns of Lee's past relationship, and everything she knew about him is questioned.

Can Roxy and Henley put the past to bed and move forward to something that might be more than what both of them had ever hoped for?

Huntley, Book 3

Daniella Knight works hard to create suspenseful and romantic tales, but after a violent interaction with a fan, she wants to hide from the world. When her house catches on fire, her and her protection dog, Tigger, are forced to rely on the help of strangers.

Huntley Young loves being in the thick of the action. Well, as long as that action has something to do with his job as a firefighter. When Huntley stops the homeowner from going back into the house, he has no clue, that he just placed himself firmly in the hero department.

As they get to know each other, Daniella's creative mind is always building on what is around her, and before she knows it, reality and fiction are hard to tell apart.

When danger strikes again, will Daniella be able to see what is right in front of her, or will her past trauma keep her safely inside her romantic fictional world?

Riley, Book 4

Riley is always the life of the party, and it's Ethan that is there to pick her up and keep her together. He knows her almost as well as she knows herself, and he knows she will never love him as he does her.

Now Ethan wants more out of life and love, but Riley denies her feelings and insists they are just friends with benefits. When a training opportunity comes up that will get Ethan out of town for months, he jumps on it. It's the only way to get over Riley and move on.

With Ethan gone and a new guy in her life, Riley finds herself dealing with several emotional issues without the help of her best friend. A family emergency has Ethan feeling lost without Riley there to lean on, but he refuses to go to her and seeks solace with another.

Will Riley make the right choices, and finally, admit how she feels, or will she find herself alone and falling further down the rabbit hole.

Kayley, Book 5

Independent Kayley Young is a real estate agent in New York and loves her life as a single woman. She's not one to get tied down, and she has no desire to have children.

Officer Cameron Sexton is new on the job, a veteran of the military, and proud of his dedication to the job. Unfortunately, he finds himself annoyed at his lackadaisical sergeant who should hang up his gun belt before getting someone hurt. When Cameron is dispatched to a burglary, he meets Kayley Young and is instantly attracted to her. Cameron has a feeling she reciprocates those feelings, except she's a little leery of the fact that he is ten years younger than her.

When Kayley's life starts taking a turn for the worse, she finds herself depending more on the attractive young man she has let into her bed for fun than she intended. Her original thought of enjoying the moment starts to last longer, but Kayley's not sure that dating a man ten years her junior is smart for the long haul. Especially with the rest of the changes that have happened in her life.

Can Kayley come to terms with the age difference, or will her family sway her away from the younger man?

Bradley, Book 6
Bradley Young is the eldest sibling of the Young family, and the only one who had previously been married. After losing his wife to cancer several years ago, he's used to caring for his two kids alone. The thought of dating is not something he's interested in, now with a busy construction business, and a family that always needs help.

Nolan Nickels needed a change, and with the help of her good friend, Kayley, she left New York and came to Millerstown to take a teaching position at the middle school. She has always been a huge tom boy and loves to fix things with her hands and play sports.

With a new house in her name, Nolan seeks out the perfect plan to get the house ready so she can bring her two daughters' home, but is her fixer-upper more than she bargained for? When Kayley finally gets Brad to stop by the house to check something, Brad finds himself more than intrigued with the spitfire, Nolan. Will he finally find the woman to spend his life with, or will she be put a halt on any type of future?

LOVING A LANCASTER SERIES

The Loving a Lancaster Series spins off of the Loving a Winston Series. In Coral's book, you are introduced to the Lancaster family while she is on vacation in Lake Tahoe. This series will consist of seven books, and stared with Leo.

Leo - Book 1

Leo Lancaster is coming home to Lake Tahoe. As a successful stockbroker and business owner, Leo has decided to open another office in Truckee and work out of that one instead of his Vegas office. Now, he must locate a house and get himself settled, and the last thing he expects to find on his return is love.

Heather McClain is a devoted mother of two teens, and a widow from Ohio. When her best friend encourages her to go on a girls trip to Lake Tahoe, she decides to take a break from the chaos at home and try to have fun. Only their antics are more than Heather bargained for.

Lucky for her, Leo is around to rescue her and the two of them quickly grow close, but is Heather ready to let go of her husband's memory and move forward into a relationship, or more importantly, are her children prepared to accept a new man into their mother's life when she surprises them with a trip to the lake?

Luna - Book 2

While Luna Lancaster loves Lake Tahoe, she thrives in the outdoors near her home in Sedona, Arizona. When Luna's good friend, Sadie, plans a visit and decides to bring a guest, Luna is excited to show them the sights of the beautiful Red Rocks around her home.

Unfortunately, Luna's friend can't make it at the last minute, and Luna finds herself entertaining Trace Hampton alone. The chemistry between them sparks the moment they meet. The problem is that Luna thinks Trace and Sadie are a couple, and she does everything possible to hide her feelings and not act on them.

When Trace reveals that he is not involved with Sadie, Luna jumps at the chance to see what they could have, but when Sadie finds out, she's heartbroken that Luna stole the man she likes out from under her.

Will Luna save the friendship and lose the chance at a happily ever after with Trace?

Levi, Book 3

Levi Lancaster is the youngest of the family, and while not as classy and outgoing as his older siblings, he works hard for his own HVAC company.

When a major snowstorm hits Lake Tahoe, Levi is enlisted to do a favor and finds himself quite taken with Diane Hampton. He's heard of her through his sister, Luna, and Luna's boyfriend, Trace, but he has never had the chance to meet them.

Diane loves her new life in Lake Tahoe, but she is not a fan of driving in the snow. When Levi comes to help her out, Diane may find herself finally ready to move on after the loss of her fiancée five years ago.

When a stranger arrives at the lake and tries to insert herself into Levi's life, Diane tries to figure out if the woman is after something, or just trying to find pieces of her past. Can Diane protect Levi or will he push her away when she is only trying to help?

Life is about to change for these two, but will it be for the better?

Still to come: Lance, Lily, Laney, and Lucas.

ABOUT THE AUTHOR

Stacy Eaton began her writing career in October of 2010 and, as each year goes by, she releases more and more novels. Stacy recently took an early retirement from law enforcement after over fifteen years of service, with her last three in investigations and crime scene investigation.

Stacy resides in southeastern Pennsylvania with her husband, who works in law enforcement, and her two dogs. She has a daughter in college and a son who is currently serving in the United States Navy.

Be sure to visit www.stacyeaton.com for updates and more information on her books.

Sign up for all the latest information on Stacy's Newsletter!

Join my Newsletter and get TWO Short Stories for FREE!

STACY'S OTHER BOOKS

Rise Again Warrior Series

The *Rise Again Warrior Series* is an intense and emotional journey through the lives of many service members, their families, and their friends. Focusing on the trials that they face after wartime is over, and they have returned home to a nation that sometimes seems to have forgotten what they were fighting for, and what all of these people sacrificed in the name of Honor & Duty. Books Include: Mission: Believe, Mission:Accept, Mission: Repair, and Mission: Courage

Loving a Young Series

The *Loving a Young Series* is a steamy romance series that consists of six books. While these books are all standalone romances, the characters will be seen across the series since this is a small-town romance series about siblings finding forever loves.

Books include: Wesley, Henley, Huntley, Riley, Kayley & Bradley

The Loving a Winston Series

The *Loving a Winston Series* is a five-book steamy romance series that spins off of the *Loving a Young Series*. Characters from both series will appear from book to book. Each book is a standalone romance with suspense, adult language and spicy romance scenes.

Books Include: Cara, Evan, Candy, Coral and Carmen.

The Loving a Lancaster Series

The *Loving a Lancaster Series* spins off of the *Loving a Winston Series* when Coral Winston meets Landon Lancaster in Lake Tahoe. Characters from previously series maybe show up in these books. Each book is a standalone romance, adult language and may contain spicy romances scenes.

Books includes: Leo, Luna, Levi, Lance, Laney, Lucas, and Lilly.

The Unexpected Series

The *Unexpected Series* is a steamy romance series where anything can happen and probably will. Each book in the series is a stand-alone happily ever after, or happy for now book. While they are stand-alone, the books are all centered around Safety Zone Security and the employees there. Characters from one book will continue throughout the rest of the series. Books Include: Unexpected Packages, Unexpected Arrivals, Unexpected Trouble, Unexpected Storms, Unexpected Desires, Unexpected Ties.

Paranormal Romance:

My Blood Runs Blue Series

My Blood Runs Blue Series is an adult Paranormal Action/Romance Series with vampires and is intended for mature audiences.

Books Include: My Blood Runs Blue, The Pulse of Blue Blood, Blue Blood for Life, Mixing the Blue Blood, Blue Bloods Final Destiny,

The Return of Blue Blood Series:

This series is 40 years in the future after My Blood Runs Blue. It is a very steamy series intended for mature audiences.

Books Included: Kristin: Blue Blood Returns, Hugh: Blue Blood Compelled, Zander: Blue Blood Reborn, Lena: Blue Blood Desired, Reckoning, Blue Blood Finale

Single Titles

Whether I'll Live or Die

You're Not Alone

Garda ~ Welcome to the Realm

Liveon ~ No Evil

Second Shield

Distorted Loyalty

Six Days of Memories

Second Shield II: The Return

Tempt Me Too

Finding the Strength

Finding Love in Special Places:

Stacy's Short Story Series

Sweet Romance about adult topics. Stories include: Finding Love on Christmas Vacation, Finding Love on the Summer Surf, Finding Love with Dear Santa, Finding Love with a Champagne Toast, Finding Love on the High Seas, Finding Love on a Dude Ranch, Finding Love at the Farmer's Market, Finding Love at the Coffee Shop

Heart of the Family Series

The *Heart of the Family* Series is a small-town steamy romance series that is best read in order. Books Include:

Mistletoe & Cocoa Kisses, Roses & Champagne Kisses, Orchids & Hurricane Kisses, Carnations & Hot Toddy Kisses,

Heal Me Series

Love Spicy Medical Romance? Check out the rest of the Heal Me Series for sexy romances that will warm your heart as they deal with life-altering medical and psychological issues. These books do contain language and open door sexual relations. While each book in the Heal Me Series is a stand-alone book, the characters cross between books and are best enjoyed by reading them in order. Books Include: Cured, Revived, Mended and Rescued.

The Celebration Series

The Celebration Series: Celebration Township is made for family, friends, falling in love, and don't forget celebrating the holidays. The first twelve books bring two people onto center stage as they overcome odds and figure out what their futures may hold. There is laughter, love, romance and even suspense when you join these couples as they each find a happily ever after over a holiday. The thirteenth book brings all twelve couples, and even a few special guests, into final focus as the first couple in Tangled in Tinsel prepares for their wedding one year after they met. Books Include: Tangled in Tinsel, Tears to Cheers, Heathens to Hearts, Rainbows Bring Riches, Sweet as Sugar, Making Mom Mad, Sparklers or Spankings, Raffles to Rattles, Flirting with Fireworks, Working Under Wheels, Masquerading at Midnight, Blessing & Beans, Velvet & Vows.

The Sometimes Series:

The Sometimes Series consists of three romances where the passion is a touch spicy and there is a hint of suspense is in the air. Sometimes You Win is a stand-alone story that ends with a Happy-for-Now ending. Sometimes you Lose, Book 2 of the series does end in a cliffhanger and Sometimes You Play the Game will finally give the couple a Happily Ever After. In all three books, you will find adult language and situations. Books Include: Sometimes You Win, Sometimes you Lose, Sometimes You Play The Game.

Pleasure Your Fantasies Series

The Pleasure Your Fantasies series is an ADULT Series with coarse language and intense sexual situations along with suspense. Books Include: Mistletoe Fantasies, Whispered Fantasies, Secret Fantasies, Conflicted Fantasies, Returning Fantasies, Arrested Fantasies, Discovered Fantasies, and Explosive Fantasies

List Updated 10/27/25

www.ingramcontent.com/pod-product-compliance
Lightning Source LLC
Chambersburg PA
CBHW031945260626
47157CB00017B/2368